KID OWNER

KID OWNER

TIM GREEN

SCHOLASTIC INC.

ISBN 978-1-338-04831-5

Copyright © 2015 by Tim Green. All rights reserved.
Published by Scholastic Inc., 557 Broadway, New York, NY 10012, by arrangement with HarperCollins Children's Books, a division of HarperCollins Publishers. SCHOLASTIC and associated logos are trademarks and/or registered trademarks of Scholastic Inc.

The publisher does not have any control over and does not assume any responsibility for author or third-party websites or their content.

12 11 10 9 8 7 6 5 4 3 2 1   16 17 18 19 20 21

Printed in the U.S.A.   40

First Scholastic printing, September 2016

Typography by Megan Stitt

For my #1 reader and super son Ty

It's not easy to be different.

They say everything is bigger in Texas, and for the most part I'd agree. Everything around me is as big as my state: our home, the truck my mom drives, the football program in our town, even my best friend—all big. That's why being known as the little guy is tough. I'm scrappy, though, and I play football like so many other kids, whether they're really made for it or not. At the end of practice the day my life took a wicked turn, the big Texas sky opened up so that we ran our sprints through a cascade of water falling from above. In August, even the rain can't deliver you from the heat, so when I got home I needed a shower pretty badly. I dried off and had dinner with my mom. Afterward, I sat in my favorite chair in the living room with *The Chocolate War*, a book our English teacher had given us for summer reading to prepare for our first assignment as seventh graders.

I was pretty well into the book and liking it when I heard the tune of my mom's phone ringing in the kitchen, where she sat at her computer, and I sensed the distress in her voice after she answered it. I let the book fall into my lap as I listened in with no idea what had happened, only knowing that whatever it was, it wasn't good. I heard her say thank you and good-bye and then her footsteps coming my way. I put my nose back into my book until she cleared her throat.

"Hi," I said, looking up. "What's going on?"

She crossed the room, weaving in and out of the dark wood and leather furniture, and took my hand. The sun had gone down, leaving a pitch-black sky. Lightning flashed in the big picture window and a rumble of thunder shook the house before she spoke. "Ryan, your father passed away."

I blinked up at her, speechless.

"I—I just thought you should know." She squeezed my hand and walked away without another word.

I didn't know what to do, or say, so I looked down at my book again and read a couple sentences before realizing I had no idea what they had said. I let the book drop again into my lap, thinking about the power of words. Two words, actually: *father* and *football*.

YEARS EARLIER . . .

These two harmless words were never spoken in my house while I was growing up.

They were the F-words. That's what my mother called them.

The father thing I understood. Everyone had one except me, so even *I* didn't like to talk about that. When I was really little, we had to draw a picture of our family in kindergarten. I'd drawn Julian off to the side so people might *think* he was my father. He and his wife, Teresa, work for us and live in our guesthouse. When my mom had seen the red Texas Rangers hat on the stick figure of a man, she'd known it was Julian, but my teacher and classmates thought it was my dad. I couldn't have really drawn my father because I'd never met him, never seen a picture of him, and knew nothing about him.

By the time I was eight years old, though, the idea of my dad had grown into something much bigger than a stick figure. I knew he was out there, somewhere. And I felt I would someday meet him, so I wanted to be worthy. My plan was to become the most important and awesome kind of person there was: an NFL football player. And I'd planned on being a quarterback. I was small—I knew that. But there were other small NFL quarterbacks, and their lack of size only made them that much more special. My father would be amazed.

I'd dreamed of one day inviting him to a Ben Sauer Middle School game. Maybe we'd be playing Eiland, our toughest rival. After a glorious win, he would wait for me outside the locker room along with the families of my teammates. I'd come out, totally exhausted from several touchdown runs. My father would see me and his eyes would grow wet. He would ache for the times he missed with me growing up. He would wish with all his heart that the two of us could now become even closer, to make up for lost time.

I would smile warmly and keep my cool, because I didn't really know the man. I grew up keeping an emotional distance from the thought of my dad mostly because I suspected he had done something wrong to my mom. Why else would he have run off? Why else would my mom avoid talking about him altogether? Why else would *father* be an F-word?

Football being an F-word was another story. I didn't get that one.

In Texas, football is a religion, but it wasn't in my house. My mom didn't like it, and that's putting it mildly.

"Too much violence," she'd say.

I mean, I was small and fast like my mom, so I understood why she pushed me to play soccer, but why couldn't we *talk* about football? *Football* being the other F-word didn't keep me from being a closet Dallas Cowboys fan, though. I'd sneak away and watch their games at other people's houses. I'd watch reruns of local sports shows featuring Cowboys players and coaches on my iPad. I even hid a box of playing cards in the garage inside a spare tire under a tarp in a far corner.

I was okay keeping my love of the game a secret because my mother and I had made a deal. If I played soccer for three years and really tried, she'd let me play football when I was older.

"How old?" I'd asked.

"Third grade." She threw that number out there probably because it seemed so far away at the time. I know it did to me.

I took those words and planted them in my heart. And they grew fast and big like the seeds of a tree. So by the time I was eight, they were as large as the monster oaks in our front yard. I never considered my mom might not know they were there.

Who in Texas *didn't* dream of being a football player?

I don't mean to knock soccer. I loved the game, and I was pretty good. But when I was at school, I couldn't get through lunch without hearing about football. So, it was lunch that killed soccer for me.

Every fall in elementary school, week after week, all the guys in my neighborhood would sit at the lunch table and talk about the Highland Knights youth football game coming up on Sunday morning. They'd be playing Carrollton or Grand Prairie or North Haven Park, and they made every week sound like it was going to be as important and monumental as World War III.

The only other kid who'd played soccer with me was Melvin Patterson. At first, we'd try to talk about our games, cramming our mouths with ham and cheese sandwiches, slurping our milk through straws. But it was never as exciting. Even our rivals sounded lame: the Innwood Spitfires or the Royal Creek Robins. So we'd sit with our heads bent low over Premier League football trading cards, uttering names like Yaya, Suárez, Messi, and Rooney, but all the while secretly listening to talk of trap blocks, go routes, reverses, and safety blitzes.

Then, in the beginning of August, during the summer between second and third grade, the day finally came: sign-ups for Premier Youth Football League, the finest football in Texas. The chatter about PYFL between my future teammates had begun months before, at the end of second grade.

It became clear to me that I'd have to cut Melvin loose and save myself. Melvin's dad would never let him play football.

That summer I'd started asking my mom to invite the guys from my class over for swimming. I may know kids with an even bigger house than ours, but I'd never heard anyone say we don't have the best pool. We have this waterworks thing in the shallow end with sprayers and hoses and a big plastic alligator that spits water. There are these gears you can crank around to change which spouts spurted, dribbled, or sprayed in crazy zigzag liquid ropes. And in the deep end is a fifteen-foot curlicue slide along with a high dive.

That summer, I'd drop hints about maybe playing football. By the time all the moms had started buying new shoes and lunch boxes, I had myself slated as a key player for the Highland Knights.

All the kids and I pretty much knew the entire roster and who would likely play where. Mr. Simpkin, Jason Simpkin's dad, who used to play for SMU, was our coach.

One night, when all the guys were having a sleepover at Jason's house, his father was in the backyard tossing a football around with us. Kids were racing each other to show their coach how fast they'd become. Jason's dad watched with interest and when I'd suggested that I race Jason—who had beaten everyone else—his father had smiled at the joke and said, "Sure. Let me see you and Jason go at it."

Jason was a cobra, lean and strong with poison in his mouth and eyes dead as glass. He had looked at me and snorted, and the gang all stopped and stared. No one challenged Jason Simpkin and won.

We crouched low and took off together.

Mr. Simpkin had nodded wisely and chuckled after I beat Jason to the swing set by two strides. "Well, you're small, but with that kind of speed, I could see you making a heck of a third-down slot receiver."

I grinned. Talk about heaven. I lay awake that entire night, staring up at the fluttering roof of the camp tent in Jason's backyard beyond the pool, dreaming of third-down plays where I'd streak into the open and make a spectacular grab. Thinking if my dad could've seen me, he'd have been so proud.

I didn't keep my mom up to speed on any of this. I probably should have told her that I was going to hang up the soccer cleats forever. But *football* was an F-word.

So I'd waited until sign-ups were being held at Williamson Elementary before I told my mom about my dream, and that we needed to go down there with my birth certificate and a check for $795.

I had planned to tell her in the car ride home from day camp at the country club, but the knot in my stomach said to wait. Then, during dinner, when Teresa was serving veal cutlets—one of my mother's favorites—as soon as we'd said grace, my mother cleared her throat and asked, "Is everything okay, Ryan?"

That had flustered me. My mom is a pretty woman, but she has these eyes that can burn into you like the desert sun through a bug glass, and that's scary. I nodded and mumbled that I was fine and quickly cut loose a hunk of veal, stuffing it into my mouth. Every swallowed bite was an opportunity to bring up football, but my tongue stayed tied.

Finally, Teresa cleared the dishes and my mom took a deep breath and a sip of iced tea and asked me what I had planned for the evening.

And then, it was go time. Sign-ups only went until 7:30, and it was already 6:53.

"Mom . . ." Her look—just a simple smile—terrified me, because I knew how quickly it could change, like a summer thunderstorm blowing up out of the desert.

"Now are you going to tell me what's wrong?" Her smile went sideways and she took another sip from her glass before tilting her head to wait.

"We have to go to my school." My words were barely a whisper.

She scowled. "Why? What's wrong?"

"For sign-ups." I still couldn't *say* football.

"Sign-ups?"

I stood up from my place. "We have to go now, Mom. It only goes until 7:30. And you need to bring a check."

"A check for what? Hey, mister." Her stern tone stopped me cold. "What's going on?"

"And my birth certificate." My eyes started to well up and I sniffed and looked at my sneakers. "Football sign-ups, Mom. Everyone's doing it. The Highland Knights. I'm gonna play this year. Remember our deal?"

I looked up at her with as much confidence as I could muster, knowing that the deal she'd cut with me three years ago might be something she'd forgotten completely. That's how adults are—they never remember the details like that.

"Football?" She'd practically snorted the word. "Ryan, what are you talking about? You're a soccer player. We've talked about this. Football isn't part of who we are. End of discussion."

I'm a pretty good kid. I know it's me saying it about myself, but other people—teachers, parents—think so, too.

And I don't get into trouble. That's because I stay inside the lines—almost always. But I have a flaw: sometimes, I blow my stack. I flat-out lose it. I can't tell you why, but sometimes it's a little thing that triggers it while big things just float on by and I stay cool. And sometimes, *ba-boom.*

And when my mom called me a soccer player, I lost it and grabbed my water glass and slammed it so hard onto the kitchen table that it shattered. I barely noticed the shards of glass on my hand when I screamed, *"I hate when you do this! You said I could! Don't lie!"*

My mother is small but tough, and she was up out of her chair in a blink. She had me off my feet, lifting me by the collar and marching me down the hall and up the stairs before tossing me onto my bed. She stopped at the door on her way out to point a finger. "You don't call your mother a *liar.* Who do you think you are, young man!"

She turned and slammed the door before I could speak, partly from surprise, but mostly from having been choked by the collar-carry.

"LIAR!" I screamed in defiance.

The word hung in the air like an exploded bomb of silence. From all the way downstairs in the kitchen I could hear the tinkle of glass as Teresa swept up the broken pieces. Then the rumble of my mother's footsteps filled the hallway, coming closer by the instant, so that when the door flew open and smashed into the wall, I was ready for it.

"Who do you think you *are*? You're acting so disrespectful!"

"You *said* third grade! I played that hot-poop sport for *three years* because you said I *had* to. You said if I played soccer and I still wanted to play football that I *could*. *That's* what *you said!*"

"This is coming out of nowhere, Ryan! You don't just drop something like this on me! Maybe, *maybe*, if you'd talked to me about this earlier, I could have *considered it*! Not now, though, mister. *NO WAY! NO HOW!* You are *not* playing football!" She slammed the door shut again. It was meant to be final.

I jumped up off my bed, fired my Lionel Messi bobblehead at the door, smashing it and putting a divot in the wood to punctuate what I was about to say.

"THEN LET ME GO LIVE WITH MY FATHER!"

PRESENT . . .

That jolted me back to the present. I must have dozed off
because my book had fallen to the side, and I realized that my
face was wet with tears. Because my father had died. I could
hear my mom talking again on her phone in the kitchen. Did
she need to deliver this news of my father's passing to family
and friends? I didn't know why when she'd barely mentioned
the man for the past twelve years. I even thought I'd heard the
words *football* and *Dallas Cowboys*, but knew that had nothing
to do with anything. I couldn't think about this anymore, and
clearly my reading wasn't getting done. My phone vibrated and
I read a text from my best friend, Jackson Shockey. He was
reminding me to ask my mom if it was okay if he came over
after football practice tomorrow. I replied that it was without

asking, and without telling him anything about the shocking news I'd just received. I just didn't want to talk about it.

I put my book away, crept upstairs to my room, got in bed, and turned out the light. The storm had passed and the moon shone in through my sheer window curtains. I just lay in bed, still thinking. Try as I might, I was unable to stop remembering back to that argument about football sign-ups.

YEARS EARLIER . . .

I'll never forget the sound my mom had made. It had been a gasp and a sob, like something someone snatched from deep inside her, the core of her heart, dropping it like a punt and kicking it high into the air.

Then she did the worst thing you could ever imagine.

I heard the soft scrape of her shoulder blades down the other side of my bedroom wall and the thump of her bottom as it hit the floor. Then, the muted crying. It hurt me, and it cleared the fog of war in my brain.

I crept across my bedroom floor and opened the door, crunching the pieces of the broken bobblehead beneath my sneakers. "Mom?"

She had planted her head between her knees and she wore her arms like a hat.

"Mom, don't cry. I'm sorry. I shouldn't have talked to you that way."

She shook her buried head and talked between her ragged breaths. "No. Don't be sorry. I'm sorry . . . I should have told you a long time ago about your father. I should have talked to you

13

when you drew that picture of Julian in kindergarten and asked me. I wanted to. Tell you. But every time I was going to, it just . . . never seemed right."

I sat down with my back against the same wall and put a hand between her shoulder blades, against the knobby ladder of her backbone. "It doesn't matter, Mom. I've got you."

"He'd be proud of you." She raised her head, her red-rimmed eyes burning. "He *may* be proud. I have no idea what he knows or doesn't know about you. And you'd be proud of him, Ryan. I really think you would. He's very successful, and he's not a bad person. He and I . . . we just . . . sometimes adults have different ideas of what life is supposed to be."

"Is he a . . . does he play? F-football, I mean?"

My mother laughed at that. "I suppose in high school he did. Not after that. He's an engineer. Very smart. But he loves the game. That I know. He *loves* that game."

I nodded my head. I liked him already. Smart. An engineer. Football fan. I was hungry for more. "Is he rich?"

She took a deep breath, uncovered her head, and looked up at me. "You and I are rich. Us. What we have, a family. And we *love* each other. That's rich, Ryan. I want you to remember that. So, in that way, no, your father isn't rich at all. Not by my standards."

"But he has a lot of money?" I couldn't help asking it.

She sighed and nodded. "And to give credit where credit is due, that's why we live the way we do."

"He pays for things?" I asked.

She nodded. "Everything."

"I thought Poppa and Nanna . . ." My grandparents lived in

Seattle, in a nice home on Lake Washington. I just figured every-one had a bunch of money. No one I knew really talked about money, so I just assumed my mom *had* it, like everyone else.

My mom laughed. "Oh, no. Not that they aren't comfortable, but your poppa? Not a dime. He didn't even pay for my college. No, they don't believe in that."

"What's my dad do?"

She took my hand and held it and pulled me next to her so she could drape an arm around my shoulders. It was one of the warm-est moments in my life, sitting there, just the two of us on the floor with the big quiet house my father bought all around us. We were like seeds in the core of some wonderful shiny red apple.

"Well, like I said, he's an engineer, but he's more than that now." It sounded to me like she admired him, maybe even liked him. "He started out as a kind of inventor on a research team for a big company that made medical devices. Then he realized that if he could get his own company going, he could do things faster, even better."

"So he just started a company?"

She laughed. "In our garage."

"Your garage? You lived with him?"

She looked at me funny. "We were married, your father and I."

"You *were*? Then how come I don't know him? How come everything's a secret?" I asked.

She bit her lower lip. "I did that for you, Ryan. I still want to do it for you. You have to trust me. It's better for you *not* to know him or who he is. It would only make things harder for you. You have to believe me. It hasn't hurt you not to know him. It hasn't hurt

15

you not to even talk about him. That's why I call it the F-word. Let's not even talk about it."

This was news that made my head spin.

Then my mother said the only thing that could have possibly taken my mind off my father.

PRESENT . . .

I woke up suddenly, my heart beating and my brow sweaty, realizing that I had tangled myself in the sheets, and now I struggled to break free. I turned over and looked at the clock. It was midnight and pitch-black around me. I had practice tomorrow, and I was already exhausted. My mom must have been, too; I could hear her voice floating up from the kitchen, still talking on the phone. I flipped over, trying to get comfortable. It was raining outside again. Shadows cast by the moonlight took on strange shapes, suggesting bad thoughts and deeds, lies and deceit and cover-ups all around me. I wanted to scream, but I kept quiet and untangled myself. I lay panting in my bed as I realized it really hadn't been the best thing for me not to know my father. Not now, not with him dead. Now I would never get to make him proud, so that even if I fulfilled my dreams of becoming a star quarterback, he'd never know. I'd never be able to tell him.

But back when I was in elementary school, my mom distracted me from the fact that I didn't know who my dad was.

YEARS EARLIER . . .

She'd said, "Let's only have one F-word we don't talk about. I'm taking football off the list. Let's go sign you up."

She'd had a twinkle in her eye, and I couldn't believe I'd come through that terrible tantrum complete with broken glass, slammed doors, and calling my mom a liar with her still willing to make me a Highland Knight.

"Thanks, Mom," I said, grinning.

I didn't say another word for fear of breaking the spell, but was on my feet in a split second and headed for the door to the garage. "Don't forget the birth certificate."

"I know, and my checkbook," she mumbled. For some reason, she sounded irritated.

But I knew the birth certificate was a must for PYFL sign-ups. The league had strict age limits on its players. I opened my mouth to explain, then stopped. It hit me why talk of a birth certificate might annoy her. Besides having my date of birth, that official government document would also probably have my father's name on it.

I rode up high beside her in the front seat of our big white truck. Lots of moms drive pickups in Texas. The inside of a King Ranch F-350 is like the living room in a hunting lodge, with big thick leather seats, the kind of place you could put your shoes up on the furniture without a second thought. I kept my shoes on the floor, staring intently at the sunbaked road up ahead but powerfully aware that the folded paper on the console between our seats very likely held the name of the man who was my father.

The thought of grabbing my birth certificate and quickly stealing a look ran wild around the inside of my head. I stuffed my hands beneath my legs and started to sweat, despite the cold blast of AC from the dashboard vent.

I looked over at my mom. She scowled at the road, lips tight. I took a deep breath.

"Mom, the league makes you bring a birth certificate to prove you're not too old to play. I'm not going to look at it."

"Oh, I don't care about that." She waved her hand in the air, but I could see her face suddenly relax.

"Okay." I gave a short nod, then turned on the radio to fill the quiet.

Ten minutes later, my mom parked the truck in the fire lane in front of the school. It was almost 7:25, and I hopped down and walked real fast, tugging her toward the main entrance. Two boys I didn't recognize walked out just as we got there. Both were big and hulking and my mom looked them over before turning to me and tilting her head in a way that asked if I was really sure I wanted to do this.

I flung open the door and held it. "After you."

In she went and we marched up to the table in the front hall of the school just outside the principal's office. The fluorescent lights above the table glowed, but the rest of the hallways were dark and eerie, and it made the whole thing seem like a dream, which made me think about how it *was* a dream, a dream come true. Me, playing football. Finally.

Jason Simpkin's dad sat on the other side of the table with a man who I thought I recognized as the father of Bryan Markham, one of the biggest, strongest—also meanest—kids in the third grade. I knew from talk at school that Bryan's dad was Mr. Simpkin's assistant and had himself played middle linebacker at Baylor. While Mr. Simpkin, the former SMU center, reminded me of a neckless rhino, Mr. Markham was more like a balding gorilla, complete with long arms and dark furry hair on the backs of his pale hands and neck. In his mouth was the unlit stub of a fat greenish cigar. The two youth-league coaches were in the process of gathering up their papers when they saw us, stopped, and looked at each other. I thought Mr. Markham rolled his eyes, but the sudden chill I felt left me uncertain of exactly what I had seen.

"Hey!" Mr. Simpkin found his smile and rubbed his forehead with a thick stubby hand. "Jason's little buddy . . ."

My mom extended her hand. "Ryan. He's Ryan. I'm Katy. Katy Zinna. We're here for football sign-ups."

Mr. Simpkin shook my mom's hand, dainty as a rhino. "Yes, well, it's nice to see you. I—"

My mom fished through her purse, then handed him my birth certificate and slapped her checkbook down on the table. "Seven hundred ninety-five dollars? Is that right? How do I make that out?"

"Well, you see . . ." Mr. Simpkin looked to Mr. Markham for help.

"Sorry," Mr. Markham grunted, adding a few more wrinkles to his thick brow, "but you missed it."

"Missed what?" My mother had that thunderstorm look.

"Sign-ups." Mr. Markham shrugged in a not-so-nice way and spoke around his stub of a cigar so that it wiggled. "We're full. Maybe next year, though. Anyway, it'll give the little guy a chance to grow."

I closed my eyes, 'cause I knew what came next. And it was not going to be good.

"Excuse me?" My mom's shrill voice could have cracked a glass.

Mr. Markham's face contorted into a mean smile and his voice got smooth, so you knew he was no stranger to nasty situations. "I'm just telling you the facts. You missed sign-ups. It's over. Sorry, lady."

I glanced at Mr. Simpkin, hoping he'd vouch for my speed and suggest I was worth bending the rules for. *I'm the third-down slot receiver, remember? You said so at Jason's party.* I wanted to say that, but didn't.

"And you're the coach?" My mom glowered at Mr. Markham.

"One of them." Mr. Markham puffed up and yanked the cigar from a picket of yellow-stained teeth.

"Good, then I wouldn't want my son being coached by a pompous jerk like you, anyway. Come on, Ryan. I'm betting there are better teams than this you can sign up for." She took my arm and we headed toward the door. Out on the sidewalk, we passed a father and his son, a boy both tall and lean.

"They closed them down, the sign-ups," my mom said, trying to be helpful.

"Oh. Yeah? Well, we'll give them a shot anyway," the man said.

My mom shook her head as if to wish them luck despite her doubts, and we climbed up into her truck. The big machine

21

rumbled to life. She put it in gear and we pulled away from the curb. As we passed the entrance, my mom slowed down and leaned my way, peering through the passenger window at the school.

"Oh, really?" she barked at the window like she was talking to someone else.

Then she hit the brakes, so only the seat belt kept me from bouncing my head off the dashboard.

She slammed the truck out of gear, turned off the engine, flung open the door, and hopped down. As she marched toward the main entrance to the school, I threw my own door open and shouted, "Mom! What are you doing?"

Caught in the horror of wanting to stop her but knowing it was hopeless, I jumped down and chased her into the school.

Mr. Markham was accepting a check from the dad while Mr. Simpkin offered back a birth certificate, along with some other papers. They froze at the sight of my mother.

She marched toward them with her arms crossed. "What do you people think you're doing?"

Mr. Simpkin stuttered without really saying anything. Mr. Markham wore that bold smile and let fly with a nasty snort. "These people already signed up. They just came back with the right paperwork. Like I said, we closed it down right before you got here."

"Mom?" I whispered. "Please."

My mother didn't hear or didn't care. She went right for Markham, got up in his face, and spoke through clenched teeth. "You can't keep my son off this team and you know it. You get that sign-up sheet back out and put his name on it or you'll have lawyers swarming you and your little mess of a football league like buzzards on roadkill."

My mother stared. Mr. Markham stared right back. Neither of them moved and I held my breath. Suddenly, Mr. Markham snorted again and rolled his eyes. "Suit yourself."

"That's exactly what I plan to do." She took her checkbook back out of her purse, along with my birth certificate, slapping them down.

The boy and his dad left without further comment. The coaches sat stiff, and what few words they uttered plunked out of their mouths like ice cubes in a plastic cup, hard and cold. As we walked away, the team schedule, fund-raiser forms, and medical permission slips clutched in my mother's hand, she held her head high in triumph.

I stole a glance back at the two coaches, who watched us like unblinking crocodiles, and wondered if, in fact, we'd won anything at all. The idea of playing for coaches who had no interest in having me on their team didn't seem fun at all, let alone smart.

We got back in the truck and my mother looked over at me and chuckled.

"I don't see what's funny. I gotta spend seven days a week with them. They're my coaches, and you just got them steaming mad before I even got my pads on."

She cranked the wheel of the massive truck and we careered around a corner with tires yipping for mercy. "Don't get between a bear and her cubs. That's the natural order of things. A *mother* fights like nothing else."

"I don't even know what that means."

My mom shook her head and I clenched my hands at the

thought of those two coaches making me run laps and do sets of twenty push-ups as punishment for all sorts of imagined violations.

"They can't threaten, bully, or intimidate me in any way, and they know it. They don't want to see my claws. They're afraid of me."

"Mom, they're the coaches."

She patted my hand as we pulled into the driveway. "They aren't going to give you a hard time. I promise."

One of the very few things I can't stand about my mom is that she's pretty much right about everything. She was right about the coaches, too. I wonder if she could have even imagined that them *not* giving me a hard time was about the worst thing they could ever do.

7

On that first day of Highland football, I had strutted around in my full uniform the moment I got home from school. The only thing I took off for dinner was my helmet. The rest of it came off only after practice, when I gleefully got hosed down by Julian to rinse the mud before I was even allowed in the laundry room. It rained in buckets during that first practice, a big Texas rain, and the coaches had us do bull in the ring right in the middle of a big mud pit down where the field drains off.

I knew what bull in the ring was because I'd heard kids talk about it in school. Everyone would circle up around a single kid. The coach would shout out numbers, and if he shouted your number, you ran full speed at the kid in the middle and *CRASH.*

I remember pulling up to the field after dinner just as the first random sprinkles of rain spotted our windshield, imagining what it would be like to be that bull.

"Oh, I doubt they'll practice when this hits." My mom waved her hand at the weather out her side window. Towering black clouds climbed over the tops of each other in their haste to get to the Oklahoma border.

"Only if there's lightning they won't." I had my hand on the door handle already, eager for her to take the truck out of gear so I could jump out.

"I don't see how you can get anything done in rain like *that*." She pointed and finally put the truck into park.

"It's *football*, Mom," I shouted back to her, and slammed the door. She'd started to say something more, but I was already gone, sprinting across the field toward my new teammates, some of whom were tossing around a ball as if there were a bright blue sky. I ran up to a few of the guys who lounged by the blocking sled, their arms draped across the big blue canvas blocking dummies like best friends.

"How about that storm coming, huh?" I hated myself for speaking, but in my excitement I felt if I didn't say something, I'd bust wide open.

"It's *football*, Zinna." Bryan Markham punched the blocking dummy like it was supposed to be me. It rattled and shook and he folded his arms across his chest. "Not *soccer*."

"I know." I nodded brightly. "I just said that to my mom."

Bryan scoffed and muttered under his breath as he snapped his chin strap and walked away. "Your mom."

Coach Simpkin gave his whistle a blast and without so much as a word, the players all took off for the sideline, running in single file around the perimeter of the field and then spilling out through the goalposts into six perfect columns spaced out every five yards on the line. I followed and stumbled into place, just doing what everyone else was doing. While my equipment suddenly felt too tight in some spots (like the forehead pad in my helmet) and too loose in others (like my girdle and all its pads drifting down my butt), excitement still won out over discomfort. I had waited so long to be here, and finally, here I was.

I stretched my hamstrings and shoulders and everything else you could stretch, barking out a ten count with the others, thrilled to be a soldier in the football army. The coaches wandered among us like generals, the wind whipping their hair. They wore shorts to their knees and shells for the coming rain. We compressed our columns to the goal line and did agility drills, running out to the twenty-yard line before re-forming and waiting to return. When the first serious drop of rain hit my helmet, I looked around for the person who'd thrown a rock. Then I heard the next tap, then another, until it was a patter that made it hard to hear Coach Simpkin shouting to us all.

"I thought this was gonna happen." Coach Simpkin cinched the strap of his floppy coaching hat as the rain pounded its brim, his voice already going raspy from raising it. "We got a lot of plays to put in and stuff, but you all know where Coach Markham and I like to go when it rains?"

"The RING!" my teammates cheered as one, already slapping one another's shoulder pads and helmets, giddy with anticipation. Coach Markham had his hood up, a stubby green unlit cigar waggling from between his grinning teeth.

"That's right, bull in the ring!" Coach Simpkin blew his whistle and pointed toward the far edge of the field where the grass dropped off to the drainage grate.

Everyone had cheered—me included, even though I'd never seen it done—and took off in a stampede, the rain pouring down on us in sheets. Just before I disappeared over the lip of the field, I looked back at the parking lot. My mom's King Ranch sat parked facing the field, headlights on, wipers slapping away the rain. I gave a quick wave and thumbs-up to the dark shape behind the windshield where my mother's face had been swallowed up by the gloom.

Then I turned, joyfully, like a lamb to the slaughter, and entered the ring.

I felt like a real football player, with those sheets of rain and the thick mud and everyone focused on chopping his feet to the tune of Coach Simpkin's whistle. We'd chanted in a huge circle, like mad prehistoric warriors, running in place to warm up for the main event. On the whistle, we'd throw ourselves face-first into the mud, then pop right back up. Our sweat mixed with the rain. We gulped for air.

Then, Coach Simpkin pointed to Bryan Markham and shouted, "Markham, bull in the ring!"

Cheers. Markham, growling, sprinted into the center, chopping his feet and spinning in place.

"Get 'em going!" Coach Simpkin followed his cry with a whistle blast.

We all started chopping our feet again, running in place.

"Seventy-three!" the coach shouted through the rain.

A lineman I knew as Big Donny Patterson took off running toward Bryan Markham with the bellow of a crazed water buffalo. Markham spun to face him, crouching and lowering his pads. The two boys smashed into each other, but Markham got his pads beneath Donny. He exploded up and extended his hands, throwing the huge lineman right off his feet to come crashing down in the mud. Everyone went bananas.

So it went, Coach Simpkin calling out numbers, players racing toward the destruction waiting at the center of the ring. After a dozen hits, Coach Simpkin changed the bull to Big Donny. When Jason Simpkin knocked Patterson down, he took over the middle of the ring. Then another player took out Jason Simpkin and so it went, each player taking a turn in the center until he was defeated.

Except me.

I'd checked the number on my jersey several times: twenty-three. A number I couldn't associate with any NFL player or college star, past or present. I kept my feet chugging, staying ready, believing after each impact that Coach Simpkin would call out my number on the very next turn. Finally, I raised my hand. Teammates around me were huffing and puffing, groaning and growling.

Coach Simpkin had looked right at me, but only smiled and winked. I'd thought about just running out there and hitting someone on my own, but it was my first day, and I knew there must be some kind of initiation I must have missed before I'd be allowed to join the fray.

The drill finally ended and we marched back up the hill for more practice. I caught up to Coach Simpkin and tugged at the sleeve of his Windbreaker.

"Coach? How come I couldn't get a turn?"

"Hey, Ryan." Coach Simpkin swept the raindrops from his face with one hand. "Oh, you'll get plenty, don't worry about that. We've got to ease you into this. You just watch and get a feel for things. That's the best way."

I felt relieved at that news, and so I watched and waited while the raindrops danced on the surface of the puddles like popping corn.

The team did tackling drills and blocking drills.

The only things I *was* allowed to do was hit dummies or foam pads and run—run through obstacles, run laps, run sprints, run forward, sideways, and backward.

That lasted a week, and at the end, I asked Coach Simpkin again. He smiled and patted my shoulder pads and suggested patience. I watched and waited a few more practices, and then a strange thing happened, something I can't explain. Something I'm ashamed to admit.

I don't know if those two coaches did it to me, or if it was just growing up in a house where physical violence was the only thing worse than an F-word. I began to *fear* hitting. I'd stopped asking to be put into full-contact drills, not because I didn't think they'd listen but because I didn't *want* to go in. I'd grown accustomed to being the shell of a football player. And no one, not even the mean kids like Bryan Markham and Big Donny Patterson, ever said a word to me. They'd tease other players for shying away, or getting knocked off their feet, but me they ignored. And I was okay with that, because I didn't *want* to hit or, most of all, *be* hit.

They let me be on the team. My teammates even let me sit with them at lunch in the elementary school cafeteria if one of the regular guys was sick or something. When that happened, I'd nod my head in agreement when they all talked big about how we'd smash whoever was our upcoming opponent. (Of course,

33

I'd never talk about smashing anyone.) I wore my jersey on Fridays like everyone else. My teammates would nod to me when we passed in the halls. And for the next four years, I got to collect the golden statue awarded to our championship team at the end-of-season banquets, same as the rest. I don't think any of our other classmates suspected I was anything but a full-blown Highland Knights football player.

My mom had no idea either because I'd even gotten some playing time. I was no starter, but our team was so good that we rarely went into the fourth quarter fewer than four touchdowns ahead of whoever we were playing. That's when Coach Simpkin emptied the bench, putting the less skilled players into the game to get their taste. Me they sent out as the Z wide receiver, where I could stand away from the rest of the crowd. Occasionally, I'd have to run a pass pattern, always a go route, straight up the field, no chance to hit or be hit.

And it was in this way that Coaches Simpkin and Markham coaxed me into a state of complete and total cowardice. I was further from a football player than if I'd never put the pads on. It went on for four years, until a few months ago, when we graduated from the Highland Knights to middle-school football.

Now, everything's changed.

PRESENT . . .

My alarm woke me and for a few seconds, I didn't even know where I was.

It all came back quickly, though—crashing down on me: the father I never knew was now gone.

Exhausted from my sleepless night, I got dressed and went downstairs. My mom sat quietly at the kitchen table with a cup of coffee, reading the news on her tablet. When I sat down, she put it aside with the half a grapefruit she hadn't touched. Teresa asked me if I wanted eggs. I said yes, strongly aware that my mother was watching me. Her eyes looked tired and her mouth sagged.

"What?" I asked.

"I'm going to the funeral later today."

I paused a moment and picked up my fork, even though I had nothing to use it on yet. "Why are you telling me?"

"Because I'm not taking you," she said. "It'll be a zoo—your father knew many, many people. Plus, you have practice anyway. I know you won't want to miss that, right?"

I shifted in my seat. It wasn't like she was even giving me the option, and I wanted to protest, but something in her eyes kept me quiet. "Well, Jackson is coming home with me after practice. Can you pick me up?"

"If I can't, Julian will. Jackson is welcome anytime. You know that."

I shrugged. "I don't know what I know," I mumbled. It was as much of a protest as I felt comfortable with.

"You don't need to know," she said. "Trust me."

Trust her? I trusted her about not needing to know my dad and now he was gone. Part of me wanted to scream, but I buried it and went to school in a daze. After practice, it was my mom who picked us up, and after a short swim, Jackson's mom arrived to take him home.

"You're welcome to join us for dinner," my mom said to his mom.

"You're too kind, but I made a tuna casserole that's waiting for us," replied Jackson's mom.

Before he left, Jackson pulled me aside. "You okay, Ry? You're acting too quiet, even for you."

"Yeah, sure," I said. I don't know why, but I still hadn't told him about my dad.

He gave me a doubtful look, then shrugged. "Okay."

I watched them pull away, then returned to the kitchen.

Teresa had dinner all out on the table. My mom sat with a napkin in her lap, sipping iced tea and watching me closely. I wasn't going to ask about the funeral. Something in me refused to make a fuss. It wasn't until halfway through dinner when my mom cleared her throat to speak.

"You're going to have to leave practice early tomorrow."

An alarm went off in my brain. "What? Mom, I can't just leave practice early."

"I'll talk to your coach, Coach Hubbard," she said. "You don't have a choice."

I dropped my fork and it clanged off my plate. Missing football practice wasn't something you just did. "What do you mean? Why?"

I watched her face turn red and then she scowled. "Am I not your mother?"

"I can't miss practice."

"For this you can."

"For what?" I wanted to know.

My mother made a fist and brought it down the way a judge hammers his bench with a gavel. Everything shook. The silverware jingled and even Teresa froze with a pot in her hands at the kitchen sink. "If I knew for certain, I'd say it, Ryan, but I don't know. Let's just say that it has to do with your father and leave it at that, shall we?"

The tone of her voice didn't allow for anything other than total agreement.

The next day, I endured the embarrassment of walking off the practice field an hour before the rest of my team. It was only after I showered and changed into the dress clothes my mother handed me outside the locker room that she was ready to talk.

"We're going to your father's office," she said as her big white truck merged into the traffic out on the highway.

"Like, where he worked?" I asked.

"Not really," she said. "It's a family office."

"What's that?" I was totally confused, because how could a family need an office?

"Just . . . you'll see," she said.

"Why are you so mad about it?"

She shook her head. "It's excessive, Ryan. Everything your father did was excessive. It doesn't even make sense when there are people, children, in the world who have nothing."

I thought that was strange. *We* had a lot, so did that not make sense? But I kept quiet because my mother was not to be questioned when she got like this, with the wild look in her eye and the tremble in her voice.

We got off the highway close to downtown and pulled into the parking lot of a building that looked almost more like an old home than an office building, with its stone walls and slate pitched roof. We went in and up the stairs. Everything and everyone was quiet. We were ushered into an enormous conference room. We met a slew of people, all somehow related to my father, including his most recent wife and some half brother named Dillon. It blew my mind. I asked no questions, just nodded politely as my mother introduced me to some, while others she just pointed out. And when we were given seats at one end of the table facing a tall window, I barely listened to everything that was being said as they read my father's will. My mind was spinning out of control because I couldn't believe who my father actually was.

Outside, a ball of late August sun glared down on the city of Dallas, melting the tar on the streets. Inside the conference room, I shivered beneath an invisible blast of frigid air. It was cold and clammy as a tomb beneath a winter freeze.

When the lawyer said "Ryan Zinna," every person in the room jumped like they'd been pinpricked, and they turned my way. My half brother, Dillon, stopped chewing his gum. His jaw slackened to reveal a mangled green wad draped over a line of molars and tucked next to his tongue. Dillon's mother pinched her lips together and scowled. In her left hand was a bottle of water, which she strangled until it cried out, crackling.

I looked over at my mom just as she reached for my wrist, the way she'd do when she was about to run a yellow light in the car. I stopped her with a desperate look and a slight tilt of the head. My mom pulled back her hand and sat primly beside me in one of two dozen high-backed leather chairs surrounding the enormous conference table. Everyone wore black.

The lawyer's suit had tiny pinstripes so fine they might have been real strands of silver to match his cuff links. He sat at the head of the table adjusting his sleek black-and-chrome glasses and then clearing his throat before he continued to read.

"To my son, Ryan Zinna," he said, repeating my name in the context of being the dead man's son, so there should be no mistake, "I leave the entirety of my ownership interest in . . ."

The lawyer looked up at me again, swallowed, and blinked in disbelief. "The Dallas Cowboys."

I think my mother uttered something like, "Oh, dear Lord."

Dillon gagged, then hocked the wad of gum onto the table where it lay like some dead sea creature, moist and alien out of its true element. His mother sucked air in through her rigid lips with the sharp hiss of a punctured tire. "No!" She slammed her palm down on the table and sprang to her feet. She stood tall and slender, quaking like a volcano. Her tan face turned purple and her pale-blue eyes glinted like ice, dancing with pins of hate-filled light.

Dillon's pale-blue eyes, on the other hand, brimmed with tears, and his lower lip, like the gum, morphed into a fat wad for all to see. Dillon is twelve, like me, even though he's as tall as any fourteen-year-old. But he *acted* more like a ten-year-old.

His face crinkled. *"But, Mommy . . ."*

His mother slammed her water bottle onto the table. "He will *not* get the Cowboys!"

It was her turn to be stared at. My mother and I weren't the only people in the room she likely hated. My father had several brothers and they all had kids he apparently remembered with some degree of fondness or they wouldn't be here to cash in on what the lawyer called the last will and testament of Thomas Peebles.

The gathering had been called at the main conference room of the family office, *their* family office. I wasn't family. Not to them, or, in my mind even to *him*. *He*, the dead man, was my father in name only, a wildly successful billionaire with enough spare money to own an NFL team, but without the emotional means—according to my mother—to love and be loved.

A man you've seen only in pictures isn't really a father, is he?

"Jasmine, please." The lawyer hooked a finger inside the collar of his crisp white shirt and tugged it to get some air. He pointed a fat pen at Jasmine's chair. "Sit down."

"You can't be serious, Jim." Dillon's mother glared at the lawyer.

"It's his *will*, Jasmine. You figure very prominently in it, I assure you."

"Prominently?" She seemed to lose her breath and she reached backward, feeling for her chair to sit. "That football team is *prominent*. It's called 'America's Team' for a reason, Jim."

"The estate is substantial." The lawyer spoke gently. "You know that, Jasmine."

Silence—well, maybe a whimper from Dillon—before the

lawyer began again. "Until the time at which Ryan Zinna shall reach a majority age, all interest in the Dallas Cowboys shall be held in trust, with said trustee, Mr. Eric Dietrich, providing guidance and assistance while adhering as closely as he can to the wishes of Ryan Zinna during his term as a minor. Upon his attainment of majority, said trust shall cease to exist and the entirety of the trust's asset shall vest in Ryan Zinna."

"What?" The word escaped me.

The lawyer nodded toward a man in the corner of the room, sitting in a chair against the wall with a painting over his head, two sword fighters ready for a duel. The man named Eric Dietrich sat upright wearing a black three-piece suit with a gray-and-black-striped tie and silver-rimmed glasses that magnified steely dark-blue eyes. He was bald but for a thin ring of snow-white hair just over his ears. He looked vibrant, tan, and fit, with the predatory smile of a jackal, but he had to be seventy years old.

"Eric Dietrich," said the lawyer. "He's your trustee, but your father's instructions are to give *you* control."

"Of the team?" I asked.

The lawyer nodded.

"The Dallas Cowboys?" I still couldn't believe it.

He nodded.

I turned to my mother, knowing her to be a source of truth, even when it hurt. "I own the Dallas Cowboys?"

For some unknown reason, my mother looked far from pleased. Her mouth grew thin as a paper cut, but still, she nodded her head. "Yes, I think you do."

My mother and I walked out of that family office in silence after they read my father's will, with the enraged shrieks of Jasmine Peebles still leaking through the thick walls.

All I could think of was that even though I now owned the Dallas Cowboys, I was still me, Ryan Zinna. I still had my two best friends—Jackson and a girl named Izzy. I was still in seventh grade and would still be on the Ben Sauer Middle School football team.

But my heart had swollen a hundred times its normal size, because this was unbelievable. There we were, me and my mom, walking through the carefully trimmed landscaping that led to the parking lot. We still climbed up into her King Ranch pickup. She still reminded me to buckle up, even though I always did that automatically. I still turned on the radio and selected the Pulse and she still switched it without a word to the Highway. And, even though I owned the Dallas Cowboys, I knew better than to switch it back.

At that moment, I made a deal with myself that things would be just the same, only better. The same because I wasn't going to sour everything because she'd kept my father a secret. I'd become an expert at tucking that away, just not thinking about it, no matter how bitter and prickly it felt. Maybe the whole missing-father thing is what caused me to break out in random angry moments from time to time, but for the most part I had kept my feelings hidden before and I intended to keep that up.

Things would be better, I knew, because my insides already felt like a county fair, colored lights and laughter and the smell of cotton candy. Better because I would now rule the school. I could see the faces of both the boys' and girls' popular lunch tables as they begged to become my friend. And better because maybe now I would have more credibility with my coaches. Maybe now they'd listen when I said I should be playing quarterback—that I *could* be a quarterback. I could imagine the shock on Coach Hubbard's face at the thought of me introducing him to the Cowboys' coaching staff and maybe a few of the star players.

"What are you thinking about, Ry?" my mom asked, breaking the spell.

"Just . . . can you believe this?" I had this vision of myself standing in front of the entire Dallas Cowboys' offensive line. Maybe I'd strike a jaunty pose, with one foot on the ball, looking up at them, expectant, with my arms folded and them staring down, waiting for orders.

"I guess I can," she said, with a tone in her voice.

"Don't sound so happy about it." I couldn't help being annoyed that she trampled the nice image in my brain.

"I'm not happy about it, Ryan. You're twelve years old. I told you years ago, my whole focus has been about you having a normal childhood and growing up into a good person."

"I'm not good?"

"Of course you are," she said. "I'd like to keep it that way is all."

"How can this make me bad?" I tried not to sound too angry.

"Okay," she said. "Tell me. Whose faces have you already imagined the look on when they hear you own the Dallas Cowboys? Jackson? Izzy? No, not your friends. You thought of your enemies, didn't you? Bryan Markham and Jason Simpkin. Or maybe their fathers, the coaches in elementary school who didn't let you off the bench until the fourth quarter? Coach Hubbard. The one you say acts like you're not there?"

"What's that got to do with anything?" I asked.

"Ryan, don't you see? You can't wait to hold it over those people, the ones you don't like. That's not a good thing. It's just negative energy."

"Can't you just be happy for me? My gosh, Mom, this is a dream come true. I love the Cowboys. I love football. You know that!"

"It's a lot easier to *love* the Cowboys than to *own* them, Ryan. I know it sounds fun, but it's a business and your . . . father had no right to hand you a billion-dollar business like it's a ten-speed bike." My mother seemed to be growing angrier by the minute, the shock of it having worn off. She slapped the steering wheel. "In fact, I don't think I'm going to allow it, Ryan."

"What? No!" I felt instantly sick. "You can't just not allow it. He left it to *me*. You can't undo that. And—and I've got a trustee."

"Oh, sure. Dietrich, his old crony. That's just great. Guidance from above. Not. Dietrich is a barracuda."

"You mean, he won't really let me control the team?" I was confused.

"No, I mean he *will*." She was growling more than talking now. "He doesn't care about a young boy growing up to be 'normal,' and he and your father were thick as thieves. Your father's company used Dietrich Die Molding to help make all those high-tech medical devices. They got rich together."

I didn't say anything. She wanted me to be a "normal" boy? What was that? Who cared about a normal boy, let alone Minna Zinna—that's what some of the kids called me—the half-pint shrimp?

I almost laughed out loud.

But they'd definitely care now, especially when they saw the headline of the sports page in the *Dallas Morning Star* the very next day.

I have to say Jackson disappointed me when I got to school the next day.

Jackson Shockey was my best friend. He'd appeared in Highland during the summer, and had shown up unannounced on the first day of football practice for the seventh-grade team at Ben Sauer Middle School. I didn't see a single kid besides Jackson who wasn't part of the graduating class from last year's Highland Knights. And boy, did he stick out. He towered over the rest of us, and looked like he would one day soon be a main event in WWE. At first everyone, including Coach Hubbard, thought Jackson had simply showed up at the wrong practice site.

But Jackson and I clicked right away. Anyway, when I saw that headline in the morning paper, the idea of sharing it with Jackson was the first thing I thought of. I was bursting with pride and I knew he'd be just as happy for me as I was. He was already that kind of friend. I took a deep breath and just stared some more at the paper, which I'd brought to school:

COWBOYS' NEW KID OWNER
WHO IS RYAN ZINNA?

Kid owner. I turned the name over and over in my mouth like a gumdrop, savoring the sugar coating and finally sinking my teeth into its juicy sweet center. I was the kid owner. I only wished they'd had a picture of me.

My mom didn't seem to share my joy. She'd read the article at breakfast and then frowned her way through the rest of the meal as she opened her laptop and scrolled through whatever screens moms look at online.

"I mean, honestly." My mom offered Teresa a look as disgusted as her voice. "Don't adults have anything better to do than to post things about a twelve-year-old boy?"

Teresa shrugged as she emptied the dishwasher. "It's the Dallas Cowboys, Ms. Zinna. They *are* America's team."

I tried not to grin.

I checked my own phone and took a peek at my mom's Facebook page. Lots of people were saying a twelve-year-old would be an improvement on things. I guess I should have felt insulted for my father, but I couldn't help feeling nothing but excitement.

On the drive to school, my mom had lectured me.

"You treat people the same as always, Ryan. Don't let this go to your head." She wagged a finger at me. "You're just like everyone else. That's how I want you to be."

"Yeah, fine, Mom." I nodded like I got it, but I was really thinking: too late.

And when she dropped me off at the curb, it started.

A pretty, dark-haired brainiac named Mya Thompson was the first one to greet me. "Hey, Ryan."

"Ryan, how you doing?" asked Griffin Engle, our team's star running back.

"Ryan, awesome, man!" Estevan Marin, our backup QB said, giving me a fist bump. "Go, Cowboys, dude."

That's all good, but get this: people were taking *selfies* with me in the background. At first they tried to be cool about it; then people just came up to me and *asked*. I smiled as graciously as I could, soaking it up like a sponge as they slung their arms over my shoulders and clicked away.

But after walking the halls, pretending not to notice the whispers, I got to homeroom. Jackson was already sitting there, and I was just waiting for him to talk about it, but he was studying for a science quiz and all he said to me was "Hi."

"Hi? That's it?"

He looked up from his book and Margaret Vespers, the girl sitting next to him, nudged him and showed him her phone with what I can only imagine was the online version of the newspaper story. I watched his lips moving silently as he read. When he turned my way, I smiled and sat up straight. His deep-brown eyes widened with concern.

"Geez," he said, "I hope you're not gonna have to miss any practices."

"Jackson? *That's* all you have to say?" I folded my arms

across my chest. I lowered my voice. "I own the Dallas Cowboys, Jackson. Think about it . . ."

He scratched his head again and shrugged. "I guess."

"You guess what?" I looked around and dropped my voice even more, to a whisper, leaning his way because my classmates had suddenly become interested in me, and Margaret Vespers was staring with an open mouth. "You *guess* I own them? Don't guess. I *do* own them. You just read it."

"I guess it's good." He looked back down at his science notes.

"It's way more than good, Jackson. Do you *guess* you'd like to watch them play the New York Giants from the *sideline*? *That's* the kind of thing the owner can do. Me and you—and maybe Izzy, too—at every Cowboys home game!" I turned my attention to my science binder and hunched over my own notes, pretending to study, but seeing nothing but the Dallas Cowboys' sideline in my mind. Hanging out with John Torres, the big-time starting quarterback rumored to have dated Selena Gomez.

That silenced Jackson for a while, but after the morning announcements and before the bell ending homeroom, he closed his science notebook and turned to me. "Are you ready for the game this weekend? I heard Hutchinson has a really big fullback who ran all over people last season."

My mouth dropped open. "Jackson, seriously? Hutchinson? The Cowboys play New York this weekend and you and me are gonna be on the *sideline*. The Giants have got Rashad Jennings. Who cares about some seventh-grade fullback?"

The bell rang, and Jackson frowned and shrugged. "I'll

catch you later." He shouldered his backpack and left for his next class. The rest of the class was sneaking peaks at me, Ryan Zinna, kid owner.

I can't say I didn't revel in it. They stared the way I'd seen people looking at Deion Sanders one time when he was having dinner at the same restaurant my mom took me to on my eleventh birthday. I'll never forget it, the way *everyone* stole glances at Deion and his family, trying hard not to get caught doing it and offering up little apologetic smiles when they did.

I grabbed my stuff and headed down the hall to my next class. I was hoping to run into Izzy on my way, and when I looked up, I saw her close her locker door and turn toward me. I puffed out my chest and gave her a cool and casual thumbs-up.

"Hey, Ryan," Izzy said. She was a pretty girl, tall and athletic with long blond hair.

"Hey, Izzy." I smiled and waited for her next comment.

"How are you?"

I deflated, caught myself starting to slouch, then stood straight, remembering who I was. "That's it?"

She stopped and gave me a strange look. "What else is there?"

"Um, didn't you hear about the Cowboys?"

"Oh, yeah. Totally cool. Sorry. We've already got a quiz in math. Percentages. I hate percentages. I've gotta go but I'll see you at lunch. We can talk about it then." She waved and headed down the hall.

What was going on? Why would my only two friends be so thick about this? I shook it off, determined to proceed on course. Let them catch up. My plan was to let the whole thing sink in, see how people reacted, then make my move to influence the world around me: most importantly, my football team.

The morning went by in a blur. I could barely concentrate in my classes. But it was lunchtime now, and I walked as tall as I could into the lunchroom, past the band kids, who pointed and whispered among themselves. At the brainiacs' table, I caught Mya smiling my way and gave her a nod. The smart kids seemed as impressed if not as excited as the kids in the band. The kids at the two popular tables weren't all there yet, but the ones who were seemed to ignore me on purpose, aware of my presence but holding their heads at odd angles to intentionally avoid looking at me. A lot of the football players sat at the boys' popular table and the girls beside them would flutter back and forth during lunch like butterflies briefly touching down on a bed of flowers.

I huffed and kept going to our table, the one where me, Izzy, and Jackson sat like the Three Amigos or the Three Musketeers.

A WEEK EARLIER . . .

The school year hadn't started out that way. It had been just me and Jackson, and our table kind of felt like the Island of the Misfit Toys, but now that Izzy was with us, it felt like something different.

Izzy wasn't going to be the most popular girl in Ben Sauer Middle because, like Jackson, she was new to the area. Still, on the first day of school she'd been welcomed by Bethany Bracewell, who had red hair, real diamond earrings, and was the queen bee of the popular girls' table. I knew who Izzy was because she sat in the front of our English class with her blue eyes bright and long blond hair pulled back in a ponytail. She'd answered all the questions, speaking with the clear and melodic voice of a bird. She was rumored to be a star athlete on the soccer field, and proved herself faster than any of the boys on the first day of gym class. She chewed bubblegum constantly and had reminded me of a flamingo, exotic and graceful in her element, but a little awkward and out of proportion just walking the hallways.

On the second day of school, Izzy had walked right past Bethany Bracewell and the popular lunch table and sat down with us.

"Hi," she'd said, then began to unpack and eat her lunch, slurping her carton of milk from a straw and looking shyly at us both through the tops of her eyelashes.

After the shock wore off, I'd noticed the table of popular girls snatching glances and giggling, having a swell time over the joke of Izzy sitting with such an odd pair as me and Jackson. Izzy hadn't looked back, but since she hadn't said anything to us, and only sat quietly eating her lunch, I knew she had to be in on their joke. She'd done a great job of not joining in on the laughter, though.

It hurt to think that a girl like Izzy, who seemed so nice, would do something so mean. I don't know about you, but I'd rather have someone say something nasty to my face than pretend to like me but all the while it's just a joke or a dare someone put them up to.

I could just imagine Bethany Bracewell with her shiny braces and her snotty smile, saying, *Izzy, I dare you to go sit with Minna Zinna and that big ogre Jackson. Go ahead. Bet you can't sit there through the entire lunch period without cracking up!*

Hurt as it did, I was used to being made fun of, and Jackson really had no idea what was happening, so I'd decided the best strategy was to ignore it, ignore her, and let the whole thing pass.

But the next day, Izzy sat with us again. On the third day, I realized that Izzy sat with us because she'd wanted to. She didn't like the popular table. She'd said it was rude how they left other people out. She'd said she knew that Jackson was new also and she made me blush when she said I seemed nice. So we've been sitting together ever since.

PRESENT . . .

I made my way to the back and sat down at our table, pulled out my lunch, and took a big gulp of milk from my bottle. I looked around for Jackson, wondering why he was late. Just then, Izzy walked into the lunchroom. She waved at Mya but otherwise marched straight for our table like usual. I caught her eye and smiled, thinking I was happy to have her sit with us whether she made a big deal out of me being the kid owner or not. She was only one table away when I noticed that Bryan Markham was headed my way from the other side of the cafeteria. Bryan and Izzy arrived at the same moment. I kept my smile, wondering if this might not be the moment when Bryan invited me to the popular table, now that I owned the Dallas Cowboys.

I tried not to let my smile be too smug. I didn't plan on moving to the popular table unless Izzy and Jackson could come, too. On that I would insist.

"Hey, Izzy." Markham spoke to her in a tone I didn't like and I made a mental note to correct him when we were alone.

"Hey, Zinna." His voice was smooth and oily, but friendly.

I smiled up at him, though, enjoying the moment. "Hey, Markham."

Then he leaned close enough to whisper in my ear. "Listen, you little shrimp. I want you to know that I see you sitting here smiling like you own the world, but I don't care."

I looked up at him and blinked at the intensity of the hatred glaring from his face. What was happening? This was definitely *not* what I expected.

"We put the pads on today, shrimp," he continued, leaning so close now that I could feel his warm breath in my ear, "and I am gonna smash that stupid smile right off your face."

14

The rest of lunch I sat in silence. Izzy and Jackson didn't really talk to me much about the kid owner stuff—they were worried about our English test later in the day—and I couldn't muster up the strength to care. Bryan's reminder had me unsettled. He was right. Later that day we would put the pads on for the first time that season. All the kid owner excitement had allowed me to forget, but Bryan's reminder filled my bones with terror. And not even my kid owner status could make that go away. I really hadn't hit anyone yet in practice; so far, we'd only been able to run around in helmets and shorts. Even a team in Texas had to have a couple weeks of practices to get in shape before the real hitting could begin.

The armpits of my polo shirt were damp and ripe by the time the final school bell rang. The image of the Dallas Cowboys line waiting for my direction was nowhere to be found.

My breath came in short gasps and my head spun lightly as I pushed through the locker room door, to be struck in the face by the stench. Many of my teammates were already half geared up. Just the odor of the pads—even the new ones with their fresh, clean, plastic smell—made my stomach turn. There was Jackson, his locker right next to mine, already fully dressed.

A sheen of sweat glinted on Jackson's honey-colored face, outshone only by his grin. "Here we go, Little Man. The big dog's gonna eat today."

"What dog? Eat what?" I fumbled with the padlock on my locker, spinning the black dial back and forth and missing the numbers I needed to open it. I didn't mind Jackson calling me "Little Man" because I knew he meant it in the friendliest of ways. He'd called me that the day we met, when I had invited him back to swim in my pool after practice. We'd laughed so hard fooling around in the pool that he threw up the two bottles of red Gatorade he'd consumed, and we'd laughed even harder when we called it the red tide.

Jackson chuckled. "Me. I'm the big dog. Gonna eat today. Pads on."

"Oh. Yeah." I finally got it right and the lock clicked open. I took out my own gear—tiny next to Jackson's—and began to pull it on.

Jackson just sat and continued to chuckle, delighted with the state of the world and himself.

"Can you get your big butt out of the way?" I nudged him with my own skinny rump so I could sit and tug on my padded pants.

"Oh, you got that fire in your eyes, Little Man. You're gonna eat, too, huh?"

"Eat?" I spat the word with disgust. "How about you eat a booger?"

I wanted to be grumpy in case Jackson ended up hating me by the end of the day, but he just laughed and slapped my shoulder pad so hard my arm went numb. He still didn't get that I was scared to death.

"I'll see you out there, Little Man. You're gonna bring the sting, I bet. It's not the size of the dog in the fight, it's the size of the *fight* in the *dog*. I know you got that bite, bet you're gonna make people bark."

I hated that Jackson was so excited for hitting, hungry for it, and I muttered to myself so no one else could possibly hear as I trembled and sweat and finished putting on my gear. "Dogs and bites? *Little* man? You big *doofus*."

If I wasn't so scared, I'd have been raving mad. But I was terrified because Coach Hubbard and his assistant, Coach Vickerson, might not be as understanding as my youth-league coaches had been about my yellow streak. My seventh-grade coaches were a little over the top. Coach Vickerson couldn't utter a complete sentence without flecks of spit flying from his mouth like buckshot. And Coach Hubbard got so excited his face turned different colors. He would actually burst little blood vessels in his cheeks, where they'd lie like tiny little red worms on the surface of his skin. Not only could I be sure they wouldn't allow me to avoid the contact drills, I suspected they might *demand* I participate.

After all, one of Coach Vickerson's favorite things to growl:

"You're only as strong as your *weakest* link, boys!"

The locker room emptied and finally, I had all my equipment on. I'd run out of excuses to delay the inevitable. I marched out of the locker room, the last to arrive on the field. Coach Hubbard gave his whistle a blast and we took off on a warm-up lap, stretched, and ran through agilities. All the while, I kept my eye out for Bryan, hoping maybe he'd forgotten about his lunchroom promise.

In the line for the shuffle run, I heard a strange noise behind me. I turned and looked and saw Jackson's sweaty face beaming like a stoplight. He shook and jiggled, laughing to himself with great delight.

"*What* are you laughing at?" I was furious.

"Hittin', hittin', hittin'," he said. "It's on."

And then he began laughing to himself again. "Jackson, what—"

"All right, get in here!" Coach Hubbard called. "Circle up. We're gonna do bull in the ring."

The team launched into screams of excitement, and Bryan Markham dashed out into the middle of the ring without even being told.

Coach Vickerson grinned. "Now *that's* a leader."

"Yeah! You *want* to hit, don't you, Markham?" Coach Hubbard slapped Markham on the shoulder pad and blasted his whistle. "Get those feet going!"

We all chopped our feet. Coach Hubbard called out numbers, and one by one my teammates broke from the circle, bolted at Markham, and received their punishment. Markham was having a swell time, and I began to think that just maybe my youth-league coaches had given Coach Hubbard a heads-up about me. Maybe Hubbard would let me slide.

Jackson, on the other hand, waved his hands and jumped up and down—which looked ridiculous as he chopped his feet in place—and grunted like he needed to use the bathroom. "Ooo. Ooo. Ooo. Me, Coach. Me. Ooo. Ooo. Ooo."

Finally, Coach Hubbard barked out his number and Jackson took off for Markham.

Jackson roared as he accelerated toward Markham, and when he hit, it was terrifying. In fact, Jackson didn't hit Markham as much as he went *through* him. Markham's body flew into the air. His feet flailed. His arms pinwheeled. He landed on his back with a thud and a bark of pain. Jackson laughed like a total maniac. He loved it. Hubbard loved it. Vickerson loved it. Everyone loved it.

Only I was horrified, but that horror was nothing compared to what happened next.

Laughing, Hubbard barked out, "Twenty-three!"

I looked around as I chopped my feet. Everyone stared at me. I looked down at my own jersey because in my fright I'd lost all sense of time and place.

I was number twenty-three.

"Twenty-three!" Coach Vickerson shouted.

"Twenty-three. Twenty-three!" Hubbard screamed.

I didn't move. I couldn't. Jackson was slobbering with delight, chopping his feet in the middle of the ring, motioning to me to have at him . . . or try.

"Come on, Zinna!" Coach Hubbard's face was purple. "Get

60

your mind back into your team. Now! I said *twenty-three*, that's *you*!"

And still I stood, my mind flooded with all the excuses I could use when I quit the team. Maybe the fact that I was kid owner of the Cowboys would be the only excuse I needed.

Then the unthinkable happened. As I chopped in place, stuck in my spot, Jackson took off, running straight at me, a charging bull elephant, with his pads lowered.

I closed my eyes.

Jackson hit me so hard, I really didn't feel it. I actually didn't feel anything. I was simply airborne, floating, until the ground punched me from head to toe with its infinite fist.

Jackson burst into laughter and immediately held out a hand to help me up. "Get up, Ryan. Come on! You gotta hit me."

"I . . . I . . ." All I could do was take his hand and allow him to yank me upright.

"You can't just stand there, little buddy." Jackson talked like it was just the two of us, but the entire team was watching and listening.

In that moment, I realized I owned the Dallas Cowboys and Jackson was making me look like a fool.

"Stupid!" I screamed.

"Hey." Jackson took a step back.

I shoved him. He stumbled, then recovered. I crashed into

him with all my might, bouncing back as if from a boulder, but he stumbled again and I went at him, smashing him with my shoulder, head, and hands.

"Stupid! Stupid! Stupid!" I pummeled and screamed, screamed and pummeled. I was out of my mind. Jackson was hitting me back now. Recoiling and crashing into me. Our pads popped and our metal face masks clanged. We were like two stags clashing horns.

Suddenly, there was a blizzard of whistles and both coaches were on us, pulling, pushing, and shoving us apart.

"Okay, okay, okay!" Coach Hubbard huffed. "Now *that's* hitting. *That's* how we play this game."

Jackson and I stood breathless, glaring at each other.

"Boys," Coach Vickerson announced, looking around with this wise and serious face, "dancing is a contact sport. Football is a *collision* sport."

"Okay," Coach Hubbard barked, "linemen with Coach Vickerson, skill players with me for individuals. Hit hard and often today, boys. Hard and often."

Coach blew his whistle and the group fell apart, big hogs going one way, the smaller, more athletic group going the other. I turned but was yanked back around by the arm only to see Jackson's big, shiny, grinning face squeezed into his helmet.

"Hey, Ry. You okay?"

"I just . . ." I faltered for a moment. "I've never really *hit* like that before. You were so hyped up about it that you didn't even care about the Cowboys, and I was, like, nervous."

"Ry, it's gonna be fine. Hey, you recovered, didn't you? You hit—hard!"

"Just because I got so mad at you for talking to me like I was an idiot."

"I was only trying to help, Ry." I knew by Jackson's face that he meant it.

"Well . . . thanks."

"You were great. Keep it up." Jackson slapped me on the shoulder pad. Best friends again, and I realized that in his mind, we never stopped being best friends, not for a single instant. In fact, it hit me that what he did was not make me look like a fool, but save me, not just from never being a real football player—a player in a sport I truly loved—but from being a wimp for the rest of my life, off the field as well as on.

"Hope I didn't hurt you." I mustered as much bravado as I possibly could.

"Ha-ha! That's it!" He winked and smacked me again and turned his gleeful face toward the rest of the linemen, jogging up toward the rear of the pack, a dog ready to dig into a pile of bones.

As I loped along on an easy jog with Coach Hubbard and the other skill players, my feet barely touched the grass. I floated to the next drill. When Coach Hubbard growled and snorted and pointed to a narrow swatch of grass between two lines of cones and shouted, "Oklahoma, boys!" I jumped right out there in the middle of the drill along with two fellow defenders. Three other players took up their position in an opposing triangle facing us, the one in the back accepting the football Coach Hubbard flipped to him.

I was at the rear of my triangle with two thick running backs in front of me. Facing us were two wide receivers and Jason

Simpkin, starting quarterback and all-around meanie. In fact, while Simpkin had tolerated me as one of the kids in the neighborhood growing up, over the past several years it seemed his disgust with me had grown with every inch he put on his own frame, and he'd grown pretty tall. And I'm sure the news about me and the Dallas Cowboys wasn't going to help our friendship.

Now Simpkin leered at me with a mocking smile and slapped the ball he held tucked into his other arm before doing the same to the side of his helmet like some kind of mad ape. I smiled right back because I knew the secret now. The secret was that if you *hit* someone with football pads on, it was nothing like *being hit*. Even smashing into a behemoth like Jackson hadn't really hurt, and even if it did, it was counterbalanced by the thrill of hitting him as well.

My hands shook, not with fear but rage, as I bent my knees and crouched into a position where I might blast up through that stupid smirk behind Simpkin's face mask. Before I had time to think anything else, Coach blew the whistle. The four players in front crashed like cymbals, shivering with noise. Simpkin faked one way, then launched himself into the small seam between his blockers.

I attacked, head low, barreling my shoulder into his midriff, driving my legs as I exploded up through him, wrapping my arms as I'd so ineffectively done to blocking dummies the past three years but never to a live person. Simpkin went up into the air and then screwed sideways into the dirt with me on top of him.

Coach blew his whistle. As I started to rise, Simpkin gave me a cheap shove.

All I did was laugh.

He could shove all he wanted.

He could call me names.

None of it mattered because every time I had the chance to smash him or anyone else on the football field, that's exactly what I intended to do.

As excited as I'd been about suddenly owning the Dallas Cowboys, this may have been even better.

Because I was finally a football player.

Even though it was a new beginning for me, if I was going to be a real football player instead of just pretending, the position I *really* wanted to play was quarterback. I mean, quarterbacks are the ones who get all the glory. Also, I knew I was never going to be one of the bigger guys on the field, and players like Drew Brees and Russell Wilson gave me hope that I could still play a key spot on the team.

My best assets as an athlete were my smarts and my speed. Some guys who get As in school aren't always the ones who are football smart. Football IQ is more than just knowing your favorite NFL teams' and players' stats. It's about knowing the strategy of the game and, even more important than that, being able to make the right decisions *fast*. A quarterback has to see all other twenty-one players on the field (his teammates as well as his opponents) and make sense out of the mishmash of bodies.

He has to see a pattern, to know what will happen next, and how he can alter that pattern since he's the one with the ball.

So, suddenly feeling like a real football player and armed with the new title of Kid Owner, I announced to Coach Hubbard during our first water break that I'd like to switch from receiver to the quarterback position.

"Yeah, sure, Ryan." Coach Hubbard barely gave me a glance. "You'll be behind Jason and Estevan, though. I can't promise you many reps."

My face burned when Simpkin snickered my way.

So, while Coach Hubbard tolerated me calling myself a QB and let me throw passes and give handoffs during the individual periods, he didn't give me a single chance during any of the meaningful drills for the rest of practice. I wanted to scream at him. I knew this was the position for me. And I *owned* the Dallas Cowboys; shouldn't that count for something?

When it was time for the offense to play scout team for the defense, Coach Hubbard told me I really should take some turns at wide receiver. "That's probably where you're gonna end up anyway, Zinna. I think it's gonna be tough for you to see over the line to throw a pass."

So, even though my outlook had changed entirely and I suddenly saw myself as a very capable football player, it was obvious that because of my size Coach Hubbard regarded me as not much more than a movable tackling dummy. But I wasn't going to accept that.

I ran my routes hard and fast on scout team offense and banged into defenders as best I could on the running plays. When I played free safety on the defensive scout team, I threw my body around like a missile. Bryan Markham never got his chance to wipe any smile off my face, because I'd already replaced it with a snarl. When we ran sprints at the end of practice, even though I was dog tired, I finished first in almost every one of them, second only a couple times to Jackson.

It wasn't perfect, but it was a good beginning.

I was done with being pushed around. I wasn't going to be anyone's dupe again. I was suddenly strong and confident, and I intended to be that way in everything I did. I'd soon learn that sometimes that attitude can get you into serious trouble.

When I got home that night, my mom listened as I excitedly told her about football practice and how well I did. I could tell something was on her mind, though, and when I finally finished, beaming at her, she said, "That's great, honey. Can I talk to you about something?"

"What?" I set my hamburger down without taking a bite. "Is something wrong?" The two of us sat at the kitchen table with Teresa at work quietly cleaning up.

"Don't worry, it's not that big a deal." She tried to play it off, but that made me worry even more because I could tell it was a big deal. "It's just that I'm going to be telling the media that you're not available for comment."

I stared at her, confused. "Wait, what media?"

"Well, after the article in the paper this morning, the phone's been ringing off the hook." She took a small bite of a pickle.

"And didn't you notice the local news van parked down the street? I even heard from your principal, saying the school had gotten calls about you. So I talked to a PR firm and they said the best way to handle these things is to tell the reporters no interviews, let things settle down, and then have a press conference to defuse everything."

"Press conference? What do you mean 'defuse'?"

"That way they'll leave you alone. We can work through the team's PR department to set it up. Mr. Dietrich wants you to go out there anyway to meet everyone, but not for a bit." She nodded and took a big sour crunching bite. "There's no hurry. The lawyers need another week to make the whole thing official anyway."

I shrugged. "Okay, whatever you say." I wasn't going to argue with my mom about it. As long as she wasn't trying to sink the whole kid owner thing, I didn't care too much about the media. Everybody in my world already knew about it.

We had a pretty regular night after that. After I finished my homework, my mom let me play Xbox for an hour before it was time to read and get some sleep. As I lay in bed, thoughts swirled in my head. It was weird—I was finally a real football player, hitting and making plays on the field. Part of me still wished my father could have seen me, could have known that I was that kind of a kid. It seemed fitting that he should have left the Dallas Cowboys to a kid who was a real football player. That was me now.

I fell asleep to visions of me playing on the Cowboys' field with Jackson and Izzy watching me from the sideline.

* * *

The next day, I was walking even more proud than the day before. I went to my classes in the morning, then strutted into the lunchroom and marched right past the popular table, pretending to ignore them completely.

The problem was that I didn't ignore them. I heard when Bryan Markham belched and told the rest of the table, "Minna Zinna thinks he's tough now. He's so tough he's got a *girl* at his table."

The rest of them chuckled and when I glanced over my shoulder, they were waiting. Markham pointed right at me. Jason Simpkin howled with delight, and the rest of them burst into an uproar of laughter. My ears burned as I approached my table. Izzy and Jackson were both already there.

"What's so funny over there?" Jackson was as innocent as he was ignorant in his question.

I was so mad, I didn't even think about my answer. "They're just a bunch of little giggling girls."

"Hey." Izzy set down her sandwich. "I'm a girl."

I looked at her and saw she was only kidding, but the laughter from the other table was hot in my ears and what Markham said did make sense to me. I mean, the popular boys didn't let the girls sit with them. They were too cool for that. But here I was, desperate for any kind of friend. This all hit me in a millisecond, and it also hit me that everything was getting ready to change for me and I didn't feel as grateful as I should have that Izzy was my friend.

So, my mouth ran away from my brain and spit out some words on its own. "Yeah, I know you're a girl, Izzy. Maybe you should find a girls' table to sit at. This table is for *football* players."

Jackson's mouth dropped open in shock. Izzy's mouth became a thin flat line.

"You, Ryan Zinna, are a jerk." With a curt nod, she packed her lunch back into her bag, got up, and left.

"Hey, little buddy." Jackson frowned. "What'd you do that for? She's really nice."

"We're *football players*, Jackson." I glared at him, strong and confident. "Don't you think we should act like some?"

Jackson's face grew dark and he stared right back, unafraid of me. "I think we should act like football players on the football field, Ryan. Otherwise I think we shouldn't act like total jerks."

Jackson and I stared each other down. I felt like I had to show him that I wasn't afraid, and I had no idea which one of us would blink first. But as we gave each other the evil eye, my bigger concern became losing the only real friend I had left.

I cast my eyes down at my hands and folded them on the table. "Sorry, Jackson. I'm going goofy. With everything that's happened, it's like I don't even know who I am. Does that make sense?"

I looked up and Jackson was back to himself in a heartbeat. He shrugged and sipped at his milk. "That's okay, but maybe you should say something to Izzy?"

I looked over at where Izzy had sat down next to Mya at the table of brainiacs, deeply regretting my words to her. "Yeah, I'll try. Let her cool off first, though."

As impressive as Jackson was on the football field, he was an even better friend. He didn't hold a grudge and he didn't miss a beat. We were soon goofing around, eating and talking about how funny it would be if we walked over to the popular table, stuck our fingers down our throats, and threw up.

"We could, like, shower them with puke!" Jackson's eyes became nothing but slits, and his teeth were bare and white as he howled with laughter.

I couldn't help but think I'd really like to do that to Markham.

On the football field that afternoon, I was like a pinball, smacking people in every direction. I wasn't necessarily knocking them down like Jackson did, but I was stinging them so that pretty quickly I became an annoyance a lot of my other teammates were happy to avoid. Only Markham really delighted in colliding with me, and he got the best of me. When you're the size of Markham or Jackson, you win almost every one of those football battles against a smaller guy. But I shy away. I walked off the practice field that day with a golf-ball-size welt on my forearm, three bloody knuckles, a sore back, and an aching head.

"Nice effort out there, Zinna." Coach Hubbard slapped my shoulder pads as we walked toward the locker room. "I wish you weren't such a peanut or you could play strong safety or something."

I glared at my coach, but he never even saw me. He marched on, handing out compliments to my teammates like they were Halloween candy. All the joy I'd had running around during practice smashing into people suddenly melted away. I clenched my teeth and my hands and felt a steady burn in my head and chest. *A peanut?*

Just like that—snap—I felt like a loser. Funny how an offhand remark by a grown-up can do that to a kid, but I think it happens more than people know. I mean, he didn't even say it to be mean, but there it was, a crater in my soul.

I changed my clothes in silence, ignoring Jackson's cheery remarks about our opening game against Hutchinson Middle, an opponent everyone figured we could beat, and slammed my locker shut before heading for the exit.

"Hey, wait up." Jackson fumbled with his book bag. "We're gonna go swimming at your house, right?"

"That's the plan," I said.

Jackson grinned at me and when he did, his bag tipped. Books and papers slipped to the floor in a mess.

I had to catch myself from calling him a bumbling bear, control my short fuse, and not insult him the way people seemed to feel they could insult me.

I'd acted like a jerk once already to Izzy and I wasn't going to do it again. Instead, I waited silently, holding the locker room door for Jackson, which had the negative effect of clearing the way for Simpkin and Markham, who strutted past.

"Hey, Zinna, at least you're good for something," Markham said. Simpkin smirked next to him as they bumped me on their way out the door.

"You're the jerks," I said beneath my breath.

Markham spun around, his faced twisted up hatefully. "What'd you say?"

"I said, 'I'm glad this works.'" I stared right back at him, the new me, unafraid. Sort of. "Me. Holding the door. I'm glad it works for you."

Markham gave Simpkin a puzzled look before he turned and kept going. Jackson caught up, out of breath. "Thanks."

"Might as well be good for something, right?" I grumbled.

"Hey, you're running around like a maniac out there. You're doing good." Jackson slapped my back, too hard.

"You see how many reps I got at quarterback?" I asked. "Three. One during team period and two during our seven-on-seven drill."

"That's three times more than one, right?" Jackson forced a smile and gave me a hearty nod.

"You see how many times we had to run that bootleg pass?" I asked. "I could've done that right the very first time. Simpkin can't read on the run. You gotta key on the free safety. If he's over the top, you throw to the tight end on the crossing pattern. If he jumps the crossing pattern, you throw deep. It's not that tough. Quarterback is about brains, not brawn."

I looked around to make sure no one could hear me. "I swear, Coach Hubbard can be so thick sometimes."

"I wondered why we kept running that play," Jackson said.

"Because Simpkin can't get it right, and I'm a half . . ."

"Half what?" Jackson wrinkled his brow.

"Nothing." I wasn't going to call myself a half-pint shrimp like some kids did. Instead, I looked at my feet and scuffed them as we went out through the back entrance of the school to where my mom would be picking us up.

When I looked up, I saw Izzy's shiny golden ponytail. She'd come out of the girls' locker room and was still dressed in her soccer uniform with grass stains on her shorts and the backs of her long, pale legs. I didn't even warn Jackson, and I didn't care who else saw me, I just bolted right for her, grabbed her arm as gently as I could, and darted directly in front of her with a half spin sort of dance move that left us face-to-face.

"Hey, Izzy. I'm sorry." I spoke the way a woodpecker attacks a tree. "Like, really, really sorry. I know you said I'm a jerk, but I'm not. I *acted* like a jerk, but I'm *not* a jerk. Markham and Simpkin and all of them were making fun of us for sitting with a girl and then I called them girls because I was so mad and . . . stupid. Please. Sit with us at lunch tomorrow, Izzy. Let me have another chance."

She looked down at me in total surprise—more surprise than when I'd insulted her out of nowhere—but then she recovered and her face turned dark.

"Please." I spoke in a sad and urgent whisper and closed my eyes, waiting and hoping.

"You're really sorry?" she asked.

I opened my eyes, wanting to read her face. Her voice didn't sound too forgiving. "Yes. I am."

"What would you do for me?" Her blue eyes were cold and hard and squinty.

"Uh, anything?" My mind whirred. "I guess."

"Read a book?"

"A . . . sure. That's easy," I said, relieved and confused at the same time.

She fished into her book bag and pulled out the book I'd seen her reading before English class. "I finished this in the locker room before practice. Here. Read it, then we'll talk."

I took the baby-blue book from her and she marched right on by. I stood and stared. "Talk in lunch tomorrow?"

"Sure." She hollered without turning around. "Can you read that fast?"

"Sure!" I shouted, grinning at Jackson, who caught up to me just as Izzy disappeared into the passenger seat of her mom's dark-blue Range Rover.

"Dude, she's kinda pretty." Jackson stared at the Range Rover as it pulled away.

"Better than that," I said. "I think she's really nice."

"That's what *I* said," Jackson pointed out.

"Great minds think alike." I studied the cover of the book, which was called *Wonder*, and saw that the childlike drawing of the face on the cover had just one eye and it was out of place. "Weird."

"Now I'm weird?" Jackson growled.

"No, not you." I stuffed the book in my own bag. "If anyone's weird, it's me. Come on. There's my mom."

Jackson was seriously disappointed with me when we got to my house. He splashed and dove and flopped around the pool, hooting joyfully and making all kinds of noise. The neighbors probably thought we were having a party. But nothing could get me out of my chair in the shade of the cabana. I sat glued to that book, ate dinner with Jackson and my mom, and jumped right back into it, barely saying good-bye to Jackson when his own mom came later to get him. It's true when I say that I didn't read the whole thing that night just because of Izzy. I could have easily faked it, right?

But this book *got* me.

I wasn't exactly sure how I felt about it either. It's the story of a kid who is seriously deformed. People see this kid and literally run or scream or both. He's just like me or you, but he's trapped inside this really bad face. Fortunately, he's got these awesome people around him who don't *care* what he looks like, and by the end of the book, everyone *loves* this kid. Not because he got some life-altering surgery, but just because people started seeing him for *him*. *Who* he was, instead of what he *looked* like.

It's pretty extreme, and the reason I didn't know what to think was because I wasn't so sure who *I* was supposed to be in that story. And the more I thought about it, the more I realized that we've all got something, some disfiguration—inside or out—that sets us apart from others. I mean, who's "normal"? Anyone? Is never knowing who your dad was "normal"? Don't think so, even though a lot of kids *don't* know their fathers. And, trust me, even suddenly inheriting the Dallas Cowboys doesn't make up for that hot mess.

Izzy wasn't trying to say we were necessarily freaks, me and Jackson, but that we were different. I think she was saying that it was okay to have a friend who was different and to sit at their lunch table instead of the popular kids'. Well, that's what I thought about when I closed that book and sat propped up on my pillows, all alone, the lights now off, and me staring out the window at some tattered ghosts of clouds as they drifted past half a moon peeking down from the trees.

It was hard to get to sleep . . . again. This was becoming a habit. But tonight, my heart thumped steadily up against my ribs, and I kept thinking about the lunchroom tomorrow, and the things I planned on saying to Izzy about the book.

I headed for my cafeteria table the next day, slicing straight through the roar of noise. In a way, it was like being alone. I didn't care about the hundreds of other kids, their antics, their food, the insults they served back and forth at one another like Ping-Pong balls. I saw only Izzy, head bowed, quietly unwrapping a peanut butter and jelly sandwich, freeing it from its plastic wrapping and taking the smallest of bites before sipping at her milk through a straw.

Jackson was nowhere to be seen—late, I assumed, since he had a math teacher who liked to keep them after the bell about every other day. I stood beside her without speaking until she looked up and smiled and offered me the chair next to her. I had to believe the popular kids were looking on, hopeful for some more fireworks. I sat down and started to eat my lunch, doing my best to mimic Izzy's finer manners.

She took another bite and then a sip before dabbing her mouth on a napkin she produced from her *lap*. "So?"

I cleared my throat. "Yes. I read it. All of it."

"And?"

I had to look at her, even though those eyes turned my insides to jelly. "Are you saying I'm Austin?"

She stared at me with those big eyes. Hypnotized, I couldn't move.

Her face erupted into a smile. "Aren't we all Austin?"

Relief flooded through my body. The tension drained through my feet. I nodded.

"I was thinking more Jason than Austin, though," she said, and now I warmed with pride and something else because Jason's character was pretty awesome, even though he started out not so great.

Was she saying that about me? I didn't dare to ask. I just soaked it up until Jackson walloped me on the back.

"Dude, it's *her*." Jackson beamed with joy, nodding at Izzy.

"She has a name," Izzy said, but not meanly.

"I told Izzy I was really sorry for being a jerk," I said, "and I finished this book she gave me to read last night. I think she's—you are, right?—sitting with us again?"

"Watch out." Jackson sat down heavily and started emptying his big bag of food onto the table in front of him. "*This* will be the popular table before you know it. Then *I'll* have to leave."

Izzy laughed and dabbed her mouth with the napkin, then suddenly stopped and stared over my shoulder. I turned around and saw Bethany Bracewell standing there with her diamond earrings glinting and her freckled arms folded across her chest, staring down in disgust. "Izzy, don't even *think* you're coming back to our table again."

I looked back at Izzy and watched the surprise on her face turn to something else. This time she didn't dab her mouth, she just laughed out loud at Bethany and her stupid lunch table. I held out my fist and Izzy gave it a bump.

"Do you like football?" I asked.

"Not at all." She shook her head, still grinning.

"Well, you'll have to start liking it, because this is the . . ." I pulled the first thing that came to mind out of my head. ". . . football superstars table."

"This is the *sports* superstars table." She stuck a thumb into her chest. "And *I'm* the best athlete we've got."

I looked at Jackson to see what he thought of that, but all he did was nod.

"I was kidding," she said. "Not about being the best athlete part, but about football. I love football, especially the Cowboys, and not just because you own them."

"Finally, you say something about it! I've been waiting for you guys to talk about me owning the team." I grinned.

Izzy shrugged. "It's cool and all, but what does it mean? What's even happening?"

I gave them a recap of when I found out about my dad, of the will reading, and how my mom was trying to schedule a press conference. "It's really still all with the lawyers to get things worked out. At least, that's what my mom says."

"I'm sorry about your dad," Izzy said.

"Yeah, me too." Jackson paused, then said, "So what changes

can you make, you know, to the team or players and all?"

"Oh, I don't know! I haven't even thought about it!"

"Well, don't you think you should?" Jackson laughed.

And as we started talking about which players were good, we moved on to the ten all-time greatest players in a friendly argument that took us to the bell. We got up and moved through the halls together, ignoring the rest of the world. It felt good to have our own small group, just like the three best friends in Izzy's book.

At practice later that day, we headed out onto the field and Coach Hubbard divided us up, telling me I should go with the wide receivers during passing drills. It frustrated me that the fact that I was the kid owner of the Dallas Cowboys didn't seem to have any impact on him. He wasn't treating me that much better than before and I wondered if he somehow might not have heard the news. It didn't seem possible. He was probably just being a football coach, focused on coaching our middle-school team. That's how they were, especially in Texas.

But now I hesitated, fearful that the change back to receiver was going to be permanent. "Coach, I'm really good with reading defenses and stuff. You might need me at QB when things get going."

"Get going?" Simpkin muttered under his breath, even though he kept throwing the football back and forth to Estevan Marin. "Take a walk, shrimp."

I looked hard at Coach Hubbard, pleading with my eyes because I knew my hands weren't much to talk about, small and hard as stones. Even the passes I got during warm-ups with other quarterbacks seemed to bounce off my hands. It was all I could do to take the snap, make a handoff to a runner, or throw a pass that didn't wobble. Catching wasn't in it for me.

"Well . . ." Coach Hubbard seemed to be thinking about it.

"Zinna, seriously? You don't question the coach!" Simpkin stopped throwing and stared at me, faking outrage and taking a step toward me as if to emphasize my lack of height. "Ever! Part of being a quarterback is calling the play you get. You don't argue when a coach tells you something. What, you think you're special 'cause you supposedly own the Cowboys? Please, that means nothing here."

Coach Hubbard scowled and looked confused before he said, "That's right! Get going, Zinna, or would you rather run a lap?"

At that moment, I wished I were Jackson. If I were, I would have pummeled Simpkin into the dirt. Instead, I just narrowed my eyes at Simpkin, turned, and jogged over to where the receivers were, a place I knew I shouldn't be.

Practices went like this for the next two weeks. And even though I was frustrated, I was still happy to be practicing out on the field. But, while I was pretty pumped up about that for the first few days of practice, wearing the bruises and cuts on my arms and hands like badges of courage around school, the pride and joy didn't last.

Now I wanted to *play*. What real football player doesn't? Practice isn't the fun part of the sport. Playing is. I got to ride the bench for the first game against Hutchinson and I began to wonder if I wasn't happier before, the way it was in youth football, hiding from contact and comfortably planted on the end of the bench without any thought of entering a game. Now, it killed me to "ride the pine." Especially since my new best friend was a monster on the field. When we needed a big play on defense, Jackson burst through our opponent's line like a bull elephant snapping twigs and slamming either a runner or a quarterback to the turf. On offense, if we needed a critical yard for a first down or on the goal line, everyone knew they'd run the ball right behind Jackson.

On one touchdown, Simpkin actually grabbed hold of the back of Jackson's jersey and got dragged across the goal line over and through a pile of defensive bodies. Simpkin spun the ball on the ground and held up a single finger like he was the hero of the day. It made me want to barf. Meanwhile, Jackson chugged right on back to the sideline for some water and a breath of air without bothering to celebrate. It was all business with Jackson.

He was amazing.

I was miserable.

Jackson and Izzy felt for me, and invented reasons for the injustice of it all. "They just don't get it." "Hubbard is a numb-skull." "Simpkin is a butt-kisser."

Bottom line, I didn't fit the profile of a quarterback and my hands weren't getting any better at catching the ball. I was too small to play anywhere else on the field. On defense, I was a hitter, but too short to be effective as a defensive back and too light to play on the line or at linebacker.

Even I saw that.

The only one who didn't mind any of this was my mom. She loved seeing me dressed in my uniform, popping pads during warm-ups for the Hutchinson game like a real football player but safe from any of the live action, where she fretted over the bodies that got helped off the field.

"You don't want to be one of *them*." She patted my leg as we drove home from the game. I looked at her hand making small circles on my leg, wanting to bite it so she'd stop trying to comfort me.

"I want to *play*, Mom. That's the point." I huffed and looked out the window.

"Your friend Izzy doesn't seem to mind whether you play or not." My mom said in a singsong voice like a songbird in spring and gave me a wink.

"Izzy could probably get more playing time than me . . . if they allowed girls." I banged my head against the window.

"She's cute." My mom tilted her head as if she hadn't heard a word I said.

"Mom, I don't care about that. I want to *play*."

"I think your coaches know their business, Ryan. There's nothing wrong with being a little undersized. A lot of great people are undersized."

I hated when she talked like that. "Whatever," I mumbled.

"Look at everything we have," she continued. "There are a lot of people who wished they lived like you." She shot a frown my way.

I wasn't sure if she meant because I owned the Cowboys or just other stuff, but neither mattered when you weren't where you wanted to be on a sports team. "Yeah, I know," I mumbled. I shrugged and sulked the rest of the way home. When we pulled through the gates, my mother gasped.

I looked up and got a shot of total excitement.

My mom said, "Oh, no."

In my mind, I said, "Oh, *yes!*"

The guy wasn't anything special. His hair was a little too long. His shirt was untucked. He had a California-wild-but-handsome kind of look, but it was the camera that excited me. It was one of those small digital video cameras with a bold little flag on it that read TMZ.

I had to try hard not to laugh out loud. This was just what I needed to pick up my spirits, a little publicity.

"You sit here." My mom's command was like a thunderclap and I froze.

She flew out of the truck and went right at the guy. I could hear her yelling through the windshield. It wasn't pretty, but needless to say, she went up one side of that kid and down the other.

"You get that camera out of my face, mister. This is private property and you are trespassing. You want to stay out of jail?

This video better not see the light of day. Your boss isn't going to be happy when TMZ is the only outfit *banned* from the press conference, so you just get back in your truck and get out of here. Go!"

The guy gave her a casual smile, but his eyes flickered like someone had tickled him with an electric shock and he got in his truck and drove away pretty fast. My mom watched him, then looked at me and shrugged, motioning to me that I could get out.

"What a rat," she said.

"Why, Mom? Why can't I be on TV? Just a little?"

"Because you're twelve years old." Her face turned to stone again. "And I'm your mother. And if I can't stop this whole thing, I can at least protect you from the worst of it, Ryan. You'll understand when you're older."

I hated that line, but she softened the situation a little by suggesting that we go to the new X-Men movie and that I invite Izzy and Jackson over tomorrow to watch the Cowboys game.

The Cowboys opened their season the next day in Chicago. I'd wanted to go, but because things weren't legally final yet, my mom wanted me to stay home. But Izzy and Jackson came over to watch on our big-screen TV, which was the next best thing. My mom didn't even come inside to check on the score. Instead, she sat by the pool, getting some sun and reading her book. That made me mad, but I kept my cool because I wanted to enjoy the game. I was rewarded when Kenny Albert, the Fox announcer, mentioned me as the new kid owner and said how everyone was waiting for my press conference. I felt like I was ten feet tall.

"Hey, they're talking about you!" Jackson shouted, spraying pretzel crumbs across the couch. "No way, man!"

I looked at Izzy. She bit her lip and gave me a nod to let me know she'd heard them mention my name on TV. I didn't know why she couldn't be more happy than that, but obviously I had no idea what made girls tick. The moment passed and we went back to rooting hard, and I got annoyed whenever the Cowboys made a bad play.

"Fusco's gotta catch that ball!" I growled when the linebacker missed an easy interception that would have kept the Bears out of the end zone. Instead, I had to watch Martellus Bennett do his orange dinosaur dance.

"You can cut him in a few weeks if you want!" Jackson's excitement was contagious. He was giddy with the power I might have.

"You gotta be fair, though, Ryan." Izzy nodded seriously, which I loved. "You can't just go cutting guys for one bad play.

Mark Fusco makes that catch nine out of ten times."

"I will." It was a thrilling promise to make.

I was taking the whole thing personally. That's how it's supposed to be, right? And sometimes I even forgot I *owned* the team. I was just rooting as a fan. It was thrilling, too, because they had the lead most of the game.

It was in the fourth quarter when things started to get close. Then, with only a minute to go, they dropped behind because of a Bears field goal. My stomach knotted up as the offense took the field. When John Torres dropped back, even I saw the blitz coming.

"Throw it!" I shouted, shocking my friends.

Torres didn't throw it. He got sacked and fumbled. After a very painful minute of pulling bodies off the pile, a Bears player emerged with the ball, holding it high like the prize it was. The referee signaled first down for the Bears and their offense danced out onto the field to kneel on the ball and run out the clock. That's when the announcers started talking about how the Cowboys' Coach Cowan hadn't lived up to expectations in the previous two seasons and that if he couldn't get them to the play-offs, this might be his last. They also talked about what a new owner might mean for all that. I waited on the edge of my seat to have them drop my name again, but they never did.

"They talked about me like I wasn't even a person!"

"Well, when the time comes," Jackson said, looking uncomfortable, "you're gonna have to get rid of someone. That you know, right? That's what everyone is grousing about. They're acting like it's your fault and you haven't even had your hands on the controls yet."

"My father did, though." It was beyond strange to be so closely associated with a man I'd never even met.

"When is that press conference your mom set up?" Izzy asked.

"She wants to wait until the deal is final. There's all this paperwork, court stuff, or something crazy like that. Once I do, though, Jackson's right. I will have to make a decision."

"That make you nervous?" Izzy asked.

I shrugged. "I don't know. I'll have you to help me, right?"

Izzy's smile outshone the sun and I couldn't wait to get the whole thing going. I wished my mom wasn't so stuffy about it all. I was going to own the team and there was no sense wasting so much time waiting for a bunch of lawyers.

The game ended and we went out back. I gave my mom a scowl when we walked by the pool, but she either didn't care or didn't notice from behind her sunglasses.

One of the other good things about Jackson is that you pretty much always have to have a good time with him. Soon we were flopping around in the pool, doing splash contests. Neither of us could come close to Jackson's torrential geysers.

We laughed and swam and then laid out on big lounge chairs with thick cushions. It lightened my mood.

"You sure know how to have fun, Jackson," Izzy said. It was like she read my mind.

"Yup," Jackson said, staring up at the sky. "Look at that cloud! It's a doggone dragon."

"Fun is his middle name," I said.

"Remember Simpkin and Markham, Little Man? What they said about swimming? What's wrong with those guys?" Jackson raised up to look at me.

"A lot," I said.

"What are you talking about?" Izzy asked.

I told her all about the first day of practice. It was the day before school started, when Jackson showed up.

A FEW WEEKS AGO . . .

He was already out on the field. I could hear the coach yelling at him, and Jackson—because he was taller than the coach—was looking down and taking it.

"This is the *seventh*-grade team, son. The middle school." Coach Hubbard lowered his sunglasses so he could lock eyes with Jackson. Coach Hubbard looked like a hippo, right down to the thick molars filling his mouth, the big belly, and the few random bristly whiskers beneath his snout.

And then he launched into a tirade about how hard we all were going to have to work if we wanted to play football for him.

As the other players filtered out onto the field, Coach Hubbard continued his speech.

"Now, I know you all are used to winning." Coach Hubbard continued to scowl. "Yeah, I saw you play. Coached by a couple fellas who know their business, so my expectations are high this year. Fact is, I don't plan on losing a single game this year with this group. And I know that means beating undefeated Eiland Middle, along with all the others."

Coach Hubbard let that sink in and surveyed his players as if daring anyone to deny his prediction.

"That's right, Eiland. Haven't lost a game in *five years*, but that's gonna be over now. *You* are gonna break them. *We* are gonna break them together. That's what this season is about: Ben Sauer Middle beating Eiland. Making history."

Coach Hubbard glared at us some more, then introduced Assistant Coach Vickerson, who basically restated everything Coach Hubbard had said, only he said it all louder.

Finally, Coach Hubbard blew his whistle and we began. They worked us hard, invoking the name of Eiland. We sweated and we ached. We breathed in dust until our snot was brown and we chopped our feet through agility drills until our sides split with pain. After half the team had collapsed, it ended. As we trudged off the field, I felt a big meaty hand on my shoulder. I looked up at Jackson.

"Hey, Little Man." He was huffing.

"Hey. You were really sweating out there. You have time to go for a swim back at my house?" I grinned.

"Okay. I'll swim." Jackson gave a curt nod like he'd made a big decision. Jackson and his mom lived by themselves, too, only in a small apartment on the edge of the school district.

"Nice."

"Can I get a ride?" he asked.

"Sure," I said.

"I can swim in my shorts, right?"

"Of course." I laughed.

We changed in the locker room and headed out. We had nearly reached the school parking lot when I realized that a cluster of teammates had surrounded us.

Bryan Markham walked along on the other side of Jackson and he chuckled before he spoke. "Hey, dude, how old are you, anyway?"

"Twelve." Jackson studied his own feet as he walked, speaking soft and low.

"Come on, bro." Bryan gave him a little slap on the arm. "You look like you're eighteen."

Jackson shrugged. "I got big bones. Hey, you guys going to Little Man's house to swim?"

"Little Man? Oh, Minna Zinna. . . . Swim?" Bryan chuckled silently. "Haven't been to his house since second grade. My little sister has pool parties."

Jackson kept looking to me. I shrugged and sighed and turned to go, eager to get away and used to avoiding confrontation. Jackson followed me while the rest of them laughed. There was nothing funny. It was just a mean and sneaky way to insult us.

The other kids gave him some space, wary of a boy so big, but Bryan wasn't afraid of anything. He stood nearly as tall as Jackson, and even though he was hardly as thick, he had muscles that the rest of us dreamed of. Bryan had been king of sixth grade and no one expected anything different in seventh.

"But you probably like that kind of thing, right, Jackson?" Bryan sneered from behind us. "You got kindergarten written all over you. That's probably why you're gonna hang out with Minna. He looks like a kindergartner and you probably act like one."

I admit that I'd felt a prickle in my spine at that moment because I knew that, muscles or no muscles, king of sixth grade or not, Jackson could smash Bryan like a roach if he wanted to. So, when Jackson stopped short and stood tall, I expected that the balance of power in the world I'd come to know was about to shift.

PRESENT...

Izzy stared with her mouth open. "Jackson beat the stuffing out of Bryan? I didn't hear about that."

I shook my head, trying not to look too sad, and continued my story. "Nah, he just asked me if I'd farted."

"What?" Izzy looked shocked and she let out a giggle.

I laughed. "I know. He said, 'Little Man, did you just fart or something? 'Cause I swear I just heard a fart.'"

"Awesome," Izzy said. "What'd Bryan do, then?"

"He just stuttered a little and muttered like the mutt he is," I said, and then I explained Jackson just a little bit more to Izzy.

Jackson didn't care one bit about whether anyone thought it was beneath his age to swim in my pool. He might as well have been in Disney World with Space Mountain all to himself. He jumped and splashed and hooted and flopped about. He *loved* the water and he loved my pool. I couldn't get him out of it, not that I wanted to.

We'd been swimming at my pool every day after practice ever since. We'd swim until dinnertime. My mom, thrilled that I had a friend who seemed to genuinely like me as much as the pool, treated Jackson like royalty, fixing us food and drinks and always inviting Jackson to stay for dinner. Could he eat? Like no one I'd ever seen. Even my mom's jaw went slack at the sight of him tearing through a second steak from the grill or polishing off an entire loaf of garlic bread.

The other nice thing about Jackson was his manners. He put me to shame. "Yes, ma'am. Thank you, ma'am. May I please have some more, ma'am? That was delicious, ma'am."

When I met his mom—she'd come to pick him up in her small battered Chevy just before dark—it wasn't hard to see where he got his politeness from. She was a big, tall woman who spoke softly and with such sincerely appreciative words that my own mom couldn't see her without asking her in for coffee, tea, or a meal—none of which she'd ever accept.

And surprisingly, my mom, who was never one to let go of things, wouldn't argue.

In sixth grade I found myself kind of on the outside, especially late in the year. So, Jackson's sudden appearance was as welcome to me as it was to my mom.

When I told Izzy that part, I looked at her and sort of blushed. I don't know why. I guess I felt a little ashamed, even though I knew she liked me anyway.

Despite his size and prowess on the football field, Jackson

had a sensitive side. He liked it when we watched corny old Disney movies like *Escape to Witch Mountain* and *Swiss Family Robinson*, or even the animated stuff like *The Lion King* or *Beauty and the Beast*. I also found out—and only by something his mom blurted out one time—that Jackson loved music. Not Jay Z or Taylor Swift kind of music. Jackson *played* the violin, which was just bizarre to me. None of the kids I knew who played in the band or orchestra were killer linemen.

Jackson only let me hear him play that thing once, and he made me swear I wouldn't tell our teammates.

When I finished, I looked over at Izzy. She had this faraway look. Jackson had his face to the sun and his eyes closed, pretending not to listen, even though I knew he was.

"That's pretty cool," Izzy said.

"Yeah, a lot of good stuff has happened these past couple of weeks," I said.

She laughed. "I guess so. You're suddenly a billionaire, you own the best team in the NFL, and you've got a super cool best friend."

I looked over at Jackson, and try as he might, he couldn't help busting into a huge grin.

I turned to Izzy. "And you."

"Me, what?"

"I got you for a best friend, too." I nearly choked on the words.

"Aww." Izzy tilted her head. "That is so sweet. Thanks, Ryan."

"Sure." Maybe it was because I felt embarrassed, or maybe it was because there's just something wrong with me. You know, that thing that makes you want whatever it is that you don't have, even if you should be enjoying the great things you do have?

Anyway, all I could think of in that moment when I should have been thinking about Izzy and Jackson and my mom and the Dallas Cowboys was how very bad I wanted to play quarterback. And, like most impossible dreams, I just couldn't see a way for that to happen.

How could I have known that the very next day someone would help me have a crack at that impossible dream?

And that the person would be Jason Simpkin himself.

The next day at practice, I was walking out onto the field when I saw Coach Hubbard off to the side. He looked like he wanted to talk to me the moment I reached the practice field, like he had something to say but didn't want to say it in front of everyone. His lips quivered, and his eyes darted back and forth from me to the ground and back.

Coach Vickerson blew the whistle and started us on our stretching routine. Coach Hubbard kept looking over my way and pacing. Finally, he wandered over while we were all laid out on the ground, one foot extended straight, the other crooked going back, doing hurdler stretches. "Hey, Zinna. How's it going today?"

"Great, Coach." I blinked into the sunshine. "Ready for a big win Saturday."

"Saturday? Yes. We all are . . . Ryan." He paused and cleared his throat. "Uh, did you see the Cowboys game yesterday?"

"Yeah. Tough loss." I felt a little jolt of electricity go through me because I already knew where we were heading.

Coach Hubbard chuckled. "And they talked about *you* . . ."

"Yeah," I said, sounding like it was no big deal, "that kid owner thing."

"Yeah . . . that. Well, congratulations on *that*. Pretty special, huh?"

"Yup." I switched legs when Coach Vickerson blew the whistle and reached for my other toe. "My mom wants everything to stay the same. Hopefully it'll be a good thing, though. I think so." I let that hang. Even though he called me Ryan for the first time ever and now knew I owned the Dallas Cowboys, I wasn't going to start badgering him about playing quarterback instead of receiver. At least, not yet.

I went through practice same as every other day. When we did tackling drills, I threw my body around like a missile. When we did blocking, I got low, exploded into people, and chugged my feet like a madman. As time went by, the whole Dallas Cowboys thing got lost in the sweat and the crack of pads. During offense, I went with the receivers, doing my best with balls bouncing off my hands like marbles on the lunchroom floor. I hated that and had to contain myself from marching right up to Coach Hubbard and demand being switched to quarterback. I felt like I could do it, too, but held back.

When we switched over to defense, I lined up at the free safety position. The offense passed on my first play in, two long routes for the receivers, a post and a go. I got right where I was supposed to be, over the top of both routes, then broke on the ball when it went to the post, but the ball sailed right over my head. The receiver caught it for a touchdown and I wanted to scream. I'm too short to play free safety and if my coaches didn't already know that, that play just proved it to them.

I should have been playing cornerback, but we already had a lot of cornerbacks. I chewed on my mouth guard, grinding the rubber on the end into a flat useless tab. I was dying to change things around, dying to take control of my football career, but something told me the time wasn't quite right.

And then, it happened

It was the second play of team period, which is kind of like a live scrimmage. Jason Simpkin rolled out on a bootleg pass. Michael Priestly came hard up the middle on a blitz. No one touched him, and Priestly built up a head of steam and launched himself. Simpkin got the pass off before Priestly slammed him, right in the ear. I think they heard the hit halfway across town. Simpkin went down like a wet blanket and flopped onto the grass, unmoving. Coach Hubbard hurried over and knelt beside him, shouting for Coach Vickerson to get the trainer. Simpkin stirred.

We had a teammate get a concussion during the first week of contact, so I knew the drill and I knew what it meant. Simpkin would have to sit out for a week at the very least. Estevan Marin would step in at first team quarterback. Simpkin got up and was helped off the field by the trainer. The coaches returned to business.

Now we'd need another quarterback. No team—not even a seventh-grade middle-school club—would go into a game without a backup quarterback.

And I had an appointment with destiny.

I saw them talking about me, Coach Hubbard with his paw hung over the shoulder of Coach Vickerson, his head bobbing up and down and the younger coach nodding in agreement before the parted.

"Ryan!" Coach Hubbard barked. "Zinna!"

I hopped to it and stood at attention in front of them both. "Coach?"

"Get in there with the second offense. We need you to be ready in case something happens to Marin. We have no idea how long Simpkin's gonna be out."

"Got it, Coach!" I bolted into the huddle and wondered only briefly if he would have given me the shot if I hadn't been the owner of the Dallas Cowboys. I thought not. I thought they would have picked Griffin Engle, our tailback—who was fast and a really good athlete overall—to fill in, but it didn't matter. This was my chance. Second-string QB didn't guarantee I'd get on the field, but it did mean I'd get reps in practice.

I looked around at my teammates.

Bryan Markham didn't even try to hide his disgust. He snorted and spit a loogie on the grass in front of him. Everyone else, except for Jackson, stared and blinked in disbelief at the sight of Minna Zinna taking over their huddle. Jackson? His face glowed and he grinned so hard that it looked like it must have hurt. He might have been happier than me, and that's saying something.

"Come on, Ryan. Let's do this." Jackson spoke like it was just the two of us getting ready to launch a bottle rocket in my backyard.

"Let's ease you in here with something simple, Ryan." Coach Hubbard looked at his clipboard, selecting a play. "Thirty-two Dive."

"Coach, I can run the dive, but there isn't a play I don't know." I turned to look directly at him. Honestly, owning the Dallas Cowboys made me feel like . . . like Superman. Things that hadn't been possible before were now. I felt like I could say what I wanted. I felt bold and confident and . . .

Coach scratched his ear and glanced down at his list of plays on the practice schedule. "Okay, Blue Right 94. Hit the 4. Got that?"

I didn't even reply and went straight to the huddle, called the play, and marched to the line like General George Patton crossing into Germany at the end of World War II. I barked the cadence, took the snap, rolled right, and threw a wobbling duck to the 4 route. It wasn't pretty, but I completed the pass.

Jackson hooted and slapped me high five, then hugged me all the way back to the huddle.

"Well . . ." Coach Hubbard looked at Coach Vickerson and shrugged. "First down. Good play, Ryan. Get a little more spin on that ball if you can."

Playing quarterback isn't always about being this super athlete. It's about knowing the offense, making the right decisions, and being able to get the ball to the open receiver. The really smart quarterbacks run the West Coast Offense, or the spread, whatever you call it, lots of passing, chipping away at the defense. You don't have to have a cannon for an arm to win games. I thought of John Torres and the way he held the ball against the blitz in yesterday's game. Even an arm as big and strong as his can't help you if you don't get rid of the ball quick.

I knew I could make all the right decisions. I was already quick. If I could just explain all that, I knew I might be able to convince Coach Hubbard that we should adapt Ben Sauer Middle's offense to some version of the Spread.

I don't know if it was luck or destiny or if Coach Hubbard was actually tuned into the possibilities, but he called a pass on the next play, too. I went to the line and read the defense. By the way they were lined up, I was sure it was a shallow zone with two safeties over the top on both sides. The play Coach Hubbard called wasn't the best for this kind of coverage. I had no choice but to run it, though.

I barked the cadence, took the snap, and dropped back. My two primary receivers ran crossing routes, but both were covered, as I expected. I checked them just in case one got wide open, but when they didn't I hit my check down pass to Griffin Engle, right away. He grabbed it and shot right up through the middle of the field for a twenty-yard gain. It was an easy pass, and the right decision.

Next play was a run. I made the handoff smooth and clean and Griffin gained seven. The following play Coach Hubbard called another pass. I dropped back and when the blitz freed up the middle, I darted outside the pocket. Instead of panicking like the newbie quarterback I was, I directed Griffin to the sideline, pointing my finger. The cornerback let him go and rocketed my way, thinking he'd have a free hit. Just before the defender reached me, I dumped the ball up and over his head. Griffin snatched it and went up the sideline and into the end zone.

My teammates cheered. Griffin tossed me the ball with a wink. Jackson slapped my back and nearly knocked me over.

I didn't stop after my first series either. I made the right decisions on every play, and even though my passes were nothing to write home about, I continued to move the offense up and down the field by completing short throws to the open receivers, making clean handoffs on the running plays, and encouraging my teammates like I was already the star quarterback I'd always dreamed I'd be.

I thought things couldn't have gotten any better for me. But, at the end of practice, just as we completed our last wind sprint—which I finished first, by the way—a big black Escalade limousine pulled into the school parking lot beside the field, its chrome grill glinting in the sun.

Coach Hubbard held his whistle halfway to his mouth,

ready to call us all in together, but everyone froze and stared at the big black SUV.

And when the rear door opened and we saw who had arrived, no one could believe it.

27

Jackson leaned into me, nearly knocking me over. "Dude, that's John Torres."

Flashing a full smile of bright white teeth was John Torres, the Cowboys' star quarterback, built like a lion. Torres wore a Cowboys sweat suit and carried a football. He was headed our way with an older man right behind him who was a thick, gray, and crusty old salt who looked like a real cowboy from the Wild West. I looked for Cody Cowan, wondering if the Cowboys' head coach had come, too.

When Torres reached an openmouthed Coach Hubbard, the star quarterback extended a hand. "What do we got here? A *football* team?"

"Yes . . . we . . ." Coach Hubbard sputtered. "I'm Coach Hubbard."

"Nice to meet you." Torres smiled and clasped Coach

Hubbard's shoulder. "Looks like you got a heck of a team here, Coach. And I'm looking for your man, Ryan Zinna."

All eyes were on me. I felt my face warming and raised my hand like I was asking a question. All my complaints about Torres's performance against the Bears melted to nothing.

"Ryan Zinna!" Torres grinned even bigger and half turned to the man beside him, who wore a three-piece suit and brown ostrich-skin boots. "You know Bert Hamhock, our general manager?"

Torres looked back at Coach Hubbard. "Can we take my man here with us? You're done with practice, right, Coach? Is it all good?"

"Uh, sure, Mr. Torres." Coach Hubbard puffed himself up. "It's all good. Thank you for coming by. Uh . . . would you maybe have a word for the team? We're 1–0 right now, so . . ."

"1–0? Wow, wish we were 1–0." Torres looked around and his face turned serious. "I do have a word, Coach."

Torres rose up to his full six-foot-six height and stared hard all around the team. "Seek the truth, fellas. Seek the truth."

He turned to me. "Come on, Ryan. We heard from Mr. Dietrich that you were coming to the stadium, so we thought we'd just come out to see you first. We got some ideas for you. Coach, good luck with your season."

John Torres put his hand on my shoulder as we walked toward the bleachers on the other side of the football field. I must have floated over there, because I sure didn't feel my feet touching anything. We sat down and John Torres kept his hand on my shoulder pad. I couldn't help looking over at Bryan Markham, whose face was a blend of confusion and hatred.

"You okay?" Torres asked me.

"I . . . yes. Sorry."

Bert Hamhock forced a smile and sat down on the other side of me, speaking in his West Texas drawl. "We wanted to welcome you, Ryan, before things get too crazy, and we thought the best way to do it was just ride right on out here after practice. . . . The Cowboys practice, that is . . . and we caught you, so, good."

I looked back and forth between them, kind of waiting. "Okay. Thanks."

"Right." Bert Hamhock slapped his knees. "Hey, no sense just sitting here like fans in the stands, you two oughta toss the ball around. What position are you, Ryan? Wideout?"

"Actually, quarterback."

"Quarterback! Hear that, John? Couple of Qs chucking it around. How'd you like that, Ryan? Pigs in a mud puddle." Hamhock glowed.

You bet I liked it. "Sure."

"Here, you stay right there." John Torres hopped up and jogged about ten yards down along the bleachers before he stopped and turned and raised the ball to throw it.

I held up my hands and when he lobbed it to me, I caught it!

He held up his hands and I threw it back.

"Move your hand back on the ball a bit." Torres tossed it back.

I did what he said and the ball didn't wobble as much.

"That's it. See?" He tossed it back and I dropped it, but I didn't care. I was playing catch with John Torres and I glanced over at my team, which had broken apart and was heading into the locker room with all necks twisted and all eyes on me.

Hamhock nodded as we kept the toss going. "This is great. See, we want you to feel welcome as hot apple pie on the sideboard, and like you can talk to me and John—me on the management side and John on the players' side—about anything you have questions about. We want to work *with* you. We know the season is starting out a little rough, but, you know, you have to stay the course with the *master* plan."

I wanted to ask what the master plan was, but felt stupid for not already knowing. Even though I nodded like I understood and caught the next pass, inside I was boiling at my mom for keeping me in the dark. Again, I could see no reason why I shouldn't have been in the thick of things, meeting the players, calling the shots. Lawyers . . . they made me sick.

"So, do you have any? Questions?" Hamhock asked.

"Uh . . ." I was thinking hard. I wanted to ask what it was like to play quarterback under an offensive guru like Coach Cowan, who'd written five books on the subject, but didn't think that was very cool. I wanted to be cool. Then it just popped in my head—something kind of cool—and I focused on John Torres as I threw him the ball. "Did you really go on a date with Selena Gomez?"

He caught the ball, chuckled. "A couple."

The minute my question came out, I wished I could've taken it back. Wow, did I feel dumb. My face got so hot I think I could've cooked an egg. Who cared about Selena Gomez? This was John Torres and the GM from the Dallas Cowboys. We were playing catch, at *my* school, and I asked about a date with Selena Gomez. I wanted to crawl in a hole.

"Oh, cool," I said, nodding like I already figured that and desperate to fill the silence.

Hamhock huffed quietly. "Look, Ryan . . . you're a *football* player, obviously. So you know that sometimes a team and a coach aren't . . . well, it's like a sow at the supper table. It doesn't work. It's the chemistry. Sometimes it's just off. No one's *fault*, it just *is*. Now, we've got a heck of a team, led by one of the premier throwing quarterbacks the league has ever seen."

Hamhock pointed a finger at John Torres.

"Well . . ." John sounded like he wanted to apologize for Hamhock being so bold, and he tossed the ball straight up before catching it.

"You are." Hamhock held up the pointing hand to cut off an argument. "Your numbers haven't been what they could be because of the system you're in. No one has ever questioned your ability. Goose and gravy, John, you run a 4.6 forty, you bench-pressed 225 twenty-seven times, and you can throw the ball seventy-seven yards. Don't be modest, son. You'd take the blue ribbon at the state fair hands down every time."

I knew all this about John Torres. He was so good, the Cowboys had traded up to get him as the third pick in the draft three years ago. So I nodded in agreement.

"Good, you see what we're getting at," Hamhock said.

I didn't see exactly, but kept nodding my head, hoping I'd figure it out soon enough. I was starting to get nervous that being kid owner was a little more involved than great seats at every game.

"I know it won't be easy, but you've got me and John behind you, Ryan. That's why we wanted to get out here and have a little visit. We're hoping we can help you through all of this. I don't think you need to tell people that, but that's what we'll do. We'll be like . . . like your older brother." Hamhock nodded toward Torres, my new older brother, before pointing a thumb in his own chest. "And your Dutch uncle. Sound good?"

"Uh, sure." What else could I say? I had no idea what a Dutch uncle was, but come on, I was standing right next to John Torres.

"You'll have your critics, we know that." Hamhock twisted his face in disgust, dismissing my critics forever. "They're like patties in the pasture. You just step by 'em and try not to get their stink on you, but that's why we're here with you. It's *your* team now, and we're all part of it."

"Why? What critics?" I asked.

"Well." Hamhock smiled and winked. "Some people will complain about it, but most people are going to pop a champagne cork."

"Sir?" I said. "I'm not sure I understand."

"When you fire him." Hamhock nodded like I was already in on the secret.

I looked at John Torres, who tossed me the ball and grinned.

"Fire who?" I asked.

"Come on, little buddy, you gotta know what we're talking about. People have been talking about it nonstop. They're kind of expecting it with the change in ownership." Hamhock winked at me again. "You're gonna fire Coach Cowan."

28

I'm the kind of fan where if there's anything negative about my team, I just don't listen. Those guys on sports talk radio, always complaining. Everyone thinking they can do better? I pay no attention.

Every game the Cowboys went into was a game I expected them to win. I didn't care who they were playing or how bad the Cowboys' record was.

But I was aware of the grumblings about Coach Cowan, and I also knew some people blamed the three-year play-off drought and the current 0–1 record on John Torres, while others blamed it on GM Bert Hamhock. Some said our star running back had lost a step. Most people ultimately blamed it on Thomas Peebles because *he* was the owner.

And now I was the owner, and I got what these two guys were doing in a blink. Trying to win me over to their side of things before I visited the team, so I'd blame Coach Cowan for the team's lack of success.

But I threw it back to them and said, "I got to talk to Mr. Dietrich about all that. He's overseeing my ownership, so I need to check with him. But I sure get what you guys are thinking."

I was pretty proud of myself for coming up with my trustee. I could only imagine their faces if I told them I would also be consulting Izzy. Torres's brow clouded over and he looked to Hamhock for direction. It seemed my response wasn't the one he was expecting, but I guess I'm not as easy to win over as Selena Gomez.

Hamhock chuckled and put a hand on my shoulder. "Ryan, Dietrich came out on ESPN Radio this morning and said he was going to defer to you entirely, which is just what your father said in his will."

I looked up at Hamhock with a knowing smile, remembering what my mom had said about Dietrich. "I only met Mr. Dietrich yesterday, but I can pretty much bet that what he says and what he does might be two entirely different stories."

Hamhock grinned and glanced at Torres. "Get our new owner, will you? How old are you? Twelve going on forty-five?"

I shrugged. "My mom taught me a thing or two."

Torres zipped the ball back at me. I had to duck as it glanced off my hands, striking Hamhock in the face.

"Darn it, John!" Hamhock held his nose and glared at the quarterback through watery eyes.

"Gosh, sorry, Bert." Torres's shoulders slumped.

I felt at least partially responsible, but the GM wasn't going to lay the blame on his new owner. "Sorry, Mr. Hamhock."

"Not your fault, kid." Hamhock forced a laugh. "Not Johnny's either. When you got a rocket arm like Johnny boy, it sometimes can't be helped. So, what do you think, kiddo? Can we take you out to the facility and show you around a bit?"

"Well, my mom's probably waiting for me." I nodded toward the parking lot beside the school. "Plus, I think we are already scheduled to see the team in a few days."

"Mom picks you up after practice?" Hamhock nodded like he already knew.

"Yes."

"Well, maybe go get changed and we can take you both out to the facility today. You and your mom. No time like the present," Hamhock said. "We'll wait and you can introduce us to her. Heck, all the ladies love Johnny Torres. Even the moms."

"Sure." I turned to go, stopping to pick up the ball so I could toss it back to Torres.

"Hey," Hamhock said before I could throw it, "you better keep the ball. It's yours anyway, right? See that? It's a Cowboys ball. Get used to it, kiddo."

I couldn't help smiling like a fool. Despite the hard choices I was going to have to make, I knew I was going to get used to it, and really fast, too.

Good things feel even better when you share them. Without a father and without brothers and sisters, I didn't always have a lot of people to share things with. As I walked into the locker room, through the stares and whispers of my teammates, I made plans in my mind to include Jackson and Izzy in this most excellent adventure. I whispered my invitation to Jackson, who got so excited he blurted out his reply: "Go to the Cowboys facility? Dude! I—" and then fell into a fit of choking.

The rest of the locker room was in awe and I soaked up their attention like a sponge, acting like it was no big deal that John Torres was waiting for me in an Escalade limo outside.

I knew Izzy would be coming out of the girls' locker room after her soccer practice, so Jackson called his mom to okay it with her, and then waited with me outside in the hallway.

"Do you think John Torres will be coming to our games?" Jackson spoke in a dreamy voice.

Before I could answer, Izzy burst into the hallway.

Her face was still sweaty and flushed from her soccer practice. "Did you hear? John Torres is outside!"

I began to snicker.

"What?" She looked at me like I'd gone crazy.

"I know." I folded my arms across my chest. "I was playing catch with him. He's waiting for me to ride over to the Cowboys facility with him and Hamhock, the GM."

"Waiting?"

I nodded. "I gotta tell my mom, but I'm sure she'll be cool with it. And I want you and Jackson to come with me."

"With you . . . and John Torres?" Her eyes got dreamy.

Jackson was yanking on my arm. "Come on, Ryan. Let's go."

"I'll text my mom," Izzy said as we walked. "*She* won't care. She says life experiences should be part of your education."

The Escalade had pulled right up along the curb with the normal fleet of family vehicles making pickups for the after-school athletes. It was perfect. Right where I wanted it, in the middle of everything. Markham and Simpkin couldn't miss it. The girls who Izzy used to sit with (many played soccer or field hockey) couldn't miss it either. I escorted my friends, opening the door and telling John Torres and the GM who they were before leaving them to gawk and heading off to the big white King Ranch to explain to my mom what was going on. She'd already climbed down from the cab of her pickup and was moving my way on the curb when I intercepted her.

"Mom, it's John Torres and Bert Hamhock from the Cowboys." I could barely catch my breath.

"The *quarterback*?" Even my mom knew who John Torres was, and she strained for a look inside the SUV.

"Yes, they're taking me to the facility for a tour—if it's okay with you—and I asked Jackson and Izzy."

"Wait, what? But we're supposed to go next week for a formal meeting."

"Mom, I own the team." I tried not to gloat. It was hard. How could she not go along?

"Yes, I know that."

"This is awesome!" I said.

She sighed heavily. "Let me double-check this with them, then I'll follow you so I can bring you all home."

"Mom." I drew the word out, punctuating it with a frown because I didn't think a kid owner needed his mom to go along with him. "You don't have to follow us."

"You're twelve, Ryan."

"I *know*. Almost thirteen. I'm not a baby, Mom."

"No one said you were." She pushed past me, heading for the Escalade. "But I'm still your mother and I'm following you. Good? Or would you rather head right home?"

I knew that look in her eye. She meant it. "Okay. Fine."

The GM and John Torres saw my mom coming and they hopped out of the SUV. My mom said hello and shook hands with them, making sure we were all set. With all my might I willed her to just leave, and finally she did. I got into the Escalade and took the captain's seat next to John Torres. Mr.

124

Hamhock sat up front with the driver, wearing mirrored sunglasses. Jackson and Izzy scrambled into the back bench. John Torres closed the door on the rest of Ben Sauer Middle School and off we went. On the highway, the big-time quarterback held out a hand and I slapped him five, the joy of that erasing the weight of my mom's big white truck tailing us.

We took the tollway north, straight out of town to where the new practice facility was, in the little Texas town of Frisco.

I was simply soaking it up, breathing deep, and was totally surprised when Izzy chirped from the backseat. "Mr. Hamhock, I liked when you traded your third-round pick to move up in the second round last April to get Mark Fusco. We were a little shaky at the outside linebacker position and Fusco's speed looks like it's helping our pass rush, too."

Mr. Hamhock turned around in his seat and slipped the mirrored glasses down on his nose to study Izzy. I wanted to melt and my hand went to my brow as I shook my head in disbelief. Who was Izzy to comment on Bert Hamhock's picks?

I was even more surprised when Hamhock burst out into a grin. "Well, little lady, not a lot of people even remember that trade. They like Fusco's two and a half sacks this season, but they forget that we would have lost him to the 49ers without that trade. You've got a sharp eye."

"Yes," Izzy said. "I know it won't mean much to you—I mean, you're doing it for *real*, I know that—but I'm in three fantasy leagues and I won two of them last year. I'm hoping for a clean sweep this season."

I went from embarrassment to pride and I gave Izzy a puzzled look. She just shrugged and said, "You never asked, and boys don't like getting beat by a girl in football, even fantasy football."

I thought about that and nodded in agreement as we pulled into the Cowboys' new facility.

I looked out the window in awe. It was as if an alien race had landed and built a base of operations. Futuristic glass, mirrors, and chrome swept across the horizon. Lush grass football fields bordered the indoor stadium, built for the Cowboys to practice in when the weather went bad and for local school teams to play when they had a big game. There was a force field of energy you'd expect from such an otherworldly site when we got out of the Escalade. I swear you could feel the power of the whole complex.

We parked and waited for my mom to join us. Even her semi-sour face as she shook hands a second time with John Torres and the GM couldn't break the magic spell. I stood tall and proud as we marched into the front entrance where Super Bowl trophies sat on pedestals in a half circle off to one side. People in the lobby pointed and stared as we marched past the reception desk and the uniformed guard into the back offices.

The hallway was lined with display cases. Inside were framed pictures and helmets signed by Cowboy greats like Roger Staubach, Too Tall Jones, Emmitt Smith, Troy Aikman, and Larry Allen. I acted like it was no big deal. Jackson's eyes were as wide as if he'd entered the gates of heaven, and Izzy's mouth hung slack.

"I can't believe this." Izzy looked around, took a quick selfie, and then stared at me. "Ryan, this is so cool."

Hamhock marched us right to what looked like an

important corner office, past a secretary with just a nod, before swinging open one of the big wide double doors and barging in.

When I realized whose office we'd waltzed right into, I was so mad at Bert Hamhock I wanted to shout.

Coach Cowan sat at his desk, watching game film on his computer.

I looked at Hamhock, remembering that this was the coach he'd just told me I should fire. I wanted to give the GM a nasty look, but even though I was feeling bigger than I'd ever felt before in my life, I guess my mom's influence still had a hold on my behavior. I couldn't just scowl at a grown-up.

Beside the coach sat a smallish young man I nearly overlooked. He wore an army T-shirt and had a crew cut that made him look like a recruit from nearby Fort Hood. When Coach Cowan saw us, he jumped up. By the look on his face, I guessed he probably knew Hamhock wanted him fired. His glance went from Hamhock to John Torres before falling on me. It was like he'd eaten a pickle but was trying to hide it.

The coach stood just under six feet tall. His dark hair was

parted on the side and he had the sharp nose of a hunting bird with dark, probing eyes. I knew he'd been a quarterback at Harvard, but only a backup, and he looked like a Harvard guy to me, despite the sweat suit. He looked smart, a cut above. I could certainly see that his demeanor didn't match the rough-and-tumble, backslapping ways of the GM.

"Uh, hello." He extended a stiff hand and I shook it. "I'm Coach Cowan. Welcome. I see you've . . ."

Coach Cowan scowled at Hamhock and clenched his teeth.

The GM only smiled back and let out a little huff of laughter before resting his hand on my shoulder. "Since Ryan owns the team, I thought, why not take John out to meet him? Who doesn't love John Torres?"

Torres looked at his feet. Coach Cowan became even more irritated. He opened his mouth to speak but checked himself and cleared his throat.

"I was just going over some film from Sunday's game with Kellen." Coach Cowan turned to the young man, who stood red-faced, looking around at the rest of us. I'd never heard of him, and obviously he wasn't important enough to be introduced.

The head coach then looked at John Torres with what I thought was more displeasure than John Torres was probably used to. "John, we've got to get you looking at that second and third wide receiver."

Coach Cowan's voice changed when he talked about football. There was no hesitation. It made me think of a hooked fish being released back into the water.

John Torres looked at Hamhock and I realized that while

Coach Cowan and the quarterback and the GM were all Dallas Cowboys, they were clearly on different sides, and if it was a secret, it was a poor one.

Hamhock snorted and called the head coach by his first name. "Cody, you've got to let John throw the rock, stretch the field. That's what he does, not dink and dunk it all afternoon. He's got a rocket. You gotta use it, Coach. You want the Cowboys to see the play-offs this year? Launch the rocket."

The GM and the head coach stared at each other for a few awkward minutes. I looked over at Izzy and Jackson, who looked uncomfortable, and just shrugged. Finally, my mom spoke up. "I'm sure Ryan will be relying a lot on Mr. Dietrich, so I don't think anyone has to worry about changes."

That got their attention, and mine, too. I wanted to ask her what she thought she was doing, but owning the Cowboys hadn't made me *that* bold. She forced a smile at them. "Where *is* Mr. Dietrich?"

Hamhock coughed. "I understood from Mr. Dietrich that he really plans to defer to Ryan on running the team. No offense to Mr. Peebles, your ex-husband, ma'am, but a lot of people think your son here might be just what we need. A fresh perspective."

Hamhock sent me a winning grin and a wink, like we were in this together. I couldn't help but like the man. Who didn't like a guy who toted John Torres around with him?

"Because even a twelve-year-old boy could run a team better than my ex-husband?" My mother frowned, but I couldn't tell if she was really mad.

No one else seemed to be able to tell either, but finally

Hamhock did something between a cough and a laugh and said, "We better let the coach get back to his film." The look Coach Cowan gave me was intelligent, serious, and doubtful. I was the owner, so I stared blankly back, doing my best not to look too confused, and gave him a nod.

On our way down the hallway, Hamhock lowered his voice and leaned my way. "I just figured we should get that out of the way. He's nothing to be scared of, just a man, like you and me. Before you break a bronco, you look it in the eye."

My mom huffed. "Mr. Hamhock, let's not get carried away, please."

"Ma'am?" He gave her a dumb look.

"He's twelve."

Hamhock bit his lip and nodded. "I have to say this, though. His dad kinda always got things the way he wanted. Anyone didn't do things the way he wanted? That dog just didn't hunt. So, if Mr. Peebles wanted Ryan here calling the shots? Ma'am, my bet is Ryan here is gonna be calling the shots. Now, that's just me."

I wanted to hug the man.

But my mom wasn't about to let that be the last word on the subject.

"Funny," she said, "my experience with Thomas was entirely different."

"Mom," I whispered. "Please."

My mom shook her head as Bert Hamhock led us into an office twice the size of the head coach's, with leather furniture and a big desk topped by a huge slab of polished green marble. One wall was all glass and it looked out over the grass practice fields as well as one corner of the indoor stadium. The other walls boasted heads of animals, most of which I couldn't name. The skin of a zebra lay stretched and flat beneath a glass-topped coffee table between two couches.

Jackson seemed drawn to an animal with curly horns, and he walked over and reached out to touch one while Izzy frowned.

"Well?" Hamhock opened his arms, signaling that all this was mine. "Impressive, isn't it? These are your digs."

"What?! Really? *My* office?"

My mother clucked her tongue.

We heard laughter from behind a door that I hadn't even noticed in the bookcases behind the desk. The sound of voices, muffled by the door, leaked into the owner's office. More high-pitched laughing followed.

The lock clicked. The handle turned. The door was flung open.

I turned and saw the faces, and I thought I might throw up.

Dillon Peebles, my dead father's other son, looked just as sick as me. Maybe there was a flash of fear in his eyes, too, like I might be some kind of rabid dog. He looked to his mother for guidance.

Jasmine's lip curled right up off her teeth and she froze. "What are *these people* doing here? Take your hands off that."

Jackson's hand dropped from the face of the strange animal he'd been poking.

My father's second wife held her chin high and directed her anger at Hamhock.

Even the all-bluff-and-bluster GM didn't seem able to hold up under her hard stare. His sunburned neck went from red to purple and he blinked, but he didn't look away.

"Uh, well . . . ma'am." He scratched his purple neck. "We were just showing Ryan and his mom around a bit. He *is* gonna be running the show, ma'am. All due respect."

Dillon recovered his wits and he too now stared at me with the kind of hatred you saved for someone who kicked a puppy.

His mom let out a harsh *harrumph*, like she knew something we didn't, before looking back over her shoulder through the open door.

Mr. Dietrich entered the room and seemed surprised to see me.

"Ahh . . . hello." He walked toward us but pulled up short of a possible handshake with anyone. He wore the kind of Popsicle-red pants you'd see old men golf in, with a lime-green and blue-plaid shirt that showed off his tan. He wore loafers with no socks and a white tennis sweater draped over his shoulders and tied around his neck.

"Actually," Jasmine sneered, "I'm glad we're all here. I've been busy with my lawyers and . . . Well, needless to say, my husband does not get to tweak my nose from beyond the grave." She looked directly at me. "And you do *not* hold a majority interest in this team. Or you won't when all the paperwork goes through."

John Torres said what I was thinking. "Huh?"

Jasmine Peebles seemed to rise up taller than anyone in the room. "Ryan Zinna is *not* the owner of the Dallas Cowboys. I am. I hope you enjoyed it while it lasted, though."

She smirked.

I looked at Mr. Dietrich, and by the way he bit his lip and inclined his head, I knew what she said had to be true.

I didn't own the Dallas Cowboys.

"All right," Mr. Dietrich said. "Jasmine, Dillon, I think it's time for you to leave. Ryan and I have some things to discuss."

After a few minutes—which included Jasmine's protests—my mom, my friends, and I were finally alone with Mr. Dietrich. He explained that there was a lot of uncertainty.

"What Jasmine is doing is, quite frankly, pretty smart." Mr. Dietrich had clasped his hands and laid them out on the table in front of him. "Texas is a community property state, so she owns half of everything they acquired during their marriage."

"She signed a prenuptial agreement!" My mom's eyes were burning and she rose up out of her seat.

I looked at her in surprise, realizing that she knew a lot more about my dad and his life than she had pretended to.

"Correct." Mr. Dietrich thumped his hands on the table. "She's challenging that, though, and I have to say that from what I've seen, I think she's got a good chance to prevail. Those agreements are always shaky and under her claim, she'd actually get *less* money."

"Then why is she doing it?" My mother burst out.

Mr. Dietrich raised his eyebrows. "Why? The team. She wants it."

"You mean, she doesn't want my son to have it." My mother went from angry to bitter.

"Be that as it may, she's in a very good position and we have to prepare for it. I'm your trustee. I'm committed to seeing your father's will carried out, so it's my job to defend your claim like it was my own." Mr. Dietrich stared at me like he was waiting for something. "You see, I don't have a family of my own. My business is my family, and your father was my brother in business."

I shifted in my chair and looked at my friends. They stared at me, too, waiting. I looked back at Mr. Dietrich. "So what happens now?"

"If she does win, then I'll have the swing vote." He cleared his throat and looked at me hard. "She'll only have half of your father's shares. You'll have the other half, forty percent each. Neither of you can control the team without the minority owner . . . me. I own twenty percent. Whoever I put my shares behind will run the team."

"You're supposed to be Ryan's *trustee*," my mom said, a disgusted look on her face, like she'd just stepped in dog doo. "Thomas *trusted* you to look out for him, and, as crazy as it sounds, he wanted *Ryan* to run the team. How could you even think about her?"

"Jasmine knows the organization. She's an adult—not one I'm overly fond of, but it would keep the organization more stable, and that's good for the value of the team and me." The room seemed to get suddenly colder and Mr. Dietrich's eyes glinted from behind his glasses. "Before you get too upset, I'm not saying Ryan *won't* prevail here, I'm just saying that nothing is certain, and if it does go Jasmine's way, I will have another duty to carry out."

"Duty?" My mother's eyes narrowed.

Mr. Dietrich smiled. "Well, you know Thomas. Very smart. An amazing chess player. I could rarely win a game. In a separate document, he gave me instructions for what to do in the event that this happened."

"Instructions? What instructions?" My mom's face hardened even more.

Mr. Dietrich brightened. "I'm not at liberty to explain it in detail, but let's just say it'll be an interesting contest."

"A contest?" I asked. "Between me and Jasmine?"

Mr. Dietrich laughed. "Oh, no. Not her. A contest between you and Dillon."

33

"Easy come, easy go." That's what my mother said as we drove home half an hour later.

I just stared silently out the window as Izzy and Jackson sat in the backseat.

It wasn't as cut-and-dried as all that. It might have been easy come, but it wasn't going to be easy go. Not if I had my way.

We were halfway back to my house before anyone said anything.

"What do you think he meant by a contest?" Izzy asked.

It annoyed me because I didn't know the answer even though I'd been thinking about it.

"Good grades?" Jackson suggested, hopefully. "You got that covered."

Izzy bit her lip. "He said he and your father played chess.

Would you have to play Dillon in chess to win the team?"

"That's pretty crazy," Jackson said.

"The whole thing is crazy," I replied.

"I think we should just forget all about this." My mom gripped the wheel and glared at the road as we cruised against the flow of the rush-hour traffic back toward the heart of Dallas. "You don't need to *own a team*. You're too young. I've said that all along."

I couldn't have disagreed more and couldn't help saying so. "You didn't seem so hot for her to take it away from me back there."

"That woman is a sack of snakes. I'm instinctively against whatever she wants." My mom seemed to forget the three of us kids were even there, and she glanced in the mirror at my friends in the backseat before putting the radio on and turning up the volume when she recognized "Colder Weather" by the Zac Brown Band. We listened to my mom sing along, one song after another, with the volume holding back any chance for conversation.

When we pulled into the circular driveway, my mom shut off the truck and chirped like a happy bird. "How about a cookout?"

"I'm definitely in." Jackson swung the door open but stayed seated.

"I can ask," Izzy said.

"You do that and let me know. Chicken and ribs. Why don't you all take a swim while I help Teresa put things together?" My mom was already on her way up the front steps, happy to be back in her own base camp and fully in charge.

I looked at my friends. Jackson licked his lips, but Izzy returned my questioning eyes with a sympathetic tilt of her head.

"Come on," I said, hopping down. "Let's go out back."

They followed me. Izzy called her mom right in front of us, so when she got denied on the barbecue because of a family dinner, I knew it wasn't her just wanting to bail on the brewing storm between me and my mom. We hung out in the back, waiting for Izzy's mom to come get her. Jackson did some stunts off the diving board, winning his own cannonball contest with twelve-foot plumes of splash. To his dismay, Izzy and I would only watch from our thickly padded lounge chairs in the shade.

"He's not very good, you know." I could tell Izzy was speaking to me, even though her eyes were on the human cannonball.

"Who? Coach Cowan?" I asked.

She shook her head. "No. The general manager. Hamhock. I made a big deal about him picking Mark Fusco because it's maybe the best move he's made since he got here. The other picks? Not so great."

"Hey . . ." I liked Bert Hamhock, even if he talked like a farmer sometimes and wanted to fire Coach Cowan. My mind raced, searching for just the right argument to quiet Izzy down. "He picked John Torres."

Izzy made me wait while she cracked open a can of iced tea and leaned forward to take a sip. "Exactly."

"You *love* John Torres." I realized the outrage I felt had crept into my words, giving them a nasty flavor.

"John Torres may be the cutest quarterback in the league right now," she said, "but that won't win games. I can think of three *backups* in the NFL who'd be better."

I barked out a laugh. "Like who? Kellen *Smith*?"

"I forgot about him. He makes four."

"Are you serious? You don't even know who Kellen Smith is," I said.

"Just because *you* don't know, doesn't mean *I* don't know." She set her tea can down hard on the little table between us, sat back, and crossed her arms.

"Okay," I said, "what was his completion percentage?"

She narrowed her eyes at me and smiled. "When? Junior year or senior year?"

I wasn't about to be outgunned on my Cowboys knowledge by a girl, no matter how much I liked her. I mean, I was the owner. Maybe. "Sophomore year."

Her smile widened into a grin and she let her head fall back like she was ready to take a nap. "He didn't play his sophomore year because of injury, medical redshirt. Dislocated his kneecap and tore the medial collateral ligament. Junior year he completed 73.8 percent and senior year it was a school record—80.1 percent, with thirty-one touchdowns and just eight interceptions. He also ran for seven hundred and twenty-three yards and eleven touchdowns."

I could tell by the look on her face that she wasn't making it up. "Yeah, I know all that. Not the exact numbers, but . . ."

I was thankful that Jackson finally got out of the pool and stood dripping wet and staring at us under the trellis of cool green vines. "What you guys talking about?"

"Just the Cowboys," Izzy sang.

"Yeah, so cool that you might own them," Jackson said. "I

mean, that you do. Kind of. Maybe. Aww, who cares? You're gonna be playing in *our* game this Saturday anyway, which is way better by far."

I wasn't so sure about that and I wasn't going to leave the field of battle with Izzy so quickly. "She thinks Bert Hamhock's not a good GM. She doesn't like John Torres."

Jackson looked back and forth between us, then froze. "Oh, no. I'm not getting in the middle of this one."

"There's no middle," I complained. "Just tell us what you think."

"I think . . . I gotta use the bathroom." He hurried off, struggling to wrap a towel around his waist.

"So . . . ," I said.

"I'm not gonna argue." She sipped her tea and squinted at the sun sparkling in the pool water. "It's your team."

"Maybe," I said.

"Well," she said, taking out her phone and sitting back in her chair, "I'm here for you if you need me. That's all."

"Thanks." I lay back, too, and took out my own phone, googling Kellen Smith and finding out Izzy knew his numbers exactly. I was impressed, but determined not to show it.

Jackson returned and sat down, too, and ten minutes later, Izzy's mom texted from the front circle that she'd arrived.

Izzy stood. "Well, let me know how it turns out with the team." She said it like we'd never let up on the conversation. "Either way, hey, you owned the Dallas Cowboys, right?"

I looked up and scowled. "Worst case, I still own part of them."

It was a bluff. They knew and I knew that a minority

interest got me nothing, except a lot of money *if* the majority owner ever decided to sell them, which might not even happen in my lifetime.

"For sure," she said. "See you guys tomorrow."

She hurried off.

Jackson puffed up his cheeks and I knew he had something to say.

"Man, she really is pretty." Jackson's eyes followed her as she disappeared around the corner, his bearlike shoulders hunched and wrapped in a fluffy towel.

"You should go out with her," I mumbled. I couldn't help being annoyed. I was annoyed with everyone and everything, but the look Jackson gave me after I suggested he ask her out took me down a couple pegs. I felt bad.

"Man, I wish." Even the thought of it seemed to hurt him. "She's crazy about you."

I shrugged. "Yeah, well, we'll see how it goes now."

The look of admiration on the face of a giant kid creates a discomfort hard to explain. "Maybe you could ask *her* to that victory bonfire they're talking about having after the game?"

"No one likes someone who's going down the drain," I said. "That sucking sound is pretty embarrassing."

Jackson rolled his lower lip beneath his teeth and nodded. "Yeah, but she's not like that. She sat with us that second day of school when she could have sat *anywhere*. She sat with us because there's something about you she likes. Then you dissed her and she *still* came back. And you weren't even second QB on our team either. Izzy was there because she likes *you*. It's like that book she had you read. She's all about what's on the inside."

This embarrassed, shocked, and scared me all at the same time. I didn't know what to say. I couldn't process it in my brain, so I tucked it into a dark corner and gave Jackson a final shake of my head, signaling an end of the discussion about Izzy.

Jackson let out a heavy sigh, but I ignored it. I returned to my phone to study more remote facts about Cowboys players, no matter how deep they were on the depth chart, not that it mattered. If Jasmine got her way, or I lost whatever crazy contest Mr. Dietrich had in mind, I wouldn't have to worry about making any decisions for anything.

I checked myself. I hated feeling this way. Negative thinking had no place if I was going to be the son of Thomas Peebles, which I now had every intention of being. And that meant fighting—for the Cowboys *and* for making bigger plays on the Ben Sauer team. And now that I was a QB—even the second QB—I was going to make things happen. One thing I knew was that regular people do all kinds of things for people who are famous; they just can't help it.

I was no fool. I knew I wasn't, like, one of the president's kids, or a pop star, but I knew there were degrees of being famous in that upper stratosphere. And as owner—part or whole—of the Dallas Cowboy, I was in it. What's the stratosphere? The part of the Earth's atmosphere that is seven to thirty-one miles above the surface. That's what our science teacher told us. You're way up there. Everyone can see you, and most of them want to be where you are, even if it's for a moment.

That's what I was counting on. Coach Hubbard wouldn't be able to resist my ideas.

I sat back, took a deep breath. I wanted to *do* something. I got up and headed for the house.

"Hey, Little Man, don't be mad," Jackson said. "I was just saying . . ."

"I'm fine," I said. "Be right back."

I returned with a book written by Bill Walsh, the famous 49ers Super Bowl coach.

Jackson looked at it. "*Finding the Winning Edge*? What's that?"

"Bill Walsh coached two of the greatest quarterbacks ever, three if you count Jeff Garcia." I sat down on the lounge chair and opened a notebook I'd also brought with me. "Neither of them had a strong arm, at least by NFL standards. They ran an offense that capitalized on their quickness—not just their physical quickness but their mental quickness."

"Nobody's more mentally quick than you." Jackson leaned toward the book. "Except maybe me."

I looked at him and laughed, because he was right about that. Already, Jackson had proven his smarts in school. He knew everything and I'd seen him helping the other players on the team with their assignments, even if we'd only run the play one time and even if it was for another position other than his. "Yeah, so let's do this together."

"What exactly are we doing?" Jackson flipped open the pages to chapter eleven. "'Preparing to Win'?"

"Yeah, that's *exactly* what we're doing," I said. "Preparing to win, on the field and off. Not only do I plan to win whatever Dietrich throws at me, but I'm gonna hit Coach Hubbard so hard and so fast with this stuff that he's never gonna see me coming."

Jasmine Peebles had some PR firm of her own do a press release about her legal challenge to my father's will. When I asked my mom about *my* press conference, she frowned and asked if I wanted to be like Jasmine Peebles. That hit home and I trusted my mom when she said a press conference would have to wait until things were final.

"Then, if you get the team," my mother said, "the time will be right. If you don't, there's no reason for a press conference, is there?"

Word quickly spread that my stepmother had suddenly put the fate of the Cowboys into question again. It was in the newspapers, on the sports channels. People, I learned, love controversy. The only thing better than a kid who suddenly inherits the Dallas Cowboys is the same kid who might lose it all. I kept my head up and played it off like it was no big deal—just a typical day in the life of Ryan Zinna.

Not much changed in the lunchroom. I still had a celebrity status that made a lot of kids sneak glances at me, and the popular group still snubbed their noses. I wasn't really concerned with what went on in school, though. It was football practice I was thinking of, and all the diagrams and plays in the back of my notebook that Jackson and I had created and that I'd perfected while my teachers droned on about long division, adverbs, and the postwar recovery of Europe.

The school day finally ended and I scrambled out of my last class, nearly skipping to my locker before heading directly to Coach Hubbard's office. I hadn't had gym that day, so this was my first time around him since he'd seen me with John Torres and the Cowboys' GM. I marched right into his office and he looked up from the desk he was writing at. He whipped off a pair of wire glasses I hadn't known about. His face actually turned red. He was embarrassed! To see me! I don't think it was the glasses either.

"Hey, Coach."

"Ryan . . ." Coach Hubbard rose and began tucking his enormous collared shirt into a pair of navy-blue coaching shorts that were ridiculously tight. "Good to see you."

Coach stuck out his hand like it was the first time we'd met. I was a new person to Coach Hubbard, no longer a half-pint scrapper who was an annoyance. I was the *kid owner*. I shook his hand and plopped my notebook down onto his gray metal desk, flipping it open to the back pages.

"I'm worried, Coach." I studied his face to see how high my stock had climbed. Before he knew I owned the Cowboys and before he'd seen John Torres in real life, I don't think Coach Hubbard could have cared less about Ryan Zinna being worried.

"Well," he said, "maybe I can help."

Coach tucked the last remnants of his circus-tent shirt into the back of his pants, briefly exposing a butt crack I could no more ignore than I could the Grand Canyon. He turned a deeper shade of red and sat back down. The metal chair creaked beneath the burden.

I sat down, too. "Coach, I know I'm not the starting quarterback."

I let that hang out there. Coach Hubbard blinked at me and shifted in his seat, sending up a flock of squeaks and rattles from the hardware below. "Okay."

"But I'm thinking that—you know—if Estevan Marin were to get hurt, I'd have to go *in*."

He nodded. "That's part of the game."

"Right, but if I have to go in, the offense we run . . ." Again, I let my words float out there between us, hoping he'd pick up the slack.

He didn't.

"So, I was thinking about Bill Walsh's book about the West Coast Offense, you know, *Finding the Winning Edge?* Kind of old school, right?"

Coach Hubbard let loose a blustery chuckle. "Bill Walsh was a genius, for sure. Joe Montana, Jerry Rice . . . *that* was a team."

Coach sighed in honor of the good old days.

"So, if I do have to go into the game, I just thought we should be ready with some plays that I *can* do, instead of trying

150

to do things I *can't*. Bill Walsh said that's one of the keys to a winning team."

"Did he say that?" Coach Hubbard's forehead rumpled like a gorilla studying a banana before I cleared my throat and his eyebrows shot up. "Yes. Sounds like him."

"Look, I know I'm short, but so was Jeff Garcia. So Walsh put in a bunch of plays that let him roll outside the pocket."

"Of course," Coach Hubbard said.

I got excited. "So I was looking at these plays of his. I copied them down. Three or four people in the pattern, and you've always got a check down . . . a safety valve if all else fails. All rollouts."

I flipped through the pages, pointing to plays I'd drawn.

Coach Hubbard's brow rumpled again as he studied the plays. He hummed and nodded as if this was all old news to him, but really, the most complicated play he'd ever drawn up was a crossing pattern under a go route, which looked like an upside-down four.

"I didn't know if you were thinking the same kind of thing." I spoke fast. Coach Hubbard might lend me his ear because of my new status, but he was still in charge. "I just thought if I drew up some plays, it'd save you some time. I hope you don't mind, Coach."

It was a bold move, me showing up in the coach's office with plays already drawn up, but if I was going to get my chance, I just couldn't let it slip by without doing everything possible to help myself succeed. If we ran the same old offense, I'd be doomed. But if Coach Hubbard even put in a couple of my plays so that I could run them if I had to, I'd stand a chance.

Coach Hubbard's small dark eyes narrowed.

I gulped. "Maybe we could try out a couple of these plays? Just an idea, Coach. Some teams do it. I know Marin's got more experience than me and I'm not saying make me the starter, but if it looks good? Boy, what a one-two combination. Like a fighter. One-two pow!"

I stopped talking and lowered my fists and waited.

Coach Hubbard scowled and wormed his pinkie into one of the tiny ears plastered to the side of his big dome. "That's a lot to learn, Ryan. Guys have been practicing these plays for weeks. Putting all these new things in would be tough to learn in a few days. I know *you* could do it, but the linemen . . ."

"I know, see?" I flipped the pages, excited. "I've got it so the line calls are all the same, color-coded like the offense we run now so everyone knows who to block. When we roll out to pass, it's really the same blocking as the zone sweep play we run right now, and all the linemen know how to block it. That's part of the beauty!"

Coach Hubbard went after his other ear now. "You've got receivers and running backs, too. They'd have to learn—"

I nodded. "I could work with those guys. Also, I was thinking about the run game out of spread formation. See, 'cause if you look, these plays all call for the quarterback to be taking a shotgun snap, and with four receivers spread wide, there's just one running back, but Bill Walsh has some awesome running plays."

"Run game?" Coach stopped drilling his ear. "West Coast is a passing offense."

"But fifty percent of the time—if you do it right—you run the ball. A lot of people think this kind of offense is all passing, but it's not. Here, look at these one back running plays." I flipped the pages again to show him. "And that's another thing I was thinking about, Coach. I mean, you probably thought of this, too, as soon as we started talking about a spread offense. We've got the *perfect* guy to be that single back."

"Griffin Engle?"

"Aw, Coach." I reached out to pat his shoulder but pulled back and tapped the desktop, not wanting to go too far. "You're testing me, aren't you?"

Before he could speak, I continued, "Jackson is so obvious. It's amazing, isn't it? A guy his size who can run like that?"

"He is amazing, but . . ."

"In a conventional offense, of course, he's a lineman, but in a spread? Wow. Who's gonna tackle him when the box is empty with the defense out covering all our wide receivers? Coach, it's really a great idea. Ha! You almost had me with Engle, and sure, he could do it, but with his speed he'll be the best of our four wideouts, a big-time weapon." I flipped a few more pages, to some running plays that used a single back. It was simple stuff: an inside trap, a cutback, the zone runs we already had only without a fullback, a simple counter, and a draw. It was stuff a barnyard animal could learn.

Coach Hubbard just blinked. Then he looked at his watch. "Mind if I keep these papers?"

"Yeah, sure. They're yours, Coach." I popped up. "I figured I'd just save you the time of copying them down from Coach Walsh's book and matching up the line protections with the ones we already have."

"I kind of like it," Coach Hubbard said as I reached for the door. "No reason we can't try a couple out and see how it goes."

"Great, Coach. Thanks!" I started through the door, heading for the locker room to change.

"Ryan."

I stopped and looked back.

"How was it? I mean, the Cowboys and John Torres and everything?"

I took a breath and shook my head, staring into space. "Dream come true, Coach. A dream come true."

Coach Hubbard had stars in his eyes, too, and he looked not at me but possibly at some kind of magical halo that he imagined over my head. "Yeah . . . I bet."

"And even if my stepmother does end up controlling the

team, I'm still going to own a pretty big hunk of it, which is kinda cool," I said.

Coach Hubbard's eyes widened and his head nodded on its own.

"See you out there, Coach." I turned and headed into the locker room, and didn't bother to look back.

37

If I could write the story I wish had happened, I'd tell you that my copied plays and the spread were a knockout success. But they weren't. *I* knew how to run the spread, and honestly, the plays we tried to run weren't that hard, but you'd have thought my teammates, and my coaches, were trying to recite the Gettysburg Address in Chinese. It was downright silly.

Guys went offside. Guys ran into each other. Guys dropped passes. Guys missed blocks. They tripped. They stumbled. They fell.

The spread died a quick death out there that very first day, and the sound of my own voice trying to pump it up began to annoy even me. It certainly annoyed Coach Vickerson. He had no patience for anything he didn't understand, and it was easy for him to laugh at Coach Hubbard when Jackson lined up at running back. Coach Hubbard raised his chin and said

156

he wanted to try something innovative. Jackson ended up slipping on the first play, fumbling on the second, and having my screen pass bounce—literally *bounce*—off his helmet on the third play. Coach Vickerson hooted and howled out loud.

"Enough innovation yet, Coach?" He gasped with laughter as he tore up a hunk of sod and tossed it for emphasis. "This isn't the winning edge, it's the edge of *doom*!"

Coach Hubbard's face went red and he gave me a dirty look like I had planned to embarrass him. "This isn't the Cowboys, Ryan. We tried, but I think it's time to go back to the old offense."

I wanted to kick Coach Vickerson in the shin. He must have read my face because he turned his scorn on me. "Minna Zinna, you trying to mess with our offense so you can see over the line? Rolling out? One back? Four wide receivers? Don't you worry yourself. Estevan Marin may not own an NFL team, but he's not going to get hurt, and Simpkin will be back next week."

Coach Vickerson turned to Coach Hubbard. "Come on, Coach. We got defense to work on."

I trudged along to a fresh spot on the turf with my head hung when someone banged into me from behind. I spun and jumped up, ready for a shoving match. It was Markham, and he stood immovable as a granite block.

"What are you doing?" I spoke with the firm tone I thought fitting for an NFL owner.

"Cut it out, half-pint," Markham growled. "I don't care if you own the entire state of Texas—you're a bite-sized dingle berry and you better thank your lucky stars you won't be out there playing quarterback Saturday, because I'll *help* the guy I'm supposed to block get in your face and smash you into the dirt."

"That's garbage. We're on the same team, Markham." I stayed standing straight, but my backbone was quickly turning to jelly.

"Team? You're not a football player." Markham snorted. "You got to hang around the past few years and watch because no one wanted to listen to your mommy crying. Yeah, you might be the 'kid owner'—or you might not be, right?—but you're not a *player.*"

"Markham!" Coach Vickerson shouted from the defensive huddle. "Get over here so we can run the play! Don't tell me you're under Zinna's spell, too! The Dallas Cowboys aren't gonna win this game on Saturday. *We* gotta do that!"

Markham gave one final snort and banged into my shoulder on his way past. I took my spot on the scout team offense with the other backup players, looking at the diagram of the play we were to run off a card Coach Hubbard held up high in our ragtag huddle. Suddenly it seemed like I'd made no progress at all. I tried, but I had failed. Now I might lose not only the Cowboys to a nasty woman but also my own middle-school team to a boneheaded coach and a bully. I bit my tongue for the rest of the practice, ran my sprints, and kept to myself as everyone changed in the locker room. Jackson gave me a sad look.

"What?" I asked.

"I *liked* being a running back in those new plays," he said in a low voice.

"Would've been nice if you could've held onto the *ball.* That's an important part of it, in case you didn't know it."

Jackson just nodded his head like it was a lesson learned. I snorted like Markham and realized what I'd done. They say that kids who get bullied become jerks themselves, and I think sometimes that's kind of true. It's like playing hot potato. You want to get rid of it, pass it on, as fast as you can.

"I'm sorry, Jackson," I said softly. I was disappointed in myself.

"That's okay." Jackson shrugged it off. "Maybe we'll get it right tomorrow. Maybe they'll realize how smart you are with the plays and all that."

"Maybe the sun will turn purple." I looked up at an imaginary sky.

Jackson wrinkled his brow.

"I'm kidding, Jackson. I'm being sarcastic. They won't realize I'm smart because they can't see it. They're not even smart enough to know they're not smart. They see you and they see a big kid who should play on the line. They see me and they see a kid too short and small to play anything but receiver, set way out on the edge of the formation, as far from the action as humanly possible."

"Yeah, but . . ."

"They're the coaches." I cut him off with a grouchy wave of my hand.

"I wish there was *another* coach, or a coach for the coaches or something. I don't know."

I perked up suddenly. "Dude, you're brilliant!"

Jackson nodded enthusiastically and chuckled, then stopped and gave me a puzzled look. "I am? Why?"

"I think I have an idea." I smiled.

My mom picked me and Jackson up from practice. When we pulled in through the gates to my house, there was a black Mercedes SUV in the circle.

"Who's this?" My mother spoke under her breath, pulling the truck right up behind the Mercedes.

I watched Coach Cowan climb out of the SUV. He wore not a warm-up suit, as he had at the Cowboys complex, but jeans, loafers, and a simple white button-down shirt. It was as perfect as it was unbelievable.

The Cowboys' coach marched right for my mother, extending a hand. "Felt like we got off on the wrong foot yesterday."

My mother blushed, a rare thing for her, but in the sunshine, wearing normal clothes, Coach Cowan looked less like a caged predatory bird and more like a minor movie star, even with those close-set dark eyes. He had a confidence about him that made you want to listen.

"It was a shock for me to see you all yesterday." He turned now and shook my hand. "I didn't expect you to stop by, and I'm sure you know that Bert and I don't see eye to eye. When a team loses—especially a team like the Cowboys—people start pointing fingers."

Before I could speak, he held up both hands. "I'm not here to do that, Ryan. I just want you and your mom to know that I'm not the aloof Ivy Leaguer some of the sports radio personalities are making me out to be. I wanted you to know that I'm somewhat of a regular guy."

"Ryan may not even own the team, you know," my mother said.

"Mom." I scowled at her.

"Maybe he doesn't, but maybe he does." Coach Cowan gazed right at her. "Funny things happen. Either way, it bothered me how I acted."

"Well, would you like to come in and have some coffee and talk?" My mother had recovered from her blush and was back in control.

"Sure. Thank you. Coffee would be great," he said, turning to face Jackson, eye to eye. "And your name is?"

"Jackson Shockey, Coach." Jackson stepped right up to the coach, grinned and nodded and shook hands.

As we followed my mom into the house, Coach Cowan looked from Jackson to me and back again. "And you're Ryan's . . ."

"Teammate," I said. "Jackson and I play football together, Ben Sauer Middle School's seventh-grade team."

Coach Cowan's eyebrows went up and I couldn't help but wonder if that was because he was surprised that a boy my size could play football, or that a boy as huge as Jackson could actually be my teammate. My mom waved us to the kitchen table, where we sat down across from Coach Cowan.

"He's twelve," I said. "Big, huh?"

"Real big."

"He's fast, too. The fastest kid on the team."

"Seriously?"

"The smartest, too. Can you imagine him running the ball in a one back set?" I folded my hands and laid them on the table.

The plan began with Jackson's idea of a coach for our coaches. Now the idea came to life right in front of me: Coach Cowan could help me *sell* the spread offense to Coach Hubbard. I could only imagine Coach Hubbard's face if he got to sit down with Coach Cowan, a real-life NFL coach. (If you know anything about coaches, they're even more impressed by NFL coaches than the players.) I had General Patton's flanking maneuvers fresh in my mind from history class. I could outflank Coach Vickerson with superior firepower in the form of Coach Cowan.

The only problem was, I had no idea if Coach Cowan would go along with it.

I had no idea if he'd even care.

A light seemed to blink on in Coach Cowan's eyes.

"You're like Ironhead, Jackson," Coach Cowan said, sounding kind of excited.

"Ironhead?" Jackson rumpled his face.

"Ironhead Heyward," Coach Cowan said. "Played for the Saints back in the nineties. I loved watching him. Big as any lineman, but fast. Used to knock people over like bowling pins."

My mom dumped some beans into the coffee maker and it began to grind and hum. She took two mugs from the cupboard and set them down next to the coffee maker. "Ryan? Jackson? You boys want some sodas?"

We both nodded and she brought us two Cokes, then sat down at the head of the table. "Coffee will be ready in just a minute. Milk? Sugar?"

"Just black, thank you," Coach Cowan said.

"I'm trying to get our coach to run a spread offense." I watched Coach Cowan closely, to see if he really cared what I thought or if he was just there on a social call to try and be our friend, protecting his job in case things went my way. "I play quarterback."

I could tell by the way he looked that he was sizing me up all over again. "You fast?"

"Real fast," I said. "And smart."

To my surprise, Coach Cowan scratched his chin and nodded his head. "Yeah, you got that look in your eyes, like you're thinking a couple steps ahead. You remind me of Kellen Smith."

"Kellen Smith? Your fourth-string guy?" I squinted and looked over at Jackson, who shrugged.

Coach Cowan laughed. "Right, Kellen. You met him in my office the other day. He's on our practice squad. Undrafted free agent out of Central Michigan. I can't get Hamhock to move him onto the active roster no matter what I say."

"Why would you?" I was shocked that the young man I'd seen in Coach Cowan's office was a football player at all. "Move him, I mean?"

Coach Cowan got a serious look on his face and leaned toward me. "Kellen is small, like you, and smart . . . like you, right?"

I nodded and felt my cheeks get warm.

"Yeah, a perfect spread quarterback. Kellen's mobile and makes decisions quick as a hiccup, but his arm strength is nothing to write home about, so there he sits, studying film with me on the outside chance he'll ever get a shot. Hamhock would rather put the ball boy out there at quarterback than

Kellen. Sometimes I think it's just so I can't be right." Coach Cowan turned those hawkish eyes on me and his voice changed slightly, as if someone had given him a little jolt. "What offense does your team run now?"

"Two backs, a pro set," I said. "Lucky if we even have two wide receivers on the field. Coach Hubbard likes to swap out a receiver for a tight end. He says with two tight ends you can build a fortress for a pocket to throw out of."

I liked the way Coach Cowan shook his head in disgust, even though he didn't come right out and say my coaches were stuck in the past. "That's simple and straightforward, like checkers. I like chess."

I nodded, wildly. "I know, and our coach wants to *be* a college coach or even an NFL coach one day."

"He'll have to get his head around some bigger ideas than a pro set and two tight ends if he wants that. It's a different game these days." Coach Cowan smiled at my mom as if he was apologizing for the football talk. It seemed like the perfect time. I didn't even stop to think twice about it. I sprang my trap. "Maybe you could talk to him."

"Who?" My mom was the one who asked, but Coach Cowan was looking.

The coffee maker stopped grinding and I spoke louder than I had to. "Coach Hubbard."

"Dude," Jackson said, "I don't think Coach Hubbard's gonna change his offense, do you?"

"If Coach Cowan makes the suggestion, I bet he would," I said.

"That's kind of devious," Jackson said. "Don't you think?

Like, tricking him into thinking he's gonna get something out of it, like it's an audition for coaching."

I waved my hand in the air. "It's not devious; it's a great opportunity to make his team better."

"Ryan." My mom frowned. "That's not really fair to ask Coach Cowan. He has a lot to do. He came here to get off on the right foot, not to help coach your middle-school football team."

"He doesn't have to coach my team, just talk to my coach." I spoke fast, wondering just how much Coach Cowan wanted to be my friend, wondering if he really thought I still had a chance to own the team.

As he opened his mouth to reply, I guessed I was about to find out.

"I love talking football." Coach Cowan's head bobbed up and down to prove his words were true.

"See, Mom?" I wanted her to get on my side.

"Well." She let the gurgling coffeepot distract her.

"If you could go over a couple basic plays, I know Coach would put them in. How could he not?"

Coach Cowan shrugged. He looked suddenly uncomfortable, and he said, "As long as your coach is okay with it, I'm happy to talk to him."

"When?"

"Ry-yan." My mom drew out my name.

Coach Cowan shrugged. "Now?"

"Now?" my mom asked.

"After a cup of coffee?" Coach Cowan tilted his head. "I'm here and it's a bit of a drive so I may as well do it now . . . if that's okay. We'd have to ask your coach."

I jumped out of my chair. "Coach Hubbard would eat his own dirty socks just to *meet* you, let alone get some ideas on the spread offense."

Jackson shook his head, but grinned. "He'd definitely like to meet you."

"What's a spread offense?" my mom asked.

"It's the new rage in football, Mom. Instead of the traditional two backs, two wide receivers, and one tight end for the skill players, you go with three or four wideouts to throw to and just one running back. It's a *passing* offense. It's fast and it's furious."

My mom huffed and gave me a look before turning to Coach Cowan. "I'm sorry—this is kind of awkward, what with Ryan maybe owning the team and you being coach. It's really not necessary to go meet Ryan's coach. Even *if* Ryan ends up somehow owning or partly owning the team, you showing up here is more than enough of a nice gesture. I'm sure you've got lots to do."

I ground my teeth together and tried with all my might to signal to Coach Cowan that my mom was one hundred percent wrong. It *wasn't* enough just to show up. If Coach Cowan helped *me*, I'd help *him* (if I could help him). I had to remind myself of that, which actually made it even better to have him in this spot because once he met with Coach Hubbard, my seventh-grade football coach would be a changed man. I saw the look in Coach Hubbard's eye when John Torres showed up and I knew that as an aspiring coach, meeting Cody Cowan would be a life-altering experience for him.

Coach Cowan wasn't a leader of men for nothing. He studied my face, then said to my mom, "Actually, after that cup of coffee, I'd enjoy it. I love talking to young coaches, especially ones who are interested in the spread offense."

I grinned and high-fived Jackson, who smiled and shook his head again.

I couldn't hear Coach Hubbard's voice on the other end of Coach Cowan's cell phone, but I could imagine it trembling with excitement. He agreed to head right back to the school and meet us in his office to talk football "Xs and Os" was what Coach Cowan said. Jackson and I rode in Coach Cowan's Mercedes and I provided the directions. When we got there, Coach Hubbard's van was already in the parking lot and we walked right into the back of the school.

Coach Hubbard was one of those people who thought that if he could fit into a smaller-sized piece of clothing, then he really was that size. His legs swelled from the hem of his coaching shorts like cookie dough bursting from a tube, and his stomach stretched the belly of his collared shirt so tight that a crescent of pale white gut peeked out at us just above his belt line. I coughed and looked away, but Jackson stared right at the sneaky gut and tugged his own shirt down as if to signal to Coach Hubbard.

Coach Cowan paid no attention. He was like a math teacher with his dry erase marker squeaking away on the board, creating angles and numbers, Xs and Os, until the entire space was covered in hieroglyphics. We were crammed into three desk chairs in the very front of our team room. Coach Hubbard scribbled notes in his book, wide-eyed and mystified.

Coach Cowan was talking fast. ". . . So, if they roll the coverage over your slot, your quarterback simply hits the back-side hook. If the linebacker plays off, he throws the check down. Both throws are very high percentage. See? You can stretch the field *and* have a back-side counter *without* making your quarterback throw dangerous passes."

Dangerous passes were long passes. (Also, coincidentally, the ones *I* couldn't throw so well, but no one mentioned that.)

Coach Hubbard's mouth hung slack and a bit of drool spilled from the corner of his lip before he swabbed it with the back of a hand. "But . . . the back is set weak, so how can it be a strong set?"

Coach Cowan gave me a quick glance and bit his lip before nodding rapidly. "Okay, you're still hung up on the formation. I get that. This stuff is complicated and I've been doing it for a long time, so sometimes I get ahead of myself. Let me go back to the formation. . . ."

And on it went, the entire school empty all around us, but the team room's lights blazing bright like a forge of football knowledge. Coach Cowan finally stopped trying to get Coach Hubbard to grasp the big picture, or even very much of the offense. He focused on teaching Coach Hubbard two run plays and two pass plays. And Coach Hubbard beamed with pride as he drew, all by himself, a Trips Left Chase Right Waggle. When Coach Cowan applauded, Jackson and I looked at each other and pitched in, too, clapping until our hands hurt.

"You got it." Coach Cowan patted Coach Hubbard on the back. "Put it in, and you'll be off to the races. I can send you a new play every week, maybe two if you'd like."

"I'd like two hundred!" Coach Hubbard was so happy, he wasn't thinking straight.

Coach Cowan laughed. "Let's go slow. Before you know it, you'll have the whole playbook down."

The sun had set by the time we walked out of the school toward Coach Cowan's Mercedes and Coach Hubbard's minivan.

"You really think Jackson here could be my one back?" Coach Hubbard gave Coach Cowan a knowing and important look.

Coach Cowan read the eager look on my face and nodded. "Of course. Remember Ironhead Heyward?"

"The Saints runner?" Coach Hubbard rumpled his brow. "Gosh, I was about eight years old then."

"Right, and you still remember him." Coach Cowan jangled his keys. "Two hundred and sixty-five pounds. Ran a 4.5. You ask Bobby Hebert—"

"The quarterback?" Coach Hubbard's face glistened with sweat.

"Yes," Coach Cowan continued. "You ask Hebert and he'll tell you Ironhead made that offense roll and that made Hebert into a multimillionaire. Sure, Jackson can do it. If he's as fast as you say he is."

"Oh, heck yeah." Coach Hubbard patted Jackson on the back like they were old friends.

"Thanks, Coach Hubbard," Jackson said, smiling.

"Coach, I gotta tell you," Coach Hubbard continued, "I appreciate this little session more than you know and I'm looking forward to staying in touch."

"Well." Coach Cowan clicked open the locks to his Mercedes with the push of a button. "If Ryan has anything to say about it, I know we will. He's a big fan of yours, Coach. That's why I'm here."

Coach Hubbard blinked as this set in and I wondered what other force in the entire universe he imagined prompted this visit if it wasn't me. If he didn't already fully appreciate that before, he sure did now.

Coach Hubbard gently placed a hand on my shoulder, squeezing it warmly. "Best thing about this offense, Coach, is that it gives a player like Ryan the ability to use his brains out there, make those reads, get us first downs."

"That it does." Coach Cowan extended his hand to shake good-bye. "Some people don't get that. Glad to know you're not one of them, Coach."

I don't think Coach Hubbard would have ever let go of Coach Cowan's hand. It seemed like he wanted to stand there shaking it forever, but Coach Cowan slipped away and he, Jackson, and I climbed into his SUV and he drove us back to my house. On the way, Coach Cowan flipped on the radio and we heard a couple of loudmouths talking about the Cowboys and how they wished Jimmy Johnson had never left the team in the nineties.

"You don't think the Jimmy is too old?" one announcer asked.

"Old? He's *still* got his hair," the other announcer said. "Do you not watch the man every Sunday on Fox? Now *that's* a coach!"

I glanced over at Coach Cowan when the announcers—I knew them from their highway billboard as the Sportz Dogz—started tearing into the current coach . . . him. Coach Cowan remained calm, but I didn't when one of the Sportz Dogz rattled a paper and said they had just received word about the status of the new ownership.

"Well, well, well," said the Sportz Dog with the newsflash, making everyone wait. "You're not gonna believe this."

"Read that thing already, will you? I'm starting to wonder if you even *can* read." The other Sportz Dog sounded as eager as the rest of us to hear.

That set them both off on a good chuckle.

"Okay, okay, okay. Here you go . . . in a surprise ruling late this afternoon, US Federal District Court Judge Abby Dobney ruled on the following injunction . . ."

"Injunction?" the other said. "Sounds like it hurts."

"Only when I laugh."

They broke out into more stupid laughter. "But seriously, an injunction is when a judge basically calls a time-out to stop the action." He rattled the paper into the microphone. "Wow, some of you are really gonna be torked about this . . ."

"Read it already." The other Sportz Dog sounded angry.

"I will." The first Sportz Dog cleared his throat and I balled my hands into fists.

I stared at the satellite radio, listening hard.

"Judge Abby Dobney ruled in favor of Jasmine Peebles, granting her a preliminary injunction against any other possible claims to the Dallas Cowboys' controlling ownership. While the court believes ownership will be split among the parties, an initial review of the facts suggests Ms. Peebles will end up with a controlling interest. The court's preliminary finding allows her to continue to control the team until such time as a permanent resolution should be found. Whew. That was a mouthful."

For some reason, both of those morons laughed some more. The first Sportz Dog rattled the paper again. "So, sounds like the kid still gets a slice of the team, but the stepmom, Jasmine Peebles, is running the show."

"And our sources tell us that Jasmine Peebles is a Hamhock fan."

"So maybe we get rid of Ivy Boy Cowan?"

"What's that? Some form of foot fungus?"

They busted out laughing some more.

I looked at Coach Cowan, whose jaw was set. I knew Ivy Boy referred to his Harvard Ivy League background.

"Doesn't sound good, does it?" Jackson asked.

The coach winced and snapped off the radio. "Well, it's just a *preliminary* injunction. Sounds like nothing is final. These court cases are like a football season. Lots of games left to play."

"It's never good to lose the opener, though," I said, trying to remember which famous coach I was quoting. "Sets a bad tone."

"Well, sorry about that, Ryan," Coach Cowan said.

"Because you wasted a trip to visit me." I couldn't help being a grump, even though I knew he must be as upset about this news as I was.

"I didn't waste anything. You'll still end up with something. Even these clowns said that."

"A *minority* owner, with no say and no swing."

"Whoa. That's sounding a little spoiled, no?" Coach Cowan laughed and snorted. "Lotta kids would be happy with a couple hundred million dollars' worth of an NFL team."

"Yeah, Ryan—that's kinda awesome anyway," Jackson added.

"I don't need money, Coach. I thought I *owned* the Dallas Cowboys. That *made* me someone. Coach Hubbard was going to build his offense around me."

"Your coach didn't care if you owned the team. He seemed pretty open to running the spread, Jackson at running back, and you at QB. I think he may still do it. It's not controlling the Cowboys, but it's something."

"Coach Hubbard will forget the plays you taught him by the time he brushes his teeth tonight, let alone be able to learn the new ones." All I could do was lean my head against the window and groan.

"Not if I keep in touch with him," Coach Cowan said.

"You'd do that?" My mouth fell open. "Why?"

"I don't know." He shrugged. "Whether or not you own the Cowboys or are kind of my boss doesn't matter. I like you, Ryan. You're a good kid. And you remind me of Kellen. I like quarterbacks like you guys. I was like that, too."

We were halfway home when my mom called. "There are TV trucks on the street. Tell Coach Cowan to drive right past them. I've already told them the first one to set foot on our property will spend the night in jail."

"Jail?" All I could think was that I needed as much positive press as I could get. Maybe it would influence the judges. I had no idea how all that worked, but it didn't seem wise to threaten the TV reporters. Besides, I was aching for a little attention.

"Yes," she said, "jail. I'll not have them harassing us."

"Mom, maybe I should just talk to them. Have that press conference?" I gave Coach Cowan a hopeful look. "People are all talking about it anyway. Coach and I just heard it on the radio."

"We are *not* commenting, Ryan." Her voice left no doubts. "*If* you end up running the team—which still sounds absolutely crazy—but if, then we'll script a press conference and

177

you can make a statement. We are not going to let the media control this."

We reached the end of my street and I could see the trucks.

"Put Coach Cowan on, please," my mom said.

I did and I watched him nod as he slowed down and turned around. "Yes, of course. I understand. Sure. I think that would be really nice. Yes, we'll meet you there."

Coach handed me back the phone. "I guess we are going out for dinner?"

"Okay," I said, trying not to sound too excited about a meal with the Cowboys head coach.

Even though it looked like I'd lost control of the Dallas Cow-boys and the whole kid owner thing was going down the drain, lo and behold, a handful of kids appeared at our table in the lunchroom the next day. One of them was the brainiac friend of Izzy's, Mya Thompson. Another, to my real surprise, was Estevan Marin. Estevan wanted to be a doctor like his dad and, although he wasn't a star athlete, he was solid and well liked.

Griffin Engle was there, too. Griffin always kept to himself, a blond-headed quiet kid who made the girls giggle. Everyone respected Griffin, though, because he did well in school and was also the fastest kid in our grade.

No one said anything about joining us. We all just sat there acting like it was normal to be there. It felt nice to be part of a group and I assumed it was all because of the Cowboys. So I also assumed it wouldn't last.

The popular table didn't like it; I could tell by the whispers and the dirty looks they threw at the newcomers to our table. I heard Jason Simpkin in the hallway before science class picking on Estevan for "kissing up" to me and saying I wasn't "worth a stack of pennies."

Estevan didn't even know I could hear through the crowded hallway, but my back straightened a bit when I heard his reply to Simpkin. "Stuff it, Jason. Ryan's cool. I don't care if he owns the Cowboys or not. He's on our team."

I was struck by the idea that maybe me owning the Cowboys wasn't the reason people sat with us. Maybe they actually liked us? Maybe they saw things the way Izzy did, that thing about what people had on the inside. That felt pretty good, I can tell you.

Honestly? It made me feel bad for plotting all those plays for when I took over Estevan's position as the starting quarterback. But he was cool with it. And really, nothing could make me feel bad enough to drop the idea. I just felt like it was my time to try and shine, and I'd been waiting more than a while. Even though the Cowboys might be slipping away, Coach Cowan's visit gave me a new hold on the Ben Sauer Middle School's seventh-grade team.

At practice that afternoon, Coach Hubbard whispered to me that he'd gotten a text from Coach Cowan. After giving me a wink, he put in the four new spread plays with me at QB. When we ran them in team period, they all worked, and I was able to convince Coach Hubbard to run some more. The whole thing made me light-headed with confidence. I felt like I could do anything and I even started changing things in the huddle like it was backyard ball instead of a highly organized offensive system.

"Jackson, this time, instead of blocking back on the Waggle play, we'll run a back-side screen. Linemen, one hit, let your guys through, then set up a wall in front of Jackson." I looked around at the faces of my teammates. Except for Markham's look of disgust, everyone else looked eager and excited.

"Okay," I said, feeling bold, "Waggle Right Screen Left on one . . ."

Markham stood straight up and hollered. "Hey, Coach! Zinna's trying to change the play! He's making stuff up!"

Everyone froze and Coach Hubbard chugged over to the huddle with his clipboard tucked under one arm. "What's this?"

My mind spun fast. I knew I probably shouldn't have changed the play on my own. I should have asked Coach Hubbard. He probably would have been okay with it. That gave me an idea. Maybe, if I gave him credit for it, he'd go along with the idea. I think his head was spinning so fast from all the new offensive stuff, he might not even remember what we had and hadn't put in.

I jumped up and pointed at Markham. "Yeah, that's what Coach Hubbard told me to do. He went over these plays with me yesterday. He's working with Cody Cowan, you doofus. Coach Hubbard knows *all* this stuff. He taught it to me and asked me to put it in if you guys were *ready*. I guess everyone's ready, Coach, except for Markham, who suddenly thinks *he's* the coach."

Markham's jaw hung open and his yellow-rubber mouth guard peeked out at us.

Coach Hubbard hitched up his shorts, tucking the shirt in around his gut. "What's your beef, Markham? You want to be a part of this offense or not? I'm sick of you griping. One more word and Sloan can start for you. Maybe you need to concentrate on defense."

Markham looked like a whipped puppy, big-eyed and stupid. He shook his head and stuffed the mouth guard back behind his lips and bent down into the huddle again, steaming, but put solidly in his place.

"I got it, Coach." I kept on pretending. "Just like you said."

I didn't dare look at Coach Hubbard because I knew that confusion would be covering his face.

We ran the Waggle Screen and Jackson ended up dancing in the end zone.

"Nice play, Coach." Coach Vickerson slapped Coach Hubbard on the back and Coach Hubbard stood proud.

That was just the beginning. The rest of the day and the next, we practiced the spread offense plays with me in there, and every day we got better. Coach Cowan didn't stop texting Coach Hubbard little snippets of encouragement and Coach Hubbard took great pride in sharing them with me.

On Friday, Coach Hubbard showed me a text he'd gotten that read, "Lead with the spread, Coach. It'll boggle their brains."

"I was thinking the same thing myself," Coach Hubbard said, nodding wisely at me.

Before practice began, he announced to the team that we'd be using the spread offense to start the game and catch our opponent, Carthage Middle School, off guard.

Everyone looked at me. Some patted my back as we began warm-ups. Even Estevan saw the sense in using such a potent weapon as the spread and he congratulated me, even though I could see he was disappointed.

Excitement swirled with fear in my gut and I could barely keep my lunch down. I looked at Jackson, who gave me a wide grin and two thumbs-up.

I was going to be the starting quarterback.

Izzy, Jackson, and I celebrated the good news by going back to my house after practice. We were hanging out at my pool waiting for dinner when Izzy suddenly yelped and looked up from her phone. "Oh my gosh, you're not gonna believe this."

"What?" Jackson and I said together.

We crowded around her deck chair and she played a link from the local Fox channel's website. The title of the video was "Kid Owner," so I thought it was about me, but when the image came up, it was Jasmine and my half brother, Dillon, ruling over the podium normally reserved for the Cowboys coaches and star players. Big blue Dallas stars covered the curtain behind them. John Torres and Bert Hamhock flanked the mother and son combo.

"What the—" I mumbled in shock.

You could see from cluster of microphones that all the local news stations as well as ESPN were there. Dillon wore a suit and tie, and stood nearly as tall as his mom. She had on a matching dark-blue pinstriped business outfit of her own over a white ruffled blouse.

I got red-hot mad. They were having *my* press conference, or at least the one I had hoped to have.

Jasmine cleared her throat and surveyed the crowd of reporters like a queen ready to pass judgment. "Good afternoon," she began in a hoity-toity voice. "You've all had fun with the term 'kid owner.'"

She looked around some more and I thought I could see her soul boiling.

"So I'd like you to continue to use the term." She turned and smiled warmly at Dillon.

"No way," Jackson whispered.

Jasmine tousled Dillon's hair and even though he shot her a dirty look, she continued to grin. "Because the Cowboys *do* have a kid owner. . . . Ladies and gentlemen, allow me to introduce the *legitimate* son of Thomas Peebles, my son, Dillon Peebles. Kid owner."

Jasmine stepped aside and I must say I was shocked and a little impressed when Dillon stepped up to the podium and glared out at the crowd of reporters with those pale-blue eyes. "My father . . . was a nice person. That's how people knew him."

Dillon's voice quavered like a tall tower of Jell-O. He gulped and it looked like he might choke. He seemed to have suddenly lost his nerve. Delight bubbled up into my nose like a soda burp. The next thing I expected out of his mouth was a stream

185

of vomit, but he surprised everyone.

"But that's *not* how you win football games." Dillon swallowed again, but he seemed to be regaining strength from his tough talk. "You win by making tough decisions, by *being* tough, and that's what I'm going to do. With my mother's guidance, I *will* make the Cowboys the franchise it was in the early nineties, when Troy Aikman, Emmitt Smith, and Michael Irvin ruled the NFL. The Dallas Cowboys are America's team, and America deserves a *winner*."

Dillon stepped away from the microphone, hands trembling but looking pleased. His mother beamed at him as she regained control of the room, leaning into the microphone. "My son is too modest."

Now *I* wanted to puke. After the news of the injunction came out, my mom said Jasmine Peebles was the kind of person who didn't know what she wanted, only that she wanted whatever other people had. My mom was right.

"Dillon is an exceptional football player himself." Her red lipstick glowed on the screen and her teeth shone like sharpened pearls. "He was his team's MVP last season and he's well on his way this year. He's played in the Eiland Elite Youth Football Program since he was six years old."

I looked across the deck chair at Jackson and narrowed my eyes. "Did she say 'Eiland'?"

Jackson's lower lip disappeared beneath his teeth and he nodded. "Yup, that's what she said."

"*He* plays for Eiland?" I was thinking about the way people said the name "Eiland"—like it was some kind of prayer—ever since I knew what a football even was. I was thinking how we faced them in two weeks, how they hadn't lost a game in *five years*, and how *Dillon Peebles* was one of their star players.

"Are you okay?" Izzy leaned toward me with a look of concern.

"Fine. Why?" I gulped down some bile.

"You look like you might get sick," she said.

Jackson hopped up off his side of the chair. "Dude, don't yak on me. One red tide is enough. That was disgusting."

"I'm not yakking on anyone." I scowled at my friend. "This is perfect. We're gonna stomp all over Eiland and now it'll be even better. I can't wait to see that big jerk's face when I light them up and you run for about ten touchdowns."

Dillon wasn't the only one who could talk tough, but, unlike the reporters listening to Dillon, my friends didn't seem to buy my version.

"Well, they haven't lost in five years," Jackson said.

"You really think you can beat them?" Izzy asked, looking worried.

"Of course," I said. "That's football. Anyone can beat anyone."

They looked at each other and shrugged.

"Yes," Izzy said.

"Sure," Jackson said.

I could smell their doubt.

Izzy brightened. "I bet Coach Cowan could help."

"Yeah." Jackson nodded with excitement. "He could. Can you imagine him breaking down film on Eiland and coming up with some plays that just crushed their defense?"

It was a beautiful ray of hope.

"Yeah," I said. "That's awesome."

"Would he do it?" Izzy said. "Help you, I mean."

"He's already helping me." I didn't want to tell them why. I didn't want to say that I thought a lot of the reason was that he might like my mom.

"So, let's go get us a big win tomorrow," Jackson said, "then talk to Coach Cowan the next time you see him about giving us some help. Good?"

"You know I'll be there rooting. You can do this, Ryan." Izzy held out a fist.

We all bumped fists and then got called in to dinner.

Not even Teresa's grilled shrimp with mango salsa over rice

could revive my appetite. I picked at it, but mostly just moved the food around my plate, hoping no one would notice. For whatever reason, the whole thing with Dillon taking over the team and playing for Eiland had me preoccupied and super nervous about my debut as a starter the next day, even though the two things had no connection. But I just couldn't shake the feeling.

My friends left, and I slept badly that night. In the morning, I was jittery and still sick to my stomach.

"You okay?" My mom tousled my hair at the breakfast table, where I tried to sip a glass of juice. "I mean, you have a lot going on—school, football, the whole mess with the Cowboys and Dillon."

"Not really." I could admit that, now that my friends weren't around. "I feel like it's slipping away, you know?"

"You shouldn't let that get to you. What will be, will be, Ryan. And maybe it's for the best."

I shrugged. "Honestly? I'm even more worried about the game today. I've never been a starting quarterback."

My mom sat down across from me with a mug of coffee in both hands. She breathed in the steam and smiled. "It's very exciting, Ryan. I know how long you've waited for this chance. I thought I'd be nervous—all those big kids chasing after you so they can smash you into the dirt—but I'm not."

"Smash me into the dirt? Great, Mom." I couldn't keep the sarcasm out of my voice.

"Well, you know how I've always worried about you getting hurt, but I looked into it. First of all, very few youth players die."

I did a double take and studied her face. "Mom! Are you serious? Die?"

She looked genuinely shocked. "I . . . I'm sorry, Ryan. I'm not doing a good job of trying to show my support. I know this is so important to you. I just wanted you to know that I am rooting for you."

I nodded. "I've got to just go do this thing." I pushed back from the table and went upstairs to my room, where I dry-heaved in my bathroom until my stomach felt like a clenched fist.

I staggered downstairs and said nothing as she drove me to the school. When I got out, she leaned over the seat. "I won't ask for a kiss or anything, but good luck, Ryan. Go get 'em. I'm going to do a little shopping, but I'll be back for the game by kickoff, and I'll be watching."

I couldn't even talk, so I just nodded again. I closed the door, slung my sports duffel bag over my shoulder, and turned for the school as my mom's truck rumbled off.

I staggered into the locker room like a zombie, trying my hardest to keep a tough-guy look plastered onto my face.

What I saw hanging from the handle of my locker made me almost certain that what was about to happen would be a total disaster.

Jackson hadn't arrived yet. I was pretty certain that if he'd been in the locker room, whoever did what they did to my locker wouldn't have dared. But Jackson was running late and there it was, taped by one corner: a pink-and-white baby diaper.

I wanted to cry, really, but knew if I did that, it would be the end for sure. I wasn't upset that someone was suggesting I was a baby girl. It was the lack of respect that hurt me. How could someone—a *teammate*—insult their own starting quarterback on the day of a big game? It cut me to the core.

Instead of tearing up, I bit the inside of my cheek and marched right up to my locker. I tore the diaper down and chucked it in the trash before dumping my bag on the bench and going about my business as if nothing had happened. As I pulled the shoulder pads over my head, Jackson arrived, wild-eyed, snorting steam, and ready for action. I stole a look at

Bryan Markham. He sat polishing his helmet and grinning at Jason Simpkin, who was dressed in street clothes, since he still couldn't play because of his injury. Neither of them looked my way, so I couldn't be totally certain it had been them who'd hung the diaper, but that would have been my best bet. I knew Estevan was upset about not starting, but we were friends. Plus, he just wasn't that kind of kid.

My limbs felt like they'd been frozen and had yet to thaw. My hands trembled as I buckled up my chin strap, putting my helmet on before everyone else, knowing that I was giving in to the urge to hide but unable to stop myself.

"Let's do this thing, baby!" Jackson smacked my shoulder pads with both fists and my head swam. "Wahoo! Big dog's gonna *eat* today! Touchdown Daddy! *Dancin'* in the *end zone!*"

I shuffled off, ignoring my friend as best I could, struck by the term "baby" even though I knew he had no idea about the diaper. He was caught up in his own craze and I just couldn't seem to find my rudder. I was drifting and floating and lucky I could even get myself out onto the field, where a handful of teammates and coaches from both teams hung around on the grass, sizing each other up from the corners of their eyes. In the stands, hundreds of people were already waiting for kickoff. This is Texas and Ben Sauer Middle School feeds into Highland High School, one of the top programs in the land, so there was a huge audience.

"Ryan!" Coach Hubbard shouted, pointing at me. "Come here!"

I jogged his way and tried to listen as he licked his lips and ran through the plays, bug-eyed with nervousness. He actually made me feel somewhat normal. He wasn't *as* shaken as me, but he was a close second. Coach Vickerson, on the other hand, joked and laughed with the Carthage Middle School coaches like they were old buddies.

Coach Hubbard peered past me nervously. "So, how you feeling?"

I cleared my throat to keep from squeaking. "Good, Coach."

He looked at me with obvious disbelief. "Yeah. Good. This spread . . . I like it. If we get the run game going, it'll be tough to stop."

I nodded and spilled out what I knew like the nervous ninny I was. "That's what the spread does. You take what they give you. They always give you something. Every defense. If we can run the ball with one back—and you know we can after what Jackson did in practice—then they'll have to choose. Either they line up more guys in the box to stop Jackson *or* they play enough guys to cover everyone who goes out for a pass and keep a free safety in the middle. You have to pick one, unless they sneak a twelfth man onto the field."

Coach Hubbard gave me a twisted smile. "That'd be a penalty."

I studied his red face. "Yeah. I know."

"Of course you know. I was kidding," he said. "Anyway, I want you to know that I'm going out on a limb here for you with this spread. There's a group of dads—actually they were your coaches in youth league—who are urging me pretty hard to stay with Estevan and our regular offense."

"Yeah, but that's youth league." I wanted to draw a bright line between Bryan Markham's and Jason Simpkin's dads and

Coach Hubbard. "They're not *real* coaches, like you . . . like Coach Cowan."

I struck the nerve I was aiming for. Coach Hubbard tucked in his shirt, stood a bit straighter, then sucked in his gut a bit. "Well, I like to get along, Ryan. It's a good way to be."

"Coach Cowan believes in this system, Coach. He believes in *you*."

"You think so, huh?" Coach Hubbard looked worried, but interested. He gripped his college ring with its deep-blue stone and cranked it around on his finger.

"I *know* it. Look at all those texts he sent you." I pointed at the phone in his pocket. "I mean, I'm not saying it'll happen, but sometimes high school coaches get their shot in the pros. Skip right over college. It happens."

"Look, Ryan." Coach Hubbard put a hand on my shoulder pad and gave me a super serious look. "Stop with the Coach Cowan thing. Do I want to move up in the coaching world? Of course I do, but I'm not taking advice from Coach Cowan because I think he'll give me a job. I'm doing this because I believe it just might be the ticket to winning this game. Jackson at running back? Who'd have thought of that? We could beat this team today. We could beat *Eiland*."

Just the name of my half brother's team made my stomach heave. I wanted to focus on today first. I looked over at the Carthage Middle School squad, which was beginning to fill up their side of the field as players streamed from the visitors' locker room. I told myself that they didn't look so terrifying. Then I saw Jackson, marching out onto the turf, hands balled into fists, a spring in his step. I could practically feel the intensity oozing from him. My heart gave a little leap.

"We're gonna smash these guys, Coach," I said. "Trust me. If it doesn't work, you can always use Mr. Markham's plan, but I am not gonna disappoint you."

"I don't think you are, Ryan." Coach Hubbard twirled his whistle and smiled.

Jackson barged into our midst. "You ready, my man? You ready? 'Cause the big dog's gonna *eat*!"

"I'm ready," I lied. This time, I was the one to slap Jackson's pads with my fists. He howled. Coach Hubbard blasted his whistle and we all fell into our places like the pieces of a clock. The gears began to turn and I was the mainspring, suddenly giddy. Suddenly fluid. Suddenly ready to be right where I was, in the center of it all. This was football. This was what I dreamed of.

I got sent out to the center of the field as a captain along with Jackson and Bryan Markham. Markham shook with rage and wouldn't even look at me. I ignored him, wondering what Jackson would do if he knew about the pink diaper. I wanted to unleash Jackson on him, but we had a game to play.

The ref looked at me and I called heads.

I won the toss and chose to receive the ball.

We'd start on offense, running the spread.

Carthage Middle School kicked.

Griffin Engle returned the ball to the forty, a good start.

"What's the first play, Coach?" I bounced on my toes, ready to go out.

Coach Hubbard looked at the field, smiling. "What do you think? I don't want any excuses, so you pick the best play you think we've got."

I almost couldn't speak because I wasn't sure he was being serious, or just kidding. I recovered quickly, though. "Trips Left Chase Right Waggle?"

"Good! It's your play. Make it happen." Coach Hubbard slapped my shoulder pad.

I nodded and jogged out onto the field. I couldn't help stealing a look at my mom up in the stands. Izzy had arrived and sat right next to her with her friend Mya Thompson. I tried not to grin as I stepped into the huddle and called the play. I marched toward the line with my teammates. I stopped in the shotgun position four yards from the center and looked at the defense, the simple 6–2 I'd expected.

"Down!" I shouted, trying to keep my voice from squeaking. "Green eight. Green eight. Set. . . . Hike!"

The center fired the ball back. I snatched it and faked the handoff to Jackson, then rolled out. Griffin Engle came wide open across the field. I fired it, hard. The ball nosedived into the turf so that the tight end had no chance to even get a hand on it.

Blood rushed to my face and my jaw tightened.

Markham bumped into me on my way to the huddle. "What the heck was *that*?"

I said nothing. Markham was right. It was pathetic, and I felt panic rising up inside me like a volcano ready to explode. I tried to breathe deep and looked to the sideline. Coach Hubbard motioned with both hands for me to settle down and signaled in a Waggle Dive play. It looked exactly like the play before, only I was to hand the ball off to Jackson, who'd run it up the middle. I wasn't sure if the play was because Coach Hubbard didn't trust me to throw it, or if he'd legitimately seen a weakness in the defense during the last play.

I called the play, forcing myself to sound more confident than I felt by thinking about that stupid diaper and getting mad.

We went to the line. I shouted the cadence and handed the ball off to Jackson.

Jackson took off like a bullet, snatching the ball from my

hands before he burst through a gaping hole and trundled down the field toward the end zone. It was incredible how easy Jackson made it look. Only one defender had a shot at him, the free safety. The defender had just the right angle and he was coming fast.

I clenched both my hands and gasped at the thrill of it.

Jackson exploded through the free safety. That kid went flying like he'd been shot out of a cannon. Jackson barely broke stride. He crossed the goal line, turned, and looked right at me, holding out the ball for everyone to see before he leaped into the air.

It was a footrace to the end zone as the rest of us swarmed Jackson. I wasn't happy that I'd muffed my first throw, but Jackson's run was spectacular and it meant that no one could argue that the spread offense wasn't working. Coach Hubbard wasn't going to let up. On the next two series he called one running play after another. Jackson answered the call, steamrolling defenders on the other team or simply outrunning them with his speed. This was all good—great, really—but I started to feel like I could use my skills to help things along as well. It was great to be winning, but now that we had a lead, I wanted to do more than hand it off to Jackson.

We were up 21–7 when I finally made a suggestion. "Coach, what do you think about a couple passes on this next series? They're crowding the line to stop Jackson and the pass should be wide open, right?"

I stared hard at Coach Hubbard's eyes, willing him to remember one of the foundations of Coach Cowan's offense: balance, the spread ultimately being half runs and half passes.

Coach Hubbard nodded and called the play like it was a reward for good behavior. "Okay, Ryan. Run that Waggle pass again. Maybe with a smash route?"

I rewarded him back with a smile. "Great call, Coach."

This time I rolled out, and saw Griffin Engle, my wide receiver, come open on a comeback. I set my feet and threw. The ball wobbled through the air on a slow arc, but it was nearly on target. Griffin snatched the ball, turned, and got another five yards before being blasted out of bounds.

I pumped a fist into the air like I was the one who had scored three touchdowns. It felt *that* good, but I seemed to be alone in my joy. My teammates took it in stride, gathering up in the huddle like a fifteen-yard pass was no big deal.

I was hungry for some real glory and when Coach Hubbard called the same pass play going the other way, it made me giddy. This time, Griffin Engle was covered. I dashed toward the line like I was going to run, the cornerback took off for me, and I dumped the ball over his head to the now-wide-open Engle. Griffin took it down to the one-yard line, where he was brought down by his heels. We huddled up and I could taste the end zone. This was my dream come true: Ryan Zinna orchestrating a touchdown drive for all to see, working the ball down the field, making great plays through the air.

When Coach Hubbard called a dive play that would send Jackson up the gut, I gave Coach Hubbard a hopeful look and made a passing motion. Coach Hubbard glared at me and signaled the dive play again. I wanted to explode. Two passes brought us to the doorstep of the end zone and now I had to hand the ball off to Jackson again? He had three touchdowns already! Didn't my coach see that? Of course I wanted to win first and foremost, but we *were* winning. Coach Hubbard obviously wasn't thinking about *me*, and wasn't this whole spread thing and running Jackson *my* idea to begin with? I knew I was being selfish, but I couldn't help it. Didn't I deserve some glory?

I growled the running play to my teammates, then broke the huddle and marched to the line.

Jackson was gurgling with laughter and muttering joyfully to himself like a little kid getting ready to trick-or-treat. "Touchdown Daddy, again. Touchdown *Daddy*."

He had no idea I was furious.

The defense crowded up for a goal line stand. I barked the cadence. The center snapped the ball and I snatched it out of the air. What happened next, I swear, I didn't even think about.

I just did it.

I guess I figured it was better to ask for forgiveness than for permission.

One thing every spread quarterback has is a favorite receiver
and a hot signal. A hot signal tells your favorite receiver
that you've read an all-out blitz and he needs to run a slant
pattern—just take off at a forty-five degree angle and get ready
for the ball to come right at him. No one else knows it's coming, just you and him. I already had a favorite wide receiver, for
obvious reasons. Griffin Engle was fast and athletic and smart.
Also, he sat at my lunch table.

I showed Griffin the hot signal on Thursday before practice
and we'd run one during Friday's practice. It pasted a huge grin
on Coach Hubbard's face to see something he never dreamed
his players could do in seventh-grade football.

"I like it!" he'd shouted. "Yes! You see an all-out blitz in a
game, you just run that hot route. Good work, guys."

The signal was me grabbing my face mask, then pointing to

my head. Griffin knew to nod if he got it.

There was no all-out blitz coming, but I looked over at Griffin, grabbed my face mask, and pointed to my head.

He gave me a look of confusion, but nodded that he understood, and I started barking out the cadence.

The snap came back and I grabbed it. Jackson took a side step, then took off toward the line on the dive play. I stepped like I was going to hand the ball to him, but didn't. I pulled it at the last instant, ran past him, and threw it over the heads of the wave of defenders swarming the line. I couldn't see Griffin. I have to admit that, but I knew right where he should be and I threw it anyway.

I won't forget that moment until the day I die.

It was every A+, every full Halloween bag, every Christmas tree bursting with presents, every birthday cake, and every last day of school crammed into one special instant.

It was my first touchdown pass.

Everyone cheered and the world seemed to stop a moment to tip its hat my way. All the images are in my head, like photos from an album. The look of confused frustration on Jackson's face melted away. His grin burned brightly at me and he hugged me and lifted me up with a howl. The rest of my teammates out on the field (except for Bryan Markham) slapped my shoulder pads and helmet. I looked up into the stands and saw my mom bouncing on her toes and clutching her hands together in a frozen clap. Izzy was right beside my mom and so happy she hugged Mya.

The thing about touchdowns is, they're like potato chips: once you have one, you're pretty much crazy to eat a whole bag. That's what I was thinking as I jogged off the field with the Ben Sauer fans still clapping. I wanted more.

Coach Hubbard was red-faced. "Ryan! We need to talk."

To his credit, Coach Hubbard didn't embarrass me in front of everyone. He took me over to the side behind the Gatorade table, whipped off his sunglasses, revealing crazed eyes, and spoke in a harsh whisper. "What was that? You *do not* run this football team."

I gulped. "I know, Coach."

"You know? So tell me what happened to the play I called? And don't even think about telling me you saw an all-out blitz! We both know better." Coach Hubbard flashed his eyes at a couple players who dared get near and they bolted for the far side of the bench.

I hung my head. "I just did it, Coach. I'm sorry."

"You 'just did it'? What does that mean?"

"I . . . I wasn't thinking," I said.

"No. You weren't thinking," he said. "And if you do that again, it'll be the last play you run at Ben Sauer."

I took a deep breath and looked hard into my coach's eyes. "Coach, I'm sorry."

"Good. That works. Now let's go win this thing." He nodded and turned back toward the game, where Coach Vickerson was sending his defense out onto the field.

I realized how close I'd come to blowing everything, and Coach Hubbard's acceptance of my apology filled me with relief. Still, I knew that if things didn't go well, I'd never get a chance like this again.

As if the gods of football were against me, a cheer went up from the visitors' bleachers. I looked up to see the ref raise his arms, signaling a Carthage touchdown.

Coach Hubbard scowled back at me from his place on the sideline. "Come on. Let's go get them again."

We received the kickoff, but incredibly, Griffin Engle muffed it. Carthage scooped it up and ran it into the end zone. In a matter of seconds, our big lead was cut to seven. With the score now 28–21, Griffin fielded the next kickoff with unusual caution and got rocked on the ten-yard line, giving us terrible field position.

Coach Hubbard grabbed my face mask and looked hard at me. "You thinking what I'm thinking here, Ryan?"

I had no idea what he was thinking, but I swallowed some of the stomach juice seeping up into my throat and nodded. I was thinking of Jackson.

"Yeah, Coach," I said. "Let's start with a 32 Dive."

Coach Hubbard looked out at the Carthage defense, swarming off their bench in a frenzy of excitement. "I like that call."

I buckled my chin strap and ran out onto the field.

The beautiful thing about Jackson was that he was unstoppable.

I called the 32 Dive and he ran for twenty-three yards. I nodded at Coach Hubbard when he signaled in a 37 Toss Sweep. Jackson got eighteen more yards. Next we ran a 33 Draw where Jackson smashed his way down to the four-yard line.

I quickly jogged over to the sideline and, hopeful that I hadn't been dreaming, suggested we run a Bootleg Pass.

"You don't want to just punch it in with Jackson?" Coach Hubbard raised an eyebrow.

"It's what they'll be expecting, Coach." I tried not to sound like a beggar, hard as it was, but things were going so well and I'd scored a touchdown on the last pass play, hadn't I? "The Bootleg should leave me untouched and Griffin wide open."

Coach Hubbard scratched his jaw. "Okay. You're right. Do it."

I jogged out onto the field and joined the huddle without looking at Jackson because, yes, I did feel like I was stealing his touchdown. But I was hoping he'd understand. Either way, I broke the huddle and set up in the shotgun position. I called the cadence, took the snap, faked a handoff to Jackson, and rolled out into the open field.

I'd been right.

The entire defense swarmed Jackson, who carried out a fake so believable that I could have waltzed backward into the end zone. I didn't, though. Like every other quarterback in the game of football, I wanted passing touchdowns, so I lofted the ball up on a slow arc so that it dropped into the waiting bread basket of Griffin Engle's arms.

Jackson was the first to hug me. "Awesome, Ry-Guy!"

"Well, you got us down here." I had to give him the credit he was due. "Sorry for the fake and just changing the whole play."

"No worries, man. You punched it in." Jackson grinned and slapped my back. "Nice pass."

Coach Hubbard met me at the sideline and gave me a high five. "Worked perfectly."

"Thanks, Coach." I fought back a grin of my own. The whole thing was almost too good to be true.

It didn't stop there. While we mostly gave the ball to Jackson to run with, Coach Hubbard obliged me with enough pass plays to make me look like a star in the making.

Twice, I was able to get the ball to Jackson as my receiver, and that made everything right in the world by giving each of us credit for a touchdown, me for passing and him for receiving. I ended the game with four touchdown passes. Jackson had four running and the two receiving.

In the end, the Ben Sauer Middle School crowd of parents and supporters cheered for us until they were red in the face. Carthage was no Eiland, but they were a respectable opponent who we ended up beating by a score of 49–24. In the locker room after the game, spirits were high and cascades of laughter rebounded off the tile walls. Backs got slapped. Jokes were made and there was lots of cheerful boasting about what we would do to Eiland the following week.

Jackson smiled ear to ear, but his pregame bluster was gone. He looked exhausted and his arms hung limp as he sat hunched over on the bench in front of his locker, breathing deep.

"Ry-Guy," he said, barely able to raise his head. "You were the man."

It was the second time he'd said that, and I grinned at him. "Ry-Guy . . . I like that."

I didn't want to even mention my old nickname: Little Man.

"Well, you are the Ry-Guy." Jackson nodded wearily. "That you are."

I gripped the thick meat of his sweaty shoulder, thinking how lucky I was that he dropped into my life. "And you're the Big Dawg, Jackson. The biggest dog on the planet."

"Woof," he said. "Heh heh."

Jackson started to slowly pull on his street clothes. I checked my phone, hoping I'd get a congratulations text from Izzy while I waited for Jackson to finish changing. My phone stayed quiet, but when the two of us walked out of the school, a crowd of parents and supporters cheered wildly. I recognized a reporter from the local paper with a camera, blushed, and looked down at my feet, thinking about how I was going to have to get used to this kind of attention if I ended up controlling the Cowboys.

As the crowd converged on us with congratulations on their lips, I struggled to find the right words to accept their praise but still come off as moderately humble. I was also worried that my mom might step in and not allow me to talk to the reporter, but hopeful she'd realize this wasn't about the Dallas Cowboys; it was about the Ben Sauer seventh-grade football team.

When I looked up and realized what was really happening, I got the shock of my life.

People brushed right past me.

It was Jackson they were there to celebrate. His six touchdowns were some kind of a league record, and so were the two hundred sixty-seven yards he'd gained running the ball. As people literally bumped me out of the way, I gulped down my disappointment.

I was a first-rate fool for thinking I was the star. That title belonged to Jackson.

Jackson's mom was there with a flashing smile. She posed with her son while the local reporter snapped pictures and people showered them with praise. Jackson's being a newcomer to the Highland area—a veritable outsider—seemed suddenly to make people even more eager to meet him and get in on the sensation that he so obviously had become in one short afternoon. This, after all, was Texas, where football was king and people started spotting future stars at our very ages.

The only two people not fawning all over Jackson were my mom and Izzy. Mya, I noticed, had positioned herself to get a quick selfie with Jackson, as did several other of our classmates. My mom and Izzy stood off to the side, politely watching and waiting for me as I slogged over to them, my head held a little higher now in defiance of all the misplaced hero worship.

"Ryan, what a super game!" My mom's excitement was genuine, although she did glance a bit nervously at the crowd around Jackson.

"I guess," I said, looking up from my phone and fishing for more compliments. "We won."

"Won? You had four touchdowns!"

I grinned and shrugged like it was no big deal.

"It's very exciting, Ryan," she said. "You must be so proud!"

"A little." I kept my eyes rigidly away from Jackson's fan club.

"And Jackson? Wow!" My mom never could let the elephant in the room go unnoticed.

It was time for Izzy to chime in and do her best. "Jackson at running back was all your idea, too."

Part of me appreciated the praise she was giving me, but another part was annoyed that she didn't use her first observation to be something about *me*. I had four touchdowns myself, didn't I? I also realized at that moment just how much Izzy meant to me. What she thought seemed even more important than what my mom thought.

"I think we ran the ball a little too much." I tried to sound as grown-up and smart as I possibly could. "We won't get away with that next week against Eiland, I can tell you that."

"Really?" My mom was confused. "It seems like it'd be hard for anyone to slow Jackson down. He's so much bigger than everyone. Faster, too. He's like some kind of speedy bulldozer out there."

"Yeah. He's good, Mom." I glanced at a couple of people who'd congratulated Jackson as they walked right past me. "Okay, let's get going. I'm worn out. Izzy, want to come over?"

"Sure. My mom's having some garden party and I have to say hello to everyone, but I'll be over after. Is Jackson coming?" she asked.

I shrugged and turned my attention back to my phone. "I guess. I'll text him and ask. Let him enjoy the moment, right?"

I sighed and looked at my phone, pretending to text. I really didn't want Jackson to come over right now. I knew I was being a bad friend, and I hated feeling this way. But I just couldn't let it go.

"It's a big stage, Ryan." Izzy frowned at me.

"Excuse me?" I said, looking up.

"There's room for you *and* Jackson. You can both shine." She softened her look and her voice became a little more patient. "Troy Aikman, Emmitt Smith, *and* Michael Irvin. When the Cowboys won their last championships, they had three stars that everyone knew."

"Yeah," I said, feeling a little ashamed but not wanting to show it. "I get it. I'm good."

"Great. I'll see you later, then." Izzy headed off toward her house, which was only two blocks away from the school.

I felt even worse now about only pretending to send a text

213

inviting Jackson over, but I still couldn't shake my disappointment. It had been a day of mixed feelings for me and I just felt like I needed Izzy to myself.

As we turned to go, I saw a group of people who *were* interested in me, but not in a good way.

It looked like the Markhams and the Simpkins had their entire clans gathered up. I don't know how many brothers and sisters, aunts, uncles, and cousins Bryan and Jason have in total, but there were at least two dozen people standing there wearing the Ben Sauer blue-and-white colors. The younger girls held pom-poms and the fathers had PYFL coaching caps on just to make sure everyone knew their importance in the hierarchy of Highland football. They didn't glare at me all at once. It was more like when you set off a firecracker string: *pop*—a glance—*pop*—a glare—*bang*—a hateful sneer—*pop*—spitting a green gob in my general direction.

It wasn't that I knew they despised me for putting myself in a position to challenge whether or not Jason Simpkin would return as the starting quarterback, it was that I *knew* they had gathered their forces and would do all they could to try and ruin me.

My mom and I marched right past them without giving them a second glance. It wasn't until we were safely rumbling down the street high up in our pickup that she frowned and said, "I hate those people, although 'hate' isn't a word I should be using."

"I hate them, too." I had no such reservations and didn't bother asking who she meant by "those people."

"They're planning something," I said.

"What do you mean, 'planning'?" She glanced my way.

"When you take over a team at quarterback, and you play well, and you win, the coaches will sometimes keep going with you, until you make a big mistake." I saw by her expression that she wasn't really following me. "Jason Simpkin will probably be back next week from his concussion, or he will now that he sees I could actually take his job. They're going to press Coach Hubbard to put him back in his starting spot. I, on the other hand, am going to do everything I can not to let that happen."

She looked at me quizzically. "You mean do really well in practice and, like, beat him out?"

I wondered if she wanted to ask if I had used my status with the Cowboys to influence Coach Hubbard. But I just said, "Yes. Beat him out."

"And you think you can?" She actually sounded excited for me, like she'd been bitten by the same touchdown bug I had.

"Yes," I said, "especially if we keep running the spread offense. I know the offense. Jason Simpkin doesn't, so Coach Hubbard needs me if he wants to keep running it."

"It worked so well." She glanced at me hopefully.

I sighed. "I wish Coach Cowan would spend another half hour with him. If Coach Hubbard felt like he had Coach Cowan behind him and some help with the game plan against Eiland . . . wow, I can't see him even thinking about going back to the old offense. Can you?"

My mom bit into her lower lip and got a faraway look in her eyes. I kept quiet, and we pulled into our neighborhood.

It wasn't until she'd shut down the engine and removed the keys from the ignition that she spoke. "I think Coach Cowan would do that."

"But I'm not the kid owner anymore, Mom. Dillon is, so why would he?"

"Yeah, well." She tossed the keys up and snatched them from the air before opening the truck door. "I think he might do it anyway."

I followed her into the house. "Mom, what are you going to do, just call him?"

She was already dialing. "Why not? The worst he can say is no."

Coach Cowan didn't say no.

The Cowboys were playing the Cardinals at home the very next day. They'd had their walk-through practice earlier in the day while we were beating the pants off of Carthage. Coach Cowan had finished his interviews with the TV network announcers and completed the finishing touches on his game plan. He said he'd be happy to meet with Coach Hubbard *and* have dinner with us tonight. He told my mom he was glad to hear about the success I had in my game and to tell me that would make it easy for him to continue to support the spread offense with Coach Hubbard, who he promised to call right away to set up a meeting.

We were out back at the pool when Izzy finally arrived. We sat three in a row on lounge chairs, soaking up the sun. I was excitedly telling Izzy the news about Coach Cowan meeting with Coach Hubbard when my mom's phone buzzed. She looked at it and scowled before telling us it was a text from Eric Dietrich.

"He wants me to call him," she said, reading it from her lounge chair next to the pool. "I wonder what he wants."

"Well, call him and find out, Mom." I nearly jumped out of my chair.

She did and after five minutes, she hung up and set the phone down. She cleared her throat and turned to us. "Mr. Dietrich has arranged for us to see the Cowboys game tomorrow from his box and to go down on the field before the game. He wants to give us a tour and let you meet some players, then discuss the whole ownership situation while we sit with him."

"What about Dillon?" I had to ask.

My mom shrugged. "He said he's got the whole thing under control and that whether Dillon runs the team or not, we're going to have an interest and we have as much right as anyone to be there."

"Wow," I said, my heart thumping. "Nice."

"The Cowboys are invading our life," she said.

"Mom, we *own* part of the team," I said.

"*You* own *part* of the team. Maybe," she said. "If Jasmine and her son are running it, I didn't think we'd be getting a tour, but to me the whole thing sounds like Eric is up to his old tricks."

"Tricks? What tricks?"

My mom's smile soured and she took off her sunglasses, signaling the seriousness of what she was about to say. "Some people are never in charge . . . but still, everything seems to go just the way they want it to. It's called being manipulative. I saw him do it with your father and if he did it to him, I imagine controlling Jasmine is as easy as tying his shoes."

"He must not control her completely." I swatted a bug off my leg, wondering if, because of what I was doing with Coach Hubbard and suggesting certain plays so I could be quarterback, my mom was trying to draw some similarity between me and Mr. Dietrich without saying it. "Otherwise she wouldn't have been going to court for that injunction thing so that *she* runs the team until they sort it out."

My mother peered at the sunshine glittering on the rippled surface of the pool. "Or maybe that's exactly what he wanted."

"Wow, just like that ancient Chinese general people are always quoting in business and sports, Sun Tzu." Izzy nodded with appreciation. Apparently she followed my mom's logic. I didn't.

"What do you mean?" I asked.

"They had an article in the *Dallas Morning Star* yesterday. I didn't tell you about it because I wanted you to focus on your game. It explained how if she breaks the will, you'll each own forty percent of the team and how you both need Eric because his twenty percent combined with one of your forty becomes the majority. So, who's really in control? Him."

"Complex strategy." Izzy gave a short nod.

"He told us that, Mom."

"I know he told us, but did Jasmine contest the will on her own? I just don't know," my mom said.

"Did he run the team when my d . . . when Thomas Peebles was alive?"

"If he did, he sure didn't take any of the blame for them not going to the play-offs, did he?" My mom raised one eyebrow. "See what I mean by clever?"

She put her sunglasses on and laid back in her chair, exhaling like she was ready for a nap. I lay back, too, listing to the gurgle of the waterfall spilling into the pool and thinking about Eric Dietrich—wondering if he was really as bad as my mom thought. I remembered Jackson thinking I was devious by getting Coach Cowan to suggest a spread offense to Coach Hubbard. I sighed and thought about Coach Cowan heading our way.

"When's Jackson coming?" Izzy asked, breaking into my thoughts.

"Uh, I think he wanted to be with his mom," I replied. It was sort of a lie, considering I never asked him, but I was telling her what I thought. I didn't like the look Izzy gave me, but I was saved when Teresa opened the back door and told my mom that Coach Cowan had arrived.

Coach Cowan stepped out onto the terrace dressed even nicer than before. This time he wore some pleated shorts and a black silk shirt and his hair was slicked back. My mom got up and quickly pulled on a cover-up over her bathing suit. They greeted each other first, shaking hands.

"We'll have to stop meeting like this," my mom said.

Coach Cowan blushed. "I think we should meet like this more."

I looked at Izzy and rolled my eyes. Izzy winked back at me.

"Something in your eye, Ryan?" my mom asked.

"No, I'm good." I bit down on my lip.

Coach Cowan said hello to me and Izzy and asked if I was ready to go sit down with Coach Hubbard.

"I called him on my way over and he asked if we could meet him at his house." Coach Cowan shrugged. "I told him that shouldn't be a problem. He texted me the address. It's on the other side of the tollway, not too far."

"Sure," I said. I never thought of Coach Hubbard having a house. I guess in my mind he was just a part of the school, like the principal's office or the wooden stage in the auditorium. It would be weird, but good for my plan of getting in tighter with Coach Hubbard. I thought it was a pretty safe bet that Jason Simpkin hadn't been there.

My mom insisted Coach Cowan have dinner with us later

as payment for his efforts and he agreed without hesitation.

"You want to go with me and Coach, Izzy?" I asked.

"Or you could stay with me, Izzy," my mom said. "I'm going to get my nails done."

I shook my head at that.

"I'd like to stay with you, Ms. Zinna," Izzy said, turning to me. "But you may need me."

I opened my mouth to say something, but the look on Izzy's face and my knowledge of her fantasy football prowess made me nod in agreement. In the middle of all this, my phone buzzed with a text from Jackson, asking me what was up. I tucked the phone back in my pocket without answering, and Coach Cowan, Izzy, and I climbed into Coach Cowan's SUV. I offered Izzy the front, but she climbed right in the back.

"This is your show, Ryan. I just want to go along."

On the way to Coach Hubbard's, Coach Cowan listened to the Highway radio station, and I wondered if he and my mom knew that about each other. I was thinking about the advantages and disadvantages of Coach Cowan and my mom possibly getting together when he suddenly turned the music down.

"So, you had a big day today?"

"It was fun. Coach Hubbard practically let me call the plays." I couldn't help feeling proud, talking this way to a guy known for his offensive strategy throughout the NFL. Even though the Cowboys were struggling under Coach Cowan as a head coach, no one doubted his offensive brilliance and the work he'd done as a coordinator. He got a lot of the credit when the 49ers won the Super Bowl and he'd been calling the plays.

"When you have a full understanding of the spread," he

said, "it's almost impossible to defend."

"Why don't the Cowboys run it all the time?" I thought I knew, but I wanted to hear him say it.

Before he could answer, Izzy leaned forward and said, "Hamhock had the team pay big money for John Torres. You can't shell out that kind of cash for a big arm and not use it. Even if he can't cut the mustard."

Coach Cowan glanced at Izzy and chuckled. "Well . . . you're right about the money, and John Torres, physically, is a superior quarterback. He's got all the tools to play in a pro set, but—it's not that he's not smart, but he doesn't process information as fast as you'd like to see, even in a regular offense, but particularly if you're running the spread."

"What about Kellen Smith? Does he process it?" I asked.

"I believe he does. I'd love to find out in a game, but like I said before, I can't get Hamhock to put him on the active roster." Coach Cowan glanced at me.

"Boy, would I love to have him on my fantasy team if he got to play," Izzy said. "I'd start him in front of Peyton Manning."

"You got Peyton on your fantasy team?" Coach Cowan raised his eyebrows and looked at her in the rearview mirror.

"Yup. And my running back is LeSean McCoy from the Eagles."

"How'd you get both?"

"Trades, Coach. Trades."

"You know about Kellen, then?"

Izzy opened her mouth to speak, but I cut her off. "If I win with this court thing—or whatever it is—I'll get him on the roster."

I could see from the corner of my eye that Coach Cowan was trying not to smile, and I wondered if it was because he was happy or if he didn't think that was going to happen.

"Let's hope you do, then," he said as we turned into the driveway of a small ranch jammed into a row of houses in a dusty neighborhood just across the tollway. "Well, this is the address."

We got out and I heard the thunder of jet engines and the sharp smell of fuel as a plane took off from Love Airfield, which was only a few blocks away. I eyed the houses up and down the street and noted the peeling paint and rust-stained garage doors. While Coach Hubbard's house was no more than ten miles away, it was in a neighborhood that was totally different from mine and Izzy's.

Coach Hubbard's wife was as skinny as he was big, but she had a giant baby on her hip who had jet-black hair like hers. She looked me over and said, "Wow, you are little."

Obviously she wasn't my new favorite person.

Beyond her rough words, I couldn't help staring at the green-and-orange tattoos all over her pale arms and shoulders.

She led us through a kitchen, where pots and pans overflowed from the sink and every kind of spill you could imagine decorated the walls, from baby formula to gravy.

"He's cute." Izzy tickled the roll beneath the baby's chin and the baby giggled and spit.

That won us a smile from Mrs. Hubbard before she shoved open a screen door in the back. She waited until it finished creaking before she spoke. "Robert's in his man cave. You can go on out back."

Izzy hesitated at the sound of a man cave, but Mrs. Hubbard said, "Go ahead. Robert gives you any guff, you tell him I sent you. That'll cool his jets."

I almost asked who Robert was, but knew it had to be my coach. I let Coach Cowan lead. We marched across a dry dirt yard littered with engine parts toward what looked like an overgrown tool shed snuggled up in a nest of crabgrass. The battered stockade fence behind it might have held up the shed, or the shed might have held up the fence. Both looked capable of collapse. Coach Cowan had to bend his head to get in through the man cave's doorway. I was fine, of course, as was Izzy. It was dark inside except for a flat-screen TV that glowed with some game tap frozen midplay.

As my eyes adjusted and I saw the walls, I knew my plan to overcome the Simpkin clan could never fail.

Covering every inch of wood paneling, shelf, or tabletop were Cowboys posters, blankets, pillows, memorabilia, and trinkets, like key chains, bobbleheads, and coffee mugs. Coach Hubbard even wore a Cowboys T-shirt. It was a shrine to my team. America's team.

Coach Hubbard sat in a musty recliner draped in a Cowboys blue-and-silver blanket. He set aside his remote and struggled to get up so he could shake hands with Coach Cowan.

"Can I get you a beer, Coach?" Coach Hubbard nodded proudly at his bar at the other end of the narrow room.

As my eyes adjusted, I realized that perched on three of the bar stools were characters who might have been from the space-bar scene in *Star Wars*: a giant bear man with a full black beard, a short round man with frog eyes and a bald head, and a skinny man, freckle-faced with red hair and buck teeth. Each wore

Cowboys shirts and caps. Coach Cowan blinked at the crew for a moment. Each of them raised his can of beer in a wide-eyed, silent toast to the Cowboys coach.

"Oh, uh, I don't drink beer," Coach Cowan replied. "Thanks, though."

Coach Hubbard scowled beneath his bright-blue backward Ben Sauer Football cap—the only non-Cowboys thing apparently allowed in the man cave—and uttered a single word heavy with disappointment. "Oh."

The skinny man stood and held up his phone. "Uh, Coach? Mind if we get a picture with ya?"

"That I can do." Coach Cowan's smile saved the day.

They crowded around him, taking selfies and then having me and Izzy use each of their phones to do group shots.

"Hey," said the bear with the thick black beard, "can we get the kid in one of these?"

"The kid owner?" The froggy man's tongue snaked out of his mouth to lick his lips before disappearing in a snap. "That's a great idea. Okay, kid?"

I shrugged and glanced at Izzy, who raised her eyebrows, before I got into the shot. I admit, it felt pretty good to be part of the excitement and no doubt, Coach Hubbard's buddies were excited. They shared their shots and tweeted them madly to friends and followers. (Though who'd follow them I couldn't even imagine.)

"So? You've got some game film?" Coach Cowan nodded at the big projection screen on the wall, and his voice had that little electric current of excitement in it.

"It's our win from this morning." Coach Hubbard swelled with pride, scooped up the remote, and pointed at the frozen players on the screen. "Used your spread. I was just telling my boys here how the game isn't just about blocking and tackling anymore. Not on certain levels, anyway."

Coach Cowan reached for the remote. "May I?"

Coach Hubbard blustered as he surrendered it. "Coach, it's an honor."

Coach Cowan plunked himself down in a wooden chair next to the recliner and began advancing the tape, then rewinding it quickly, back and forth. He did this for several minutes, burning through half a dozen plays before he spoke. "Did they stay in this zone on you?"

"Yeah. Can you believe that? It's like they never saw a spread before." Coach Hubbard chuckled and sank down into his chair before looking back at his posse, who had reluctantly returned to their bar stools. "You guys see okay?"

"Oh, sure," they all said at the same time, nodding in agreement and drinking their beer.

The skinny guy was secretly positioning his phone alongside his beer can to snap yet another picture of Coach Cowan's glowing face. Coach Cowan paid no attention if he saw it. He was dialed in on the game film, running it and rewinding it, fast, over and over. It was hard for even me to keep up, and I had played in the game.

"Yeah," Coach Cowan said, pointing at the screen, "but the next guy—if he watches this film, anyway—you know what he's gonna do, right?"

"Play man free," Izzy said, her face also intent on the film. "And, yes, their coaches will be watching this film, if they haven't already."

No one said a word. Coach Cowan looked back at Izzy. Who ever heard of a girl knowing about man-to-man coverage with a free safety in the deep zone *and* knowing the terminology to call it "man-free zone"? I wanted to melt.

"Oh," Izzy said, looking around the man cave. "Sorry?"

Coach Cowan broke out into a grin that put everyone at ease. "Don't be sorry. You're absolutely right. They're gonna play some man free for sure. You gotta be ready for that, Coach. I mean, if the next team is any good and have cornerbacks fast enough to play man coverage. Are they?"

Coach Hubbard snorted. "The team we play next week is as good as it gets. They haven't lost in five years."

"You haven't beaten them in five years?" Coach Cowan froze the tape to look at Coach Hubbard.

"*No one* has beaten them in five years." Coach Hubbard looked kind of offended.

Coach Cowan bit his lip. "Well, can you show me their film? Maybe I can give you some ideas."

Coach Hubbard struggled out of his chair, chuckling and trembling as he put a new disc in his player. "Coach, if you'd do that, I would owe you big time."

Coach Cowan gave me and Izzy a secret wink and said, "That sounds good."

Coach Hubbard started the film, still chuckling. "Eiland isn't gonna know what hit them, I can tell you that."

"Eiland?" Coach Cowan's face dropped and even in the

light of the screen I could see that it had lost some of its color. "Wait, that's Dillon Peebles's team?"

"Well, yeah," Coach Hubbard said. "He's their best player."

Coach Cowan was on his feet quick and he gently set the remote down on the chair he'd been sitting in. "Uh, okay. Well, I better go on that note."

"Wait, why? You can't give us just a couple ideas?" Coach Hubbard looked like he might cry.

Coach Cowan shook his head. "No way. I'm sorry. I had no idea."

Everything crumbled right then and there, my entire plan of making the spread offense a weapon so potent that Coach Hubbard just couldn't cave in to the Simpkins.

Coach Cowan turned to me. "Sorry, Ryan. I can't do something directly against Dillon Peebles. If his mom wins this case, she'll be my boss. I had no idea. Come on, guys. We'd better go."

Even as we walked toward the street, people were approaching, neighbors and friends of the Hubbards on the street, snapping off pictures of Coach Cowan. A couple kids ran up with footballs to be signed. Coach Cowan signed them as we walked and got into his SUV, firing up the big engine and waving people off as they knocked on his window.

"Sorry." He shouted through the glass. "Gotta go."

They were like zombies, pouring in on us from every direction.

"Hey!" some guy shouted, pointing at me through the window. "It's the kid owner!"

Coach put the SUV into gear and eased away. My disappointment was so great I couldn't even speak until we crossed over the sunken tollway.

"You said you'd help." My tone of voice made what he'd

done sound like a major crime.

"Oh, no. I like you, Ryan, and I like your mom, but I'm not ending my career with the Cowboys so you can star in a middle-school football game. No way."

"Ending your career?" I was hot. "I could *save* your career!"

"Whoa, settle down." Coach Cowan shook his head. "Ryan, the Vegas odds of you having control of the team are five to one."

"Vegas odds? What are you talking about?" I shook my head in frustration.

"Betting," Izzy explained from the backseat. "They bet on everything in Vegas."

"You heard those people," Coach Cowan said. "That 'kid owner' thing is catching on, whoever that kid ends up being. People are talking. They're laying odds on who'll end up with the team, you or your half brother."

Coach Cowan glanced over and saw my frown. "Look, Ryan, can you imagine if Hubbard's friends start tweeting about me giving Ben Sauer Middle a game plan to beat your half brother? It'd be on *SportsCenter* by seven."

I knew now what he was afraid of, and I didn't blame him. Jasmine and Dillon? They'd fire Coach Cowan in three seconds for sure if he helped me.

"But they say there's a chance Jasmine and Dillon might *lose*, that this injunction is going to go away." I tried not to beg, but it was hard. "I heard *that* on *SportsCenter*."

He shook his head. "Too risky, Ryan. Plus, if you win, you'll keep me as head coach anyway."

"I might not, you know." I flared my nostrils at him even

though I knew he was right.

"Yes, you will." He spoke with absolute certainty as he turned the SUV in through our front gates. "You are a good kid. You believe the same things I do because it's your life, brains over brawn. Besides, just because I can't help you, it doesn't mean I can't help you."

"What? That doesn't even make sense."

"Well, it will when I explain." He pulled into my driveway and turned off the engine, but didn't get out.

I let my own hand drop away from the door handle. "I'm all ears."

58

"You understand why I can't have your coach and his buddies getting all giddy about me giving him a game plan, right?" Coach Cowan asked.

I would only shrug.

He huffed. "Look, I can *give* him a plan, but not there in the land of Cowboy fever. I had to do what I did so they'll tell all their friends what a jerk I was and how I *wouldn't* help Coach Hubbard. That way, I'll be safe if you *don't* win this court thing."

"You probably won't be safe anyway." Izzy couldn't help chiming in from the backseat, and when we both turned, she held her hands up in surrender. "I'm just saying."

"She's right," I said. "Hamhock is probably out there some-where right now, giving Dillon a foot massage."

Izzy snorted a little laugh and it made me smile.

"Safer than if I'm seen as the guy who sided with you," Coach Cowan said. "The truth is, you'd be the best owner for this team. I know you care about the team. Dillon? I think he and his mom don't care much about anything but themselves. I think your dad would be proud of you, Ryan."

"Okay." I was still doubtful, but bursting with pride at the mention of my dad. "So how *do* you help?"

"We let the dust settle, then ask him to come over here. I watch the tape—it'll take me all of half an hour—and I give him a handful of plays you all can practice this week that'll shred this Eiland offense."

"Shred . . ." I let the word hang on my lips so I could savor it.

"Can your coach keep a secret?"

"If you asked him to be a blocking dummy for the Cowboys, I think he'd do it. He's sure going to keep a secret if you ask him to."

"He'll be able to contain himself?" Coach Cowan asked.

"Coach Hubbard likes the spread and I think he's like all you coaches . . ."

Coach Cowan raised an eyebrow.

"He wants to be in charge. It's his team and he's not going to *want* people to know the game plan came from you. You're pretty safe with Coach Hubbard." I opened the door and got down.

We went inside and I think Coach Cowan went over his plan to secretly help Coach Hubbard with my mom. The two of them stayed inside for a few minutes together talking, while Izzy and I went outside and sat on the big wicker couch under the shade of the trellis next to the pool.

Izzy fanned her fingers out to look at her nails. "I probably should have gone with your mom and gotten my nails done. We barely got to watch any film."

"Nails? I'm surprised to hear you talk like that," I said. "Who cares about fingernails?"

"Ryan, a girl can be an athlete and still wear a dress or get her fingernails done. People can be a lot of things at once. Don't you know that?" She stared at me and never looked so pretty, so even though I wasn't totally sure, I gave her a nod.

She smiled, and I put my hands behind my head and sat back with my feet up, just enjoying her company.

"You know," she said, "you don't have to compete with Dillon Peebles."

"What's that supposed to mean?" I sat up to study her face.

She adjusted her sunglasses without letting me see her eyes. "Eiland hasn't lost in five years. There are things at work here a lot bigger than you. Just don't put so much pressure on yourself, that's all."

"He's a creep and a jerk," I said.

"Ryan, you don't even know him. All you know is that his mom wants the Cowboys. If you guys met under different circumstances, you might be friends. Maybe Dillon isn't really *that* bad."

I wanted to pull the hair out of my head. Me and Dillon, *friends*? I loved the way Izzy was so nice and forgiving with me, but saw no reason why she had to be that way with a jerk like Dillon. "Well, I want to beat Eiland, Dillon or no Dillon."

"Okay," she said. "That I get. Just don't make it you versus him. You're better than that."

I felt a hot spring in my stomach. "What's that mean?"

She shrugged. "You're you and that's all you need to be. For me, anyway. Jackson, too. Hey, where is Jackson?"

"Huh?" I couldn't help stuttering. "I . . . I don't know. I never heard back from him."

Suddenly, her smile melted into a dark scowl. She pulled her sunglasses down on her nose so she could peer over their tops.

"What?" I said.

"Ryan," she said, "did you lie to me about texting Jackson to ask him over?"

I took a breath, kind of annoyed that I'd been caught and had to explain myself, but knowing deep down I was wrong and also not wanting to sour our friendship over it. "I'm sorry. I guess I just felt like being alone with you. You know, so we could . . . talk."

She sharpened her focus on me and I felt like she could see right into my mind. Even if she could see, though, I don't know what she *would* see. My mind was a jumble of all kinds of things. I liked Izzy, not just as a friend, but maybe something more. Even admitting the possibility of that made me shake like a wet dog.

"Is this about the bonfire?" She seemed suddenly forgiving and excited.

I *knew* about the bonfire. Everyone in school was talking about it. Every year the student council put on a bonfire event after the Eiland game. It was a tradition. But, despite talking to Jackson about it a couple times, I hadn't been thinking seriously about even going, let alone with a date. The way Izzy was looking at me, though, let me know I'd better do something or she'd be upset. Besides, it was a good way to explain my behavior toward Jackson. I really didn't want to tell her I was jealous of the attention he'd gotten after the game.

"Well, sort of."

Izzy blushed and looked down with a shrug. "Are you, like, asking me?"

I had no idea where to go from there and I really didn't deserve a quick and easy escape, but my phone rang and it was Jackson.

"Where've you been? I, like, texted you five times," said Jackson.

"Yeah, I got a lot going on. Sorry. Hey, awesome game." I wanted Izzy to see me being a stand-up guy.

"Thanks to you, dude. I still can't believe Coach Hubbard's letting me run the ball. . . . So, what is up?"

"I'm trying to keep the spread offense alive here, Jackson. I got Coach Hubbard hopefully coming over to meet with Coach Cowan."

Jackson whistled over the phone. "Dude, you *own* Coach Cowan, right?"

"I don't own anybody, Jackson." I lowered my voice. "I don't even own the team for sure, but I think Coach Cowan likes my mom and if I *do* end up owning the team, I think he wants me on his side."

Talk of Coach Cowan "liking" my mom made my face hot with Izzy sitting right there. "Anyway, let me work on this thing. I don't want Coach Hubbard going back to the old offense if Simpkin comes back."

"Would he?" Jackson asked.

"I saw Simpkin's parents after the game and I didn't like the way they looked at me. I think because they run the youth team that people listen to them," I said.

Izzy whispered in my ear. "Tell him about the Cowboys game tomorrow, right?'

I nodded like it was the next thing on my mind. "Hey, and Jackson, do you want to go with me and Izzy to the Cowboys game tomorrow? We got sideline passes and if we've got this owner-type status, I bet we're going to get to go in the locker room."

The phone went silent, but I thought I could hear Jackson breathing.

"Jackson?"

"Dude, are you serious? If you are, I'm gonna have to check my drawers."

"Drawers?" I wrinkled my face.

"My shorts, dude, in case I just messed them."

"Jackson, that's gross." I laughed. "No one's gonna want you in the locker room with a mess in your shorts."

He laughed. Izzy made a disgusted face and shook her head.

Jackson said he'd have his mom drop him off and agreed to let me try and work my magic with Coach Hubbard.

"Ry-Guy?" Jackson said.

I liked the new nickname. "Yeah?"

"You're the best friend I ever had, dude."

That hit me hard. Jackson was intense about everything and I knew he meant it for real. I had the feeling he'd do anything for me, like support me calling pass plays near the end zone to build up my stats. But I couldn't be totally sure. I guess it was because I wasn't used to having such a good friend. I *wanted* to trust that he'd be on my side, even if it cost him a few touchdowns here or there, but I just couldn't. I knew I was safe keeping him in the dark, working my game with Coach Hubbard and solidifying my spot as the number-one quarterback.

I felt bad, though, especially for not inviting him over because I was mad he'd gotten all the attention after the game. It kind of made it hard for me to talk and what I said came out as a little sound that embarrassed me even more.

"Me, too," I squeaked.

"Okay. See ya tomorrow," he said.

"Tomorrow," I said, trying to sound casual and tough, and hung up.

Izzy smiled. "I really like how you guys are such good friends. It's cool."

"You and me, too." I suddenly felt a tingling in my head.

She tilted her head at me and gave me an amused, warm smile. Her voice was soft. "We are friends, aren't we? Good friends, right? Really, really good friends?"

"Sure." I could barely speak.

"Well," she said, swallowing, "I'd like to know how you'd define really, really good friends. Like, what's it mean? To you?"

A few weeks ago, I never would have thought a girl like Izzy would have any interest in me at all, but as the kid owner, anything was possible. A thrill went through me and the idea that I might ask her if she wanted to be my girlfriend perched on my lips like an eagle ready to swoop.

I couldn't do it.

I wanted to. I think she would have said yes. The look on her face and the sound of her voice practically asked *me* out. I knew what Jackson would have told me to do. But, in the end, I froze.

"Hey, Ry," my mom said, opening the back screen. She and Coach Cowan saved me from too much torture by appearing and sitting down in the big wicker chairs on either side of the couch.

"Well," Coach Cowan said, "it worked. Your coach is heading over here with the Eiland film. I think he understood. Not sure about that completely, but I'll watch some film with him and give you some plays that should work."

"That's great." I looked over at Izzy to see if she realized how well this was all working out for me, but she frowned and looked away.

Coach Hubbard got there so fast I wondered if he took a rocket ship. I thought it was strange that Izzy stayed with my mom outside while I went in with the two coaches to watch the Eiland film in our game room. I pretended it was more about her not feeling comfortable being the only girl rather than any issues about the bonfire.

Coach Cowan got my mind off Izzy darn quick. He was amazing. I could see why people called him a football genius. He watched Eiland's defense for about twelve plays before he shut it off and proceeded to explain to me and Coach Hubbard everything they were doing and how we could pretty easily destroy their defense with the spread offense. He gave us half a dozen plays, each an extension of the other that looked very similar, but each attacking the defense in a different spot.

"See?" Coach Cowan pointed with his pen to the notebook he'd put in front of Coach Hubbard on the coffee table. "They'll drop their other safety to get double coverage on both sides. They have to, and when they do, you run the read option play where Ryan either hands the ball off to the big guy or keeps it depending on what the defensive end does. It'll shred them."

There it was again, the word "shred." It sent a shiver down my back.

We kept strategizing for another hour. Coach Hubbard apologized that he couldn't stay for dinner when my mom asked. "My little lady makes a mean beef stroganoff and she likes to get the baby down by seven, so I'm off, but Coach . . ."

Coach Hubbard shook his head and clasped Coach Cowan's

hand. "I don't even know what to say."

"Well, just keep it between us and that'll be all the thanks I need, Coach." Coach Cowan patted him on the back as we saw him to the front door.

"I'd never say nothing to no one, no how, Coach." Coach Hubbard's face was shiny with sweat and sincerity. He gazed at Coach Cowan for a long moment before climbing into his car. We said good-bye and watched Coach Hubbard's vehicle cough blue smoke as it passed through the gates.

Coach Cowan sighed. "Well, we'll see."

"Thanks, Coach."

"Hey, my pleasure. It's fun, really." Coach Cowan scratched his neck and looked through the house back toward where we'd left my mom and Izzy. "I can't believe Eiland is as good as they are running a defense like that. They've got some pretty serious players, and they're even more impressive when you see how bad their scheme is."

I didn't know if Coach Cowan was trying to remind me of my half brother or not, but that's what he did. I thought of how tall and mean-looking he was, and obviously very good at football, not just because of all the awards I'd heard about. On the film we'd watched, I'd seen Dillon firsthand, chasing down running backs and blindsiding quarterbacks. He was all over the field. It made me a bit uncomfortable, but at the same time, it made me kind of mad. My father—Thomas Peebles—had left that team to me, hadn't he? That's what he wanted. Maybe he knew his other son was a jerk?

Or maybe he felt bad for me, that he was never there, that I was fatherless, undersized, and with no outward chance to be associated with the highest levels of football unless I hit the jackpot. Well, I'd show everyone that I was meant for the game as much as Dillon Peebles, and not just as a kid owner, but as a real player. We won my first game as a starting quarterback, right? My numbers were impressive. What if I had a real coach, one who knew the spread the way Coach Cowan did? What would my limitations be then?

I might not have been tall and fast and mean in a predatory way, but I was smart, on the field and off. I must admit, I felt rather proud of myself and actually had a slight taste of confidence.

"They have great players, Coach. They're bigger, faster, and stronger." I held up the notebook I'd been writing in all the while that Coach Hubbard was being schooled. "But Dillon's team will be playing checkers. We're gonna play chess."

Coach Cowan got a laugh out of that. "Hey, speaking of your half brother, let's make sure you don't let on about all this either, right? You're sure to see him tomorrow at the game."

"You think?" I asked. I hadn't even thought of that.

"Yeah," Coach Cowan said. "On the sidelines for sure."

I had no desire to see Dillon and I'd hoped the stadium was a big enough place that we wouldn't have to run into each other.

I'll admit that I designed a couple missiles I would have ready to launch if Dillon said anything nasty to me on the sidelines the next day. But of all the things I thought he'd say, I was in no way ready for what he really did say.

I walked out into the huge open space of the field with my mom, Jackson, and Izzy. Sunlight spilled in through the open roof, heating the turf so that the baked scent of it filled the air. We marched straight to the Cowboys bench, where we found Mr. Dietrich. The four of us stood with him in a clump even with the fifty-yard line in front of the Cowboys' bench. Around us, men the size of water buffalo swarmed, some huffing from the effort of warming up, others rotating arms and legs like the first turns of a windmill. Faces like John Torres, DeMarco Murray, Jason Witten, and Sean Lee jumped out at us, faces we'd seen plenty on TV, the internet, and billboards around town. Excitement was high. Energy steamed up out of the turf, making us light-headed.

Mr. Dietrich seemed at ease in his flannel gray pinstriped suit, looking not only rich but intensely serious. The tension of the upcoming contest with the Cardinals seemed to weigh as heavily on Mr. Dietrich as it did the players.

Dillon must have been waiting for him to step away because it wasn't more than five seconds after Mr. Dietrich escorted my mom to the back of the bench to have a chat with the TV announcer, Joe Buck, when Dillon appeared. He, too, wore a suit that made him look five years older than me and my friends. I felt suddenly silly in my dress shirt rolled up at the sleeves with my thin tie, khaki pants, and sneakers.

It became clear that it was Izzy he had eyes for. "Hey, girl, you are way too good-looking to be with this guy. What's your name?"

I was ready for every kind of direct insult you could imagine: things about my father finally getting it right with a panther-like son, my mother being unmarried, me being short, my school having inferior sports teams, Coach Cowan being overrated as an offensive strategist and downright incompetent as a head coach. I was ready for anything that jerk Dillon might say to me. Everything but trying to kiss up to Izzy.

Izzy wasn't ready for it either. Her face turned red and her back straightened. "I . . . Ryan and I are friends."

"You just got prettier in my book. You feel bad for the little fella. A girl with feelings." Dillon grinned like a wolf and he stepped closer.

When he reached out to touch Izzy's hair, I felt outraged and helpless at the same time.

"Wow." Dillon smiled at Izzy.

I hadn't known Izzy that long, but I'd never seen her unable to speak. She wore the expression of someone who'd dropped her toothbrush in the toilet bowl. She stepped back and swatted his hand.

"Feisty." Dillon gave her a short nod. "I like it."

He turned to me. "Zinnia, that's a flower, right? Enjoy the view from down here while you can. My mother and I are planning to keep the sidelines clear before the games, no minority owners or anything like that. Try to keep the little kids from getting hurt and the team getting sued or something. Ha-ha. Just kidding, buddy."

Before I could find a single word worth saying, he removed an iPhone from his pocket, which he got seriously interested in. He began typing something as he sauntered away just before

Mr. Dietrich appeared without my mom. "Getting caught up with your brother?"

I didn't know if he was serious, but I had to say something. "Half brother. Yeah, he's a charmer."

Mr. Dietrich tilted his head. "Your father always liked to be unique."

I waited for him to continue.

He motioned his hand toward me, then toward Dillon, who was now right out in the middle of the field talking to John Torres like they were buddies. "Having a kid run an NFL team. It's his way of showing how little he cared about the game. The Cowboys were like a fancy car for him, or a yacht: big, flashy, but not something that entered his consciousness on a daily basis." Mr. Dietrich snorted. "I promise you, there were times when he didn't ask a single question about this team for weeks. Think of it."

I looked at my trustee's cold blue eyes, glowing in their frame of snow-white hair and tan bald head, and I realized that he never really cared for my father at all. They were business partners, period. So his next words didn't surprise me.

"I'm different." Mr. Dietrich got a faraway look. "I care about this team. I was a lawyer working for a developer and I did the closing on Don Meredith's mansion. He invited me for a barbecue. That's the kind of guy he was. You don't even know who Don Meredith is, do you?"

His eyes seemed a bit damp from his favorite memories and I stared at him, hard, talking fast to cut off Izzy because it would be just like her to chime in at this moment. "I think my favorite Don Meredith moment was against Washington in '67.

They were down 14–10 when he hit Dan Reeves for a thirty-six-yard touchdown pass to win it."

There was a flicker of light in Mr. Dietrich's eyes, but then it was gone. "You can google anything these days, right?"

I didn't bother to point out that I hadn't googled anything. Dietrich was no dummy. He knew I didn't google it. I just couldn't imagine what he had going on behind those glinting glasses and cold blue eyes. I felt like he *should* be on my side, but that he wasn't.

I didn't have time to think about it, though, because first my mom reappeared and then Coach Cowan did, too. He was jittery and glazed in sweat, acting like he'd had too much coffee. The calm, confident coach I'd come to expect was entirely gone.

"Gotta get this one. Big one today. Big one. Good to see you Mr. Dietrich. Ryan." He patted us both on our shoulders, chewing gum a mile a minute and then tugging on his Cowboys cap like it itched his head. He turned to Jackson and Izzy. "Hey, kids. Have fun."

He saved my mom for last and his face seemed to relax for the five seconds he spoke to her. "Katy, how are you? Lots of excitement, right? I hope you enjoy the game. Have fun. I'll see you later."

Then he was gone, moving through the crowd of players, who were now beginning to filter back toward the tunnel that led to the locker room.

Mr. Dietrich raised an eyebrow. "Anyone you kids want to meet? Take a picture with?"

No way was I going to look like a rookie, but Jackson

couldn't contain himself. "Can we get a picture with the cheer-leaders?"

"Cheerleaders? Really, Jackson?"

"Well, they're kind of famous," Izzy said.

I looked at Izzy with disbelief.

"How about John Torres *and* the cheerleaders?" Jackson suggested.

Mr. Dietrich smiled and seemed to like Jackson's choice.

Other Cowboys players passed us on their way into the locker room, smirking and clapping and laughing at the sight of us all.

"That's that kid owner," I heard one of them say.

"Naw," said another as they jogged past, "kid owner is that Dillon boy with the hot mom."

I nearly pointed to my own mom and shouted at the player, "How about her, you fart head! You think Dillon's mom's hot?"

Of course, I said nothing. Maybe if I owned the team, I'd cut that guy. I didn't recognize him, but I memorized his jersey number.

I was so flustered by Dillon and the dumb photo with a gaggle of cheerleaders that I honestly couldn't enjoy the tide of fans, or the hustling TV cameramen, or my proximity to the giant players cracking each other's pads. By the time my blood started to cool, the players had all migrated to the locker room without me even really enjoying the spectacle. With Mr. Diet-rich as our guide, though, we got to follow the team through the tunnel and into the locker room. I looked over at Izzy and Jackson. They both seemed as jittery with excitement as I was.

There was no fun waiting for us in the locker room, though.

Instead, it was a quiet and hostile place. The only thing missing was the tick, tick, tick of a time bomb. Players strapped on their last pieces of equipment like soldiers getting ready to jump from a plane onto the battlefield. Coaches ground their gum or gnashed their teeth. It was eerily silent.

When I saw Dillon Peebles standing in the far corner, surveying the scene like some kind of emperor, I wanted to barf.

Mr. Dietrich ended the discomfort with a knowing nod and directional wag of his head intended to signal our departure. We followed without a word and I glanced at my friends' faces as we advanced down the concrete tunnel toward a reserved elevator.

From the light in their eyes, I knew that excitement burned bright in their hearts and minds, and that frustrated me. I didn't *care* that I'd been out there in the bustling midst of *America's Team*. I didn't feel it. Like well-chewed gum, the flavor of excitement was gone.

It had been worn down like a pencil by Dillon's appearance and my inability to dust him from the scene. He was a dark cloud that hovered over everything. As we shot up the elevator into the luxury level of the stadium, Mr. Dietrich's cold gaze made me feel like some furry little animal who'd been trapped in a cage. The luxurious surroundings of an owner's box, the trumpets and smoke, columns of fire and thundering cheers from the crowd mean nothing if you feel small and weak.

As we all sat down and the coin toss went off, Mr. Dietrich left my mom and my friends at the buffet table and escorted me to the edge of his box where the two of us could talk alone. With an arm draped over my shoulders and a firm grip on my collarbone, my father's old partner sighed with cheerful anticipation.

"Ryan," he said, "I want to explain to you exactly what's going on and tell you what you're going to have to do if you want to control this team."

This startled me. "I . . . I can control it?"

"Yes, you very well may," he said.

I looked into his smile and realized the bluish-white teeth were entirely porcelain, not his own in any way.

"Okay," I said, waiting.

The stadium announcer welcomed everyone and began to announce the visiting team. Boos and catcalls erupted in a good-natured way.

"I like you, Ryan." He spoke clearly over the jeers.

I glanced back at my mom and friends, who stood holding plates piled with food.

"Thanks."

"Yes, you're a good kid. Less spoiled than I imagined."

I could only guess that I outscored Dillon in this category by double digits and I nodded politely and without reply in an attempt to seem *very* unspoiled.

He sighed heavily and removed a letter from his inside breast pocket and unfolded it. "I should have known things wouldn't be that simple with your father."

"What do you mean?" I scowled at the letter.

The booing grew louder as he held it out. "You can read it if you want, or I can tell you what it says."

"You can tell me." For some reason, I didn't want to take the letter. The paper was heavy and cream colored with legal lettering and a seal stamped into the bottom.

Mr. Dietrich laughed at that and gave me a little shake. His eyes twinkled. "It's from your father."

"My . . ." I was shocked and scared and confused.

Mr. Dietrich glanced at the letter. "He directed his lawyers to wait until after the will had been read before sending it to me. He wanted the maximum impact, I think."

"Maximum impact on what?" Now I was totally confused.

Mr. Dietrich grinned. "Your father liked to stir things up. He liked competition. For example, he enjoyed having a coach and a GM who couldn't stand each other. Vicious competition interested him."

"Why are you saying this?" I asked.

"Your father *knew* Jasmine would contest his will. He *knew* that—as his wife—she could break it by asserting her right to half of everything. He also knew that she'd want *her* son to be in the spotlight. He *knew* I would then hold the swing vote, enough shares to support one side or the other to give you control."

I didn't like the look on his face. "And you're choosing Dillon?"

He laughed. "*I'm* not choosing anyone. All he asked me to do is set up the competition. He's given me total discretion in that. He only asks that it be a clear and fair competition."

I shook my head, thinking of crazy things. "What? Like, arm wrestling or something?"

He nodded. "I guess, although I hadn't thought of that. I think he meant possibly a standardized test or a game of chess. Maybe how much money you could raise for a charity?"

I felt relieved, not because I was certain I could beat Dillon at chess, but because I was certain I couldn't beat him in anything physical.

Mr. Dietrich bit his lip and tilted his head. "It's almost like he knew, but he couldn't have known. His death surprised us all."

"Knew what?" I was sick of the guessing games. I wanted to know what I had to do to get my hands on the NFL football team that was surging out onto the field below to thundering applause that made me have to shout to be heard.

"That the competition is already in place!" Mr. Dietrich shouted back, the crowd so loud now that it hurt my ears.

"What competition?" I yelled.

"A football game! You versus Dillon! Next week. You're playing *head to head*. Mano a mano. I love it, and the media? Ha-ha! One winner. One kid owner. It's all about *football*!"

I stood there in shock.

The stadium went silent for the national anthem.

Mr. Dietrich acted like the song didn't matter to me and him. "Did I ever tell you I played the game? Sure, back east. Williams College. Oh, football was a big deal at Williams."

I had a wad in my gut. Immediately, all I could think of was educating Mr. Dietrich on the fact that Dillon's team hadn't lost in the last *five* years, to *anyone*! I imagined Dillon, standing with fists on hips, eyes black-painted like a death mask beneath his football helmet with muscles bulging under a skintight uniform. Behind him I envisioned a handful of coaches who were like superheroes, each with an amazing skill set, ready to match wits against me and . . .

Coach *Hubbard*.

Was this what it would really come down to? Was there no

punch line? No back slap? No chortling with my friends about the way Mr. Dietrich had played me?

"That's not fair." The words dribbled from my lips.

"Oh, it's entirely fair. It's the most fair thing I could ever come up with," he said.

"What if I don't even *play?*" I tried not to choke on my words. "I mean, I'm not the starter and if Jack Simpkin gets cleared, I might not even be involved."

"If you're not good enough to play, certainly you're not good enough to win," Mr. Dietrich scoffed.

I studied his face. He was dead serious.

I don't know if my mom snuck up on us on purpose, or if she was just trying to get a better look at Dustin Lynch singing "The Star-Spangled Banner." Whatever the reason, she must have heard what Mr. Dietrich had said and she pounced.

"*What* do you think you're doing, Eric?" She got right up in his face, and I'll give Mr. Dietrich credit, he didn't flinch.

"Talking to your son," he said, then added, "to Thomas's son."

"Thomas." If ever a word was spit, that was it. "Thomas had a son on paper. That's not a son."

"In any event, I've been given a job." Mr. Dietrich seemed bored. He held the letter up briefly before tucking it back in his pocket without showing her.

"Yes, you always did his dirty work." My mother sneered.

I took hold of her arm. "Mom."

She shook free. "They're *twelve-year-old boys*! You want to play with them like this? Win a stupid *football game*? To own the Dallas Cowboys, just win a *middle-school football game*? If

260

it wasn't you saying it, I'd laugh. I know it'd be a sick joke, but not with you, Eric. I think you really mean it."

"And I do mean it." Mr. Dietrich stayed dead calm. "It's fallen on me to determine which of these young men will run this team. I have my instructions. This isn't about me. Thomas knew that I'd take what he wanted with complete seriousness. It was his team. This is what he wanted. I'm fine with that. It's not my place, or yours, to judge."

"Do you know the kind of *pressure* you're putting on these boys?" My mother could barely talk she was so mad.

Mr. Dietrich smiled wide. "You think if your son ends up running this team, he won't feel pressure?"

"You expect me to believe that? My son's not going to run this team, even if he wins. Not really." My mother snorted.

"Do you know when I formed my plan for Dietrich Die Molding? I was *twelve*, Katy. *Twelve.* I had no parents and no home. I lived on the street, but I had a plan. I got a job at *twelve* sweeping shavings from a factory floor to earn enough money to eat. Don't tell me about twelve. Twelve is plenty old enough," he said. "What do you want him to do? Quit? Run away? Is that what you want to teach him?"

My mom's face shook. I thought she might hyperventilate, but she slowly calmed herself by breathing deep.

"No," she said. "I guess I don't."

And she walked away.

To my mom's credit, we stayed to watch the whole game. She glared and glowered and snarled, but we stayed. The Cowboys won the game and spirits were high. Fans cheered for each other and tugged at their shirts to more fully display their John Torres jerseys. As we crawled behind our police escort out of the stadium, other drivers honked merry tunes on their cars' horns.

"Well, it's nothing I shouldn't have expected." My mother shook her head as she drove.

"We have a *police escort*." Jackson's fingertips clutched the headrest of my seat and his head peeked into the front in order to feast his eyes on the flashing lights.

"Technically, it's not our escort." My mom shot a quick glance at Jackson to make sure he understood. "It's for the TV announcers, so they can get to the airport."

"Are you gonna get this every week?" Jackson nudged me, winking.

"Right now, it's up in the air whether I'll even be allowed in the stadium," I said, annoyed that Jackson hadn't put two and two together. I'd told him and Izzy everything Dietrich said as we sat watching the game.

Jackson's eyes never left the cop car, except to take brief note of a motorcycle cop holding back an artery of traffic and saluting us as we swished by. "All we have to do is win—and I got you covered on that front because we will beat Dillon's backside. Besides, even if a miracle happened for him and we didn't win, you're still gonna own *some* of the team. That's what they said on *SportsCenter*, anyway. Right?"

"I told you what Dillon said. If he runs the team, we are not going to be welcome here."

"Well, I know Izzy's gonna be welcome. *Riiigghhhttt, Izzzzyyy?*" Jackson let go of my headrest to flop back into his seat and torment Izzy.

I can't say if I was more sad or surprised when Izzy slobbered on her pointer finger and wiggled it into Jackson's ear.

"Gross! Awww!" Jackson frantically tried drying his ear canal with a corner of his shirt. "What'd you do that for?"

"'Cause you asked for it." Izzy sat looking mad and straight ahead as if she'd done nothing.

The police escort sprang us out onto the open tollway and my mom beeped her horn to thank them as we swished past before she stomped the pedal like she always does.

"Did you ever think it might have been a compliment? That guy liking you?" Jackson kept screwing a pinkie into his ear as he watched the fading police lights over his shoulder.

"Who?" My mom looked at Izzy in the rearview mirror. "Dillon?"

"He was kind of a jerk," Izzy said.

"Yeah, *but.*" Jackson let his ear alone and folded his arms across his chest, smirking at Izzy.

"But what?" I asked, turning in my seat so I could see Izzy's face.

When she blushed, my stomach sank to the bottom of its tank.

"Go ahead, Izzaroo. Tell Ry-Guy what you did." Jackson had no idea the pain he was causing me. To him it was all fun. He didn't get it.

"I didn't *do* anything." But her face was burning cherry-red and she was definitely *not* looking at me.

"Do what?" I asked, both afraid and desperate for the answer.

"Didn't you see?" Jackson laughed and then answered his own question. "Oh, no. I forgot. You were too busy with the *cheer*leaders."

"I wasn't busy with anything. What are you talking about?" I scowled at Jackson to signal that this was no time for joking around.

"It's not a big deal. Dillon asked me to friend him."

"*Friend* him?"

"Well, just to accept his request. On Instagram."

"*That* guy?" It felt like a trapdoor opened under my feet and I was dropping into a bottomless pit. "You didn't, *did you?*"

"Ryan, he was standing right there on top of me and I had my phone out. I felt rude."

"Rude! *He* was rude! He, like, grabbed your hair and you slapped him down!" I wanted to pull my own hair out of my head. This was unthinkable.

"I know." Her lower lip disappeared beneath her teeth, then she turned mad. "Just stop talking about it already. I friended him. No biggy. I didn't feel like I could say no."

"Well, you can unfriend him, right?" I said.

"He'd know. It's rude," she said.

"Who cares?" I said.

"My mom says a polite person is polite to everyone, Ryan, not just the people it's convenient to be polite to." Her tone said she wasn't going to budge.

My mouth must have looked like a fish desperate for food. I gurgled, choking on any words that might have come out. I looked at my mom. She glanced over and some knowledge tugged half her mouth upward by an invisible string. She shook her head ever so slightly, signaling for me to let it go, and that she'd try and explain, later.

"Whatever," I mumbled. I folded my arms across my chest, but when I stole a look into the backseat, I saw that Izzy sat the same way as me.

Everyone got interested in his or her phone and my mom turned up the Highway. Keith Urban sang "Tonight I Wanna Cry," but I tuned it out.

266

We dropped Izzy off at her house, an enormous modern building with lots of glass, before skirting the edges of Highland, where Jackson got out in front of a clapboard three-story structure in a small army of other clapboard three-story apartment houses with white plastic railings and shutterless windows.

He poked his head back into the truck before closing the door. "Yo, Ry-Guy, this was amazing. Just unbelievable. Thanks, man. And thank you, Ms. Zinna."

"You're very welcome, Jackson. I do appreciate your manners. Please give your mother a hug from me."

"Yes, ma'am." Jackson nodded and closed the door with more perfect manners before sneaking me a crazy face with his tongue sticking out sideways and his eyes crossed.

I was in no mood to laugh, and I canceled out his puppy dog smile with a grimace before turning to my mother. As we pulled away, I asked her in a state of complete confusion if she knew what in the world was going on with Izzy.

My mom sighed.

"What?" I was annoyed with her now, too. "What does *huuugh* mean?"

"Ryan, honey . . ." She shook her head, and tightened her grip on the wheel, smiling sadly. "These things are so hard. You're too young to be worried about girls."

"I'm not worried about *girls*. I'm talking about Izzy."

"And Izzy's a girl."

"I know that, but this isn't a girl issue."

"Oh?" She raised an eyebrow but kept her eyes on the road.

"Mom, this is about that butt brain Dillon. This is about loyalty. Friendship." I clenched my hands and teeth to keep from spitting inside her truck. "I gotta beat him and his team. If I do, I'll *own* the Cowboys."

"You'll probably never own the Cowboys outright, Ryan.

Nothing's that simple."

"Okay, I'll *control* the Cowboys. Then I'm the one who can ban *Dillon* and his nasty mother from the sideline. I can't have Izzy Facebooking with that creep. Instagramming. Whatever. What if she talks about Coach Cowan? Mom, this is a disaster." I pounded a fist on the dashboard. "This doesn't have anything to do with girls."

"Not the definition of 'really good friends'?" My mom puckered her lips, referring to my last conversation with Izzy at my pool.

"How do you even know about that?" I asked.

She shrugged. "Izzy mentioned it. Not directly."

"Mom. It's stupid. Who cares? Friends or really good friends or really, really good friends? I can't even think about that junk. I've got to win this game next Saturday." I chewed on a knuckle. "Maybe I should call Coach Hubbard. Maybe I should go over there. He needs to *know* this stuff."

"Not a bad idea."

"You think?" I looked sharply at her. "Good. I will."

"I want you to win, Ryan. I want you to get what you want," she said.

I was suspicious. "Yeah, but you've been grousing about the Cowboys and me from the beginning."

"Right," she said. "It's complicated. I'd rather none of it happened in the first place, but it did happen and I'd rather not see the whole thing stolen out from underneath you. That might be the worst thing of all."

"Why do you say that?"

"It's human nature, Ryan. We all do it. It's like with Izzy.

You didn't care about the bonfire, maybe you didn't even want to go? But when Dillon simply asked her to accept his friend request, you panicked. No one likes to lose something of value and when they do, it's hard to forget about it."

"Izzy's a thing of value?" I snorted like that was funny.

"You're getting to be that age, Ryan. It may not be Izzy, but it'll be someone. Some *girl*." She shrugged.

"Mom!"

"That's life, big guy. You fall in love. It just happens. You don't get to decide." She scratched the outside of her knee. "Trust me."

"That's what happened with you and my dad?" I didn't think about the question, I just asked it.

She tilted her head at the road. The sun shot thin beams through the trees on our street and she kind of sparkled. "Yeah. That's what happened."

"Then you fell *out* of love?"

"No. We changed. I think when you really love someone you never fall out of love." She sighed. "But things change, people change, and then the life you're in starts to rub one of you, or both of you, the wrong way and it's time to get out."

"Oh." I looked down.

"Look, Ryan. Your father was a good man, but his own father treated them pretty badly. I think it scared him. It was like he didn't trust himself and I couldn't have you grow up like that. Nothing was, or is, more important to me than you."

"You thought he'd hurt me or something?" I asked.

"No. Not ever." She shook her head violently. "But he was going to abandon you, and I don't mean because he had a girlfriend. I saw it the day you were born and it broke my heart. He wouldn't pick you up, wouldn't touch you. He wouldn't even look at you, and I think that hurts worse than not having a father at all. That's what I believed. It's what I still believe."

I sat there listening to my own breathing for a few minutes, forcing everything she just told me out of my mind.

"Mom?"

"Yes, honey?"

"I gotta win this thing."

"I know you do." She sounded so sad.

"I'm gonna call Coach Hubbard to work on our plan," I said.

"Leave no stone unturned," she said. "That's the way to do things."

Mom told me because it was Sunday afternoon to make sure I apologized for calling him on the phone, and I did. Coach Hubbard said it was no problem, but told me that he was at a barbecue with his wife's family and suggested that instead we meet before school started in his office the next morning.

I hung up, panicked, because this thing was more important to me than it was to my coach. I wondered if it was because he thought Simpkin would return. That would ruin everything, and I began to fret.

"Relax," my mom said. "Just do everything you can do. He said he'd meet you early tomorrow. That's good, right?"

"Yes," I said. "Better than nothing."

I decided there was nothing I could do about Simpkin. I had to carry on as if that just wasn't going to happen. I worked all night, reviewing and memorizing plays, and the next morning my mom dropped me off early as planned.

Coach Hubbard and I got after it. No messing around. We hit the grease board, diagramming Eiland's defenses and drawing up our own plays against them, proving to each other like math formulas how they could work. We looked for weaknesses in their strategy, as well as ours, making little adjustments even beyond what Coach Cowan had suggested that could be the difference between winning and losing.

"If they move Dillon up to the line on the outside," Coach Hubbard said, circling the X on the board that represented my half brother and drawing an arrow that moved him to the line, "you'll have to check to the toss going the other way."

"I can run the boot right at him, Coach." My face felt hot with excitement. "I can juke him out or throw it right over his stupid head."

Coach Hubbard's shoulders slumped. He turned and looked at me. "Ryan, don't let your pride get in the way. Dillon is the best player we're gonna see this whole season. He's big and fast as a cat. You see him, you run Jackson the other way. No questions, okay?"

I couldn't hide my disappointment.

"Hey," he said, "am I letting Coach Cowan help me with this plan? Yes, I am. Now, if I put my pride in front of my good sense, I'd tell him to leave me alone. But I want to win, and when you want to win, you put yourself second. Understand?"

I nodded but didn't understand completely, to be honest.

I didn't have time to think too much about it, though, because Coach Hubbard shut down the lights and played some Eiland game tape for me, pointing out the keys to their defense and rewinding plays over and over so I could get a feel for what they were doing and how it would look. It was impossible not to notice Dillon. He stuck out like a swollen thumb on a hand, big and bold and in your face. He flew around, smashing people and popping up from the ground to lord over his victims. Just watching him made me furious, but also that much more determined to defeat him.

After my session with Coach Hubbard, I marched around the hallways with my head high. When I saw Izzy, I acted like nothing was wrong even though I couldn't stop being a little mad about her friending Dillon. At lunch everyone was talking about the big game. If we won, the student council was definitely going to have a bonfire that evening. Jackson made fun of Griffin when he learned that he'd asked Mya to be his date to the bonfire. Mya's face turned red and she stared at the table.

"We're really, really good friends." Griffin looked defiant.

Jackson had a mouthful of milk and he snorted so hard it shot out his nose. "*Really, really good?* Dude, you sound like you're talking about a piece of *candy.* Saturday is the biggest game of the season, maybe the biggest game of your life. You gotta be in the right frame of mind."

I couldn't help snickering, but I hid it behind my sandwich because of the furious look on Izzy's face. I suspected the "really, really good friends" thing was code for boyfriend or girlfriend.

"Leave him alone, Jackson. The bonfire isn't until after the game." Izzy scolded him with a finger. "It's nice, Griffin. I admire you for asking Mya. Who wouldn't want to take Mya to the bonfire?"

I looked down and studied my shoelaces. I retied them

three times before I got them just right and by that time Estevan and Jackson were entertaining everyone in the cafeteria by having a contest to see who could hold his breath longer. Both were turning different shades of red. Thankfully the bell rang before either of them passed out and I scrambled for my next class, glad to have escaped.

In gym class, I ignored the talk I overheard between two teammates about Jason Simpkin being cleared by the doctor to play again. I felt just a quick pang of worry before I shucked it off. I couldn't waste my time thinking about Simpkin. I had Eiland to think about. I trusted that between Coach Cowan's help and my extra work that Coach Hubbard was fully on my side.

Jason was small potatoes, right? I was in the big leagues now. In my mind, I was getting ready to play for all the marbles: not just owning the Dallas Cowboys, but my own football career, too. It was like if I dominated this game and we won, all my dreams would come true. I felt like I had it under control. Coach Hubbard's upbeat excitement that morning had given me a turbo boost. I could tell I had nothing to worry about when it came to Coach Hubbard.

All was well until I walked out onto the practice field.

When I saw who was standing there having an intense conversation with Coach Hubbard, my knees buckled.

Maybe to remind Coach Hubbard exactly who and what he was, Mr. Simpkin had a dark-blue cap with gold letters reading PYFL COACH tugged down on his thick head. Built the size of Coach Hubbard, but more evenly proportioned with bulging arms and a neck of concrete rather than flab, Mr. Simpkin cut an imposing figure, the way you'd expect a rhino to impress you more than a hippo. Mr. Simpkin's arms were short and stout and his thick hands fluttered at Coach Hubbard, adding punctuation to the words he spit through tight white lips.

They stared hard at each other and the players who were already out for practice had shied away to other parts of the field, so they stood isolated on the fifty-yard line. I was drawn to the scene the way people need to see what comes out of a crushed car in a traffic accident. I actually heard a few snatches of Mr. Simpkin's snarled words, like *"when I was at SMU," "because of injury," "pip-squeak," "tough luck," "this program,"* and *"my son."*

When the two of them realized they weren't alone, they stopped talking suddenly and glared at me.

"Ryan, we're having a private conversation. I'll be with you in a few minutes." Coach Hubbard sounded nothing like the man I'd met with in his office that morning.

Desperate to remind him of our unspoken deal, I blurted out the next best thing to invoking Coach Cowan's name as I backed away. "I was just . . . those new plays you put in . . . to ask you about . . . against a cover two . . . I . . ."

They both battered me with their scowls until I turned my back and jogged off toward the end zone, where I distractedly played catch with Jackson while he prattled on too loudly about how *unbelievable* it was to have been in the Cowboys locker room! Normally, I would have enjoyed Jackson's praises because of the respect it injected into my teammates by reminding them of my rise in the world of football, but now, with my fate being discussed by two thick-necked football coaches, none of that seemed to matter.

I realize that's because the things you *have* aren't half as important as the things you *are*. I wanted to *be* a football player. More than a kid owner?

Absolutely. Not even close.

I couldn't tell anything at all by the way the two men parted company. Mr. Simpkin chugged away kicking up little puffs of dust from the dry turf. I watched him through the fence surrounding the field. He climbed into his Tahoe truck and backed out of his spot, the windshield flashing a blinding light from the sun's reflection before it disappeared from the parking lot. Coach Hubbard was busy with Coach Vickerson. The two of them were studying the practice plan and making notes beneath the hot sun.

Off to the side, Jason Simpkin sat on his helmet talking to Bryan Markham like he hadn't a care in the world.

I had a bad feeling.

We warmed up, stretching and doing agility drills. Next was individual drills and Jason Simpkin stood tall, firing passes and making loudmouth remarks whenever he had a good pass.

"Feel *that* heat?" Simpkin snorted with laughter. "No more ducks, boys."

I know he was referring to my wobbly throws that barely made their mark.

I reared back and did my best on the next throw. It wasn't bad, a hard throw, but wobbly I have to admit. Simpkin snorted again. Everyone around us only watched and waited to see how things would play out.

We did team defense first, which was torture because the question I had wouldn't be answered until Coach Hubbard called for the first team offense. Part of me couldn't believe he'd risk the connection with Coach Cowan, the new and improved offense, and my kind regards as owner (in whole or part) of the Dallas Cowboys.

We toiled through team defense with Coach Vickerson making the calls and Coach Hubbard showing us the scout team cards so we could mimic Eiland's offense. I took the first reps at quarterback on the scout team, but Simpkin didn't even seem interested. It was like he *knew* what was going to happen, and still, I also knew Simpkin was the kind of jerk who'd act like he was the starter even if he wasn't.

Defense ended and Coach Hubbard hollered for us to take a break at the water horse. We jogged off to where a long plastic pipe with holes punched in it sat, so ten at a time could take a drink. Simpkin muscled into the front of the group, swallowed big, then stood up with a huge belch too hard to ignore. He strutted around through the team like a tom turkey, his helmet raised and tilted slightly back like some kind of space-age crown. I looked at Jackson and rolled my eyes. Jackson only shrugged.

I was too uptight to do more than rinse my mouth with water. I thought whatever I did swallow might come right back up on me.

Coach Hubbard blasted his whistle. "Okay! First team offense, here we go!"

Estevan stood still, knowing he was the second-string quarterback whoever went in first. I took off like a jackrabbit, buckling my chin strap as I went, but saw Simpkin from the corner of my eye, running toward where the first team offense was to huddle up just like I was. We arrived at Coach Hubbard's spot on the grass like whistled-in dogs, panting and eager.

I couldn't read Coach Hubbard's expression to save my life.

He looked back and forth between us both and consulted his practice plan, as if he needed it to find the answer.

When Coach Hubbard opened his mouth to speak, I swallowed so hard that I nearly choked on my tongue.

I knew what Coach Hubbard was going to say before he said it.

He couldn't even look at me as he cleared his throat. "Simpkin, you run with the first team. I can't have a player losing his starting spot because of an injury. That's just not how it's done in any big program, even the pros and college."

I stood frozen. I could feel the fury building up inside of me like hot lava, melting everything else away, vaporizing my manners, my self-control, and my good sense.

"You got it, Coach." Simpkin jogged off to take over my huddle.

Then it happened. I blew a gasket. I lost it.

"Simpkin's *dad* got to you?" I screamed. I whipped off my helmet and slammed it on the ground. "I *saw* it! I *know*!"

"Excuse me?!" Coach Hubbard's face was red with rage and he brandished his clipboard at me like it was a battle-ax.

"You're *way* out of line! You don't own *this* team! You're out for the day. Keep it up and you'll be out for the Eiland game! Now, hit the showers!"

"Ahhhhh!" I pulled my hair and shrieked with rage and stomped off toward the locker room without my helmet, without my starting job, and without a thread of sanity to keep me from trashing my locker like a cyclone. If I didn't play in that game, I'd lose the Cowboys for sure. *I* had to win that game, not Ben Sauer Middle School. If I was on the bench, it would be like a forfeit. Mr. Dietrich had been clear about that.

I went wild.

I yanked everything out and threw things as hard as I could against the opposite bank of lockers, screaming all the while. As the snowstorm of papers from my science folder cascaded down from their explosion on the ceiling, my vision cleared and I realized my life was in total ruin.

Did I cry?

Let's just say I sniffed and wiped something from my eyes that could have been sweat. It was like an oven in there.

I went into the bathroom and puked in the toilet and it seemed to empty me of a lot of poison.

Anyway, I picked up the mess I'd made in the locker room and steeled myself to do the right thing, which was to march out onto the field and apologize to my coach and hope and pray that he'd make me do a thousand up-downs until I puked myself (again) and then let me back onto the team. I wasn't going to be known as a quitter or a whiner or some spoiled brat. If I had to ride the bench forever and endure the sneers of everyone, I wasn't going to quit. They wouldn't be able to say that about me.

My helmet lay where I'd thrown it. The team was in full swing of the offensive practice, with Jason Simpkin running the old offense like he hadn't missed a beat. As I reached down into the grass and wiped the dirt off my mouth guard, Simpkin launched a pass close to fifty yards in the air to a wide receiver in the end zone. It was something I could never do and it stung like soap in my eyes to see.

I walked over to Coach Hubbard. He ignored me until I tapped him on the arm. He signaled a play to a smirking Jason Simpkin before he took a deep breath and spoke without looking at me. "I thought I sent you to the showers."

"Coach, I'm sorry. I never should have yelled at you. I don't know what happened to me. I lost it. I'm . . . Can I come back?"

Coach Hubbard made me stand there, suffering. He looked at his sheet and signaled in another play to the huddle as if I didn't exist. Simpkin threw another long touchdown pass.

Coach Hubbard sighed. "Take five laps and then get out there on the scout team at cornerback."

"Yes, sir!"

"And Zinna, if you ever talk to me that way again, you are done."

I nodded and bolted for the perimeter of the field before he could change his mind, taking off like a jackrabbit for the second time that day.

I ran until I was dizzy. A knife of pain jabbed my ribs and my lungs felt like bags of acid. If I had anything left in my gut, I would have lost it, but I already left my lunch in the locker room. I was gasping and wheezing, but I jumped right out onto the field to relieve the scout team cornerback. He happily jogged off to the sideline for a break.

I noticed now that Jackson was on the scout team playing defensive end, and between plays I whispered to him. "What happened? Why are you not on offense?"

He shot me an angry look. "I mouthed off about how you should be our starting quarterback, and they benched me."

"What?" My voice was barely more than a hiss.

"I didn't go for that bull." His nostrils flared and he glanced over at Coach Hubbard, who was busy instructing Simpkin on something while the rest of the offense watched. Coach Vickerson marched away from us after having shown the scout defense the card for the next play. "I told them *you* were the only quarterback who could beat Eiland."

I felt an uncomfortable mix of joy and horror. "Well . . . thanks."

"You'd have done it for me, too," he said.

I swallowed, thinking of the touchdown I'd stolen from Jackson and how I'd been mad at him for getting all the attention after our game. "Jeez, Jackson. You're the best. I feel . . . kind of bad."

"What are you talking about?" he asked. "Why?"

I swallowed. My mouth was all dry, but I felt like I had to tell him. "Well, I changed the play during the Hutchinson game so I could score instead of you. I got bent out of shape that you were like the hero. That's not a good friend."

He grinned and slapped my back. "Aw, you're just a competitor. I don't care about stuff like that. There are enough touchdowns to go around."

I nodded in amazement. Jackson was the best friend ever. All I could do was whisper another thanks before I got into my position.

"Okay," Coach Hubbard suddenly shouted at the whole team. "Five plays to end it. Live scrimmage! LIVE SCRIM-MAGE! I WANT TO SEE SOME HITTING! WE GOT A BIG GAME SATURDAY! WE GOT EILAND! LET'S GO!"

The whole team let loose a roar. Live scrimmage was the real deal. We got to hit each other full speed, blocking, tackling, the works, and it was just what I needed to vent some excess rage.

The offense marched to the line and Simpkin roared out the cadence. He dropped back to pass; Griffin Engle and I smashed into each other before he sidestepped me and raced down the field. I fell back into coverage, running alongside Griffin, each of us slapping at the other's hands for position.

When I heard the crack, I stopped in my tracks and turned to look along with everyone else.

What I saw, I couldn't believe.

Jackson was stomping around bellowing and throwing his fists at the ground as if he were trying to shed the sleeves of some invisible winter coat. The rest of the team stood frozen in shock. Coach Hubbard's mouth hung open. Coach Vickerson gripped his head like it might fly off his neck.

Lying in a stone-still heap on the turf was Jason Simpkin and the football that had spilled from his hands.

"Yes!" Jackson snorted and thumped his helmet, still flush with the excitement of a monster hit. "Big dog gotta *eat*!"

Coach Hubbard began blowing shrill notes on his whistle, as if enough ear-shattering blasts might turn back time. They couldn't, and he finally stopped and rushed over to Jason. For a moment, I was shocked—I won't honestly say afraid—at the idea that Jackson had killed Simpkin, but Simpkin began to groan and twist on the ground.

"Water! Get me water!" Coach Hubbard waved his hand like a magician, and Coach Vickerson broke free from his own trance and scooped up his personal water bottle from the sideline. Coach Hubbard cradled Simpkin's head like a baby's while Coach Vickerson fed sips of water to our fallen quarterback.

Simpkin sputtered and came to life and looked around, clearly confused.

Coach Hubbard proceeded to ask him what hurt, going over every part of his body until it was clear Simpkin had his bell rung and no more.

Coach Hubbard bared his teeth and snarled up at Jackson. "*Jackson*, what the heck were you thinking?"

The question rained on Jackson's parade and he stood still with a blank look on his face, thinking for a moment. "You said 'live scrimmage,' Coach. So I went live."

Everyone waited to hear the answer to that unsolvable riddle, but none was coming.

"Glad he got cleared by the family doctor," Coach Hubbard said. He gave Coach Vickerson the harsh look a coach usually reserves for his players when they mess up, I think to make sure the two of them were covering each other's backs if Simpkin's dad went nuts about him getting hurt.

"He did." Coach Vickerson nodded wildly. "That's what the dad said. I saw the note. You *have* the note."

Coach Hubbard patted his pocket and nodded, as though he sensed a possible lawsuit in the air and was relieved to know that they were on the same page. They helped Simpkin up and over to the bench. You might think practice would end, but then you probably don't play football in Texas. In Texas, anything short of a roiling black tornado and you finish football practice.

So Coach Hubbard suddenly had another big decision to make, and because of my earlier tantrum, it was a tough one.

He could either go with the old offense and install Estevan Marin as the starting quarterback, or fall back on me and Jackson and the spread playbook Coach Cowan had given him. Going back to me would create a political nightmare, but choosing Estevan wouldn't give the team the best chance to win.

I had no idea what Coach Hubbard would do.

But I probably should have known.

This was Texas, and all that mattered in football was winning.

"Zinna, get in at quarterback." Coach Hubbard straightened as if daring any single one of us to even mention his seesaw strategy. "Give me that starting spread!"

Coach Hubbard hammered out a note on his whistle and everyone jumped into place. He grabbed a bar on my face mask and yanked me close enough to whisper. "Just call our three best plays."

"Got it." I didn't wait to give him a chance to change his mind.

Jackson beamed at me from his spot in the huddle as running back. He practically danced with delight. "We got this, Ry-Guy. We got this."

Jackson and I fist-bumped. I called a throwback screen. We scored a touchdown on the first play, ran for thirty-seven yards on the second, and punched in another touchdown with a short pass to Griffin Engle on the third. Coach Hubbard lined us up to run ten exhausting cross-field sprints, then dismissed us after a chant as if nothing unusual had happened at all.

I couldn't help glancing at Jason Simpkin as I walked past his place on the bench. It was hard, but somehow I managed not to smile.

Coach Hubbard never mentioned the temporary Simpkin take-over and I never asked. Jason was hurt, and two concussions in a row made him strictly unavailable, and I was the quarterback. There really wasn't anything he had to say. Everyone knew how it went, even the Simpkin clan. It was football.

Practice for the rest of the week went so well, it made me nervous. My receivers darted around like water bugs, especially Griffin. Just as I threw the ball, they'd turn their heads, or I'd throw it and they'd make the break I expected. My passes weren't strong, but they were accurate. And Jackson? Jackson was Jackson, a raging bull in a barnyard of cows, pigs, and chickens. He was unstoppable. Confidence was high, almost too high.

But I was prepared—not only for the game and making middle-school history beating a team who hadn't lost for five years, but also to win the Dallas Cowboys in my contest with Dillon.

The Dallas Morning Star ran an article about the game in its Wednesday online edition, complete with photos taken of me and Dillon talking on the sideline from the Cardinals game. No one knew how much was at stake. People just thought it was rich that the two kids battling in court over who'd control the Cowboys were facing off on the gridiron. They probably wouldn't have believed it if someone told them the ownership would be determined by who won a middle-school game and I wasn't going to be the one to tell. I had enough pressure on me as it was.

Still, interest was high. Local TV stations showed up for practice and interviewed Coach Hubbard. Even if my mom hadn't banned anyone from interviewing me, Coach Hubbard said the school policy was no player interviews. We were too young.

With all the attention being given to us and the game, and all the pressure because of what was at stake, by Thursday, I was having a hard time keeping my food down. On Friday, I stopped eating altogether. My stomach was a jangle of nerves.

So the last thing I needed when I closed my locker and turned toward homeroom was to see Izzy scowling at me with her arms firmly folded, blocking my path.

"What?" I asked.

"You know what, Ryan. If you all win tomorrow, there's that bonfire. Mya and Griffin are going as really, really good friends."

"Tomorrow is the biggest game of my life, Izzy."

"Well, the bonfire is after the game. Life goes on, you know. I thought maybe we were really, really good friends and we could go together, too, and then you got all weird about it and any time it comes up it's like you can't even look at me."

I was, in fact, looking at the floor at that moment. I forced my eyes up into hers. "What? I can go—if you want."

She smiled at me.

It was weird. I mean, when I heard about Griffin and Mya, I wanted to go with Izzy. I just had no idea how to go about it, and now it was just happening. "I mean, if you'd really want to go with me."

"Hey," she said, shrugging and then smiling to let me know she was teasing, "you're the kid owner."

I gulped down some bile. I wanted to tell her that I might not be the kid owner, but the bell rang and she started to slowly back away, heading for homeroom.

The rest of the day was a blur. I have the dim memory of Jackson howling with delight and mocking me gently at the news I'd be going to the bonfire if we won. At practice, we had a simple walk-through, going over the last-minute details of our game plan without even putting pads on.

That night, I couldn't fall asleep. I didn't drop off until sometime very early on Saturday morning. The last time I remembered checking the clock from my tangle of damp sheets it said 3:12 a.m. I dreamed of winning and when I woke, even though I can't say I was rested, I was upbeat and ready to go. I choked back a yawn and poked my fried egg with the tines of my fork, making enough of a mess that my mom wouldn't know I'd eaten absolutely nothing.

"Is that all you're going to eat?" she asked.

"Big game, Mom." I liked the sound of my voice. It made

football seem as important in our kitchen as it was across the state.

"I hope you aren't too nervous, Ryan. It's just a game—it's not life. If Dillon wins, you'll still own part of the Cowboys. Remember that."

"Mom?"

"Yes, Ry?"

"I'm not a kid anymore, right?"

"Well," she said, "you're not a *child*. No, you're a young man."

"So, I appreciate what you're trying to do," I said, "but I think I'm old enough to know how big this is. I don't want to pretend that it's not and I don't want you to pretend. If I win this, my wildest dreams come true. If I don't, I lose."

I let that word hang between us like dirty laundry, then I spoke quietly. "I hate it, but it's the truth and I don't want to pretend it isn't. Okay?"

She looked at me with a serious face and spoke in a quiet voice, too. "Yes, Ryan. I understand, and I'm proud of you."

As we pulled into the school parking lot, my mom's phone rang.

"Oh, hi." Her voice bubbled and her face blushed just a bit. "Yes, he's right here. I'm sure he'd be happy to talk to you."

She gave me a funny look and handed over the phone. "Coach Cowan wants to wish you luck."

My chest swelled. "Hello?"

"Hey, Ryan. You ready?" he asked.

"I am."

294

"Make sure you take time to get your pre-snap reads. That strong safety is gonna give away the coverage with these guys every time, right? And watch out for Dillon. You'll know when he's blitzing. That kid's got no discipline whatsoever."

"Right," I said. "Thanks, Coach."

"We just finished practice ourselves and I'm gonna be there watching, so . . . make me proud."

"Thanks, Coach."

I handed back the phone, dizzy with excitement but wildly sick from nerves. My mom talked for a minute, then got off. "Well, that's impressive. Fun, right? The coach of the Cowboys wishing you luck."

"Fun and scary. I mean, you know . . ."

My mom put a hand on my leg and squeezed. "Like I said, Ryan. It's just a game. You need to have fun."

"The only fun in football is when you win, Mom."

"Says who?"

"I don't know. Somebody said it."

"Well, it's a game, Ryan." She pulled her truck into the school parking lot. "I want you to win, but it is a game. It's not life or death."

I didn't argue with her, even though I felt differently, so I grabbed the handle and flung the door open. "Okay, Mom. Thanks for the ride."

"Ryan?"

I stopped before closing the door. "Yeah?"

"Go get 'em, Ry-Guy." She made a fist and held it up. "I'll be cheering for you."

"Thanks, Mom." I closed the door and marched toward the locker room.

I was pretty sure that it was going to be the most important game of my entire life.

Have you ever been bodysurfing, going along, riding out these awesome waves, and then all of a sudden the ocean just tosses you like a salad? You have no idea what's up or down, whether it's light or dark, if you can breathe or if you can't. When that happens, you know the next thing is that you're going to be bounced off the sand, seeing stars and hearing the crunch of your own bones.

That's what I felt like, dressing in the locker room with Jackson going berserk and the rest of the team feeding off his mania with chants and growls, barks and cheers. I floated on their excitement, out onto the field for warm-ups. The hot smell of the watered turf snuggled up inside my nose. A slight breeze steamrolled the thick heat and the sun stared down without a blink. Sweat poured from every spot of skin.

The home stands were nearly full, but the visitors' stands

overflowed with the orange-and-black Eiland colors, spilling them all the way along the fence to either end zone. Their colors looked mean and tough next to the Ben Sauer Middle blue and white. I spotted three cameramen and wondered if they were all local or if ESPN might have sent a camera as well. Either way, it only increased the pressure.

The Eiland team had white jerseys because they were visitors, but their black helmets and black pants with orange stripes made them look even bigger than they already were. I spotted Dillon immediately in the middle of their team circle, already leading warm-ups with military jumping jacks that ended in a ferocious cheer. Dillon leapt into the air, swinging his arms like weapons and bouncing off his toes like a frantic puppet.

I sought out Jackson and exchanged shoulder slaps. "We can do this, right?" I asked, more to convince myself that we stood a chance against these guys.

"Heck, yeah, Ry-guy!"

They might be bigger across the board, but no one could rival Jackson's size and probably not his craziness either. I got caught up in the excitement and the nervousness and didn't look into the stands until I removed my helmet for the national anthem. When I did, my eyes went right over my mom and Izzy and Mya to the upper reaches of the stands. There, by himself, stood Mr. Dietrich. He held a straw hat over the heart of his flouncy white shirt. His reddish pants reminded me of strawberry taffy. His face was serious behind a large pair of sunglasses and his lips were unmoved by the patriotic song.

He may have seen me looking because when the song ended the first thing he did after replacing the hat on his bald head

298

was raise a pair of binoculars and direct them right at me so that I quickly pulled on my helmet. I worried that maybe I should have acknowledged him, but I worried even more when I saw Dillon across the field waving into the stands, turned, and saw Mr. Dietrich waving back with a smile. It was like the two of them knew how this would turn out before it even started. Worry is the wrong word for what I felt. I got sick, for real.

I made a break for the back of the bench and dry-heaved onto the strip of grass skirting the track. When I looked up, Coach Hubbard was scowling at me.

"You okay, Ryan?"

I nodded and he consulted his clipboard. "You got the first five plays memorized, right?"

I only nodded because the acid from my stomach had scorched the back of my throat and I didn't trust how my words would come out.

Coach Hubbard looked up and eyed me now with suspicion. "Right?"

"Yeah," I croaked.

"Well, okay."

We won the toss and that meant that I would be out of my misery sooner than later and that was better. The only reason I was even aware of how badly I was sweating was because I felt like I could barely get a grip on the ball as I took a few more practice snaps from my center. Our kickoff return team got stuffed by a mob of insane Eiland players, and I jogged out onto the blazing hot field under the thunderous boos from the black-and-orange section of the stands. I'd never seen fans booing in a middle-school game before, but I'd never seen Eiland.

The first play was a rollout pass with receivers at two levels, a third breaking into the deep center field and a throwback to Jackson in an emergency.

It was an emergency.

An instant after I took the snap, I saw Dillon from the corner of my eye, coming like a lightning bolt, straight up through the gut of our offensive line.

I thought I could hear Dillon's breathing, even through the noise. I ducked and he shot over me like a missile. More Eiland defenders were coming though and Dillon pounced from the turf like a panther. In a panic, I heaved the ball back to Jackson.

He caught it and did his thing, rumbling up the gut, breaking a tackle and heading for the thinner defensive population on the far sideline. Players chased, but couldn't catch him until an Eiland defensive back tangled himself in Jackson's ankles. It was still a twenty-three-yard gain and now the Ben Sauer fans cheered like maniacs to let Eiland know that Highland football was something to be reckoned with, too.

Jackson went wild. He slapped high fives and shoulder pads and banged his helmet against mine in his joy.

"Easy, Jackson!" I glared at him. "I gotta think."

Jackson just laughed.

"Okay, let's huddle up, guys. Come on! I love twenty yards, but we got a long way to go to win this thing. Get in here!" I surprised even myself with how I took control, and the flicker of the father I never knew danced across my brain. Maybe he had been that way?

I called the next play, a run to Jackson, and he took it to the seven-yard line. The third play was a draw play, fake the pass and hand it to Jackson, but I swapped it out with the fourth play, a swing pass I couldn't miss on. If the defense kept blitzing—and I knew they would—it would be wide open.

I went to the line and got up under the center. Dillon was no more than six feet from me. His eye twirled like pinwheels and he snorted and growled like a junkyard dog. I tried to ignore him, but a shiver jiggled my spine. It was like I knew he was coming for me on a blitz, and of course, he was. I thought maybe I should have stayed with the game plan and not skipped one of the plays Coach Hubbard had given me. It seemed the right thing to do, but now, not so much. The problem was that the play clock was ticking down. I had no time.

I barked out the cadence, took the snap, and started to roll out. My right guard fired out at Dillon's knees and should have cut him down like a blade of grass, but Dillon leapt right over the guy and before I could even think about making the throw, he had me by the collar with a mighty paw. Even knowing how fast Dillon was, I still couldn't believe he'd gotten to me as quickly as he did.

My feet left the ground and my body floated for the briefest moment in the air before that wave smashed me to the turf. I felt its shock in my teeth. Stars ignited and burst. I have no idea what happened to the football, but I sensed the action moving away from me in the opposite direction at rapid speed like a fading dream.

I stumbled to my feet just in time to see the referee signal an Eiland touchdown on the other end of the field.

Dillon jumped into the air, celebrating with his teammates and holding my fumbled football high in the air for everyone—fans, cameras, Izzy, my mom, and Mr. Dietrich—to see.

He may as well have ripped out my heart and held that high, too.

The really good things about ourselves, or the really good things we do, we like to pretend came from our own personal well of talents and gifts. Usually, it's not the case. Usually, what makes us special can be attributed to our mom or dad. I think my own relentlessness came from both. It's just how I'm hardwired. I didn't learn it or develop it because of some great teacher or coach who sat me down and told me, "This is what you have to do if you want to have a chance to succeed." I'm just that way.

So, even though it looked like everything was going against me and that the entire day—and then my whole life—were going to fall apart, I dug in my heels. It actually made me more determined, and the doubt I saw in my teammates' eyes enraged me.

I grabbed Jackson's mask, yanking his glum and sweat-soaked face so close he had to blink and wince at the tiny flecks of spit jumping from my mouth alongside my words. "Don't you dare quit!"

I released him and he stumbled back. The other players on my team and even Coach Vickerson stepped back to give my crazy rant room to breathe. I shook my finger all around.

"We are *not* going to lose this thing! That was one bad play! We *will* not lose!" I glared at them until their faces softened with the possibility that this wouldn't be a blowout; then—head held very high—I marched through them to get a slug of Gatorade before replacing my helmet, moving to the edge of the field, and cheering on our kickoff return team.

Griffin Engle got pummeled deep in our own territory again, but I bounced out onto the field like a cricket in a frying pan, shouting and clapping my hands. "Let's go! Let's go! Here we go!"

I think there is a joy in fighting that's not quite like anything else—fighting for something that's right, fighting against a wrong, or just fighting for something. Sometimes it hurts, yes, but there's something so primal about it, like there's this secret inner part of our hearts and brains that was built just for that.

So, we battled.

I stopped worrying about looking good for my mom, or Izzy, or the fans, or even Mr. Dietrich, and instead eagerly agreed with Coach Hubbard that we had to give the ball to Jackson almost exclusively.

In the huddle, on our first play back on offense, I snarled at Jackson. "They need a taste of the Big Dawg! You gonna eat?"

Jackson's eyes rolled in his head and he bellowed like a lunatic. Our teammates shifted in discomfort, not sure if he'd lost his mind completely. I called a run play, right up the gut. We broke the huddle and I whispered to Jackson. "You see that Dillon? He's looking right at you. He's *growling* at you! What are you gonna do about it?"

Jackson couldn't even speak. A howl tore through his chest and he smacked his own helmet. I went to my spot behind the center.

Dillon crept up close to the line, sneering at me. "Gonna wipe you up again, Tiny!"

"Nice." I sneered right back, knowing that he was about to get a mouthful of Jackson Shockey.

"Blue 27!" I shouted. "Blue 27! Set! Hut, hut, hut!"

I took the snap and handed it to Jackson.

I should have carried out the fake, but I just couldn't. I had to watch. Jackson shot through a gap and Dillon met him in the opening.

SMACK!

Helmet to helmet, they hit. Dillon literally flew through the air. More defenders poured toward Jackson, but he quickly dipped his shoulders and blasted through them, too, leaving a trail of bodies until he got tripped up and dragged down by three Eiland players. He burst from the pile, an exploding volcano, and stomped back to the huddle, pointing at Dillon all the while. "I'm comin' for you, hotshot! I'm comin' for you. Big Dawg gonna eat all day!"

I have to say that I loved it.

Passing became a counter to the steady diet of runs up the middle, off tackle, and around the end. We gave Eiland more than they wanted of Jackson Shockey. The only touchdown I had was on a play action fake to Jackson. I pulled the ball from his gut, stuck it to my hip, then bootlegged around the end, tossing an easy pass over the head of Dillon Peebles before he smashed me into the turf. I got up with a hunk of sod hanging from my face mask. I peeled it away, filling my nose with the fresh hot scent of dirt and grass, and saw Griffin holding my touchdown pass up in the end zone.

"That's all you got?" I laughed right in Dillon's face.

Still, for every score we had, they answered with one of their own. While Dillon was a defensive player first—fast, aggressive, and mean as a snake—he also played tight end for the Eiland offense, and had two touchdown catches. Added to that was a running back quick as a hiccup, built low to the ground, and powerful enough to shake half the tacklers who got ahold of him.

Back and forth we battled. The game was close and we were down by three with time running out when Jackson exploded around the right side of the line. He made it past midfield when two Eiland cornerbacks tangled themselves up in his legs like shoelaces tied together. Still Jackson lurched forward. That's when Dillon Peebles caught up to him.

I can't say for certain that it was intentional, but I think it was. Dillon launched himself at Jackson's knees and when he hit, he turned his body and rolled so that Jackson went down face-first with his knees twisted beneath him.

"Jackson!" I screamed.

His howl made me shiver and I ran over to him.

He lay on his back, wincing in pain, gritting his teeth, and breathing fast and shallow. "My knee, Ry-Guy. They got my knee."

Tears welled in his eyes and it scared me.

The coaches and trainer swept me and everyone else aside. They helped Jackson up and carried him to the bench. The crowd politely applauded.

"Ry, don't worry about me. We're so close. We can't stop now."

I nodded and looked at the scoreboard.

We were down by three and out of time. The clock read :07.

It was fourth down. We had just one play to win or lose the game.

In that brief moment, I thought about who I was and what I'd proven that day. The times I got smashed into the dirt, I bounced back up. When I had twisted an ankle, I walked it off. When blood poured from the missing chunk of flesh on the back of my hand—removed courtesy of Dillon Peebles's helmet in the third quarter—I had ignored it as Coach Vickerson wrapped it in tape. I proved to my teammates that day, and even more to myself, that I belonged there. Would I end up as an All-American or in the NFL?

No idea. The odds were against me, but I was a football player through and through.

But then there was the contest between Ben Sauer and Eiland, me and Dillon. If the TV cameras hadn't made that clear, Mr. Dietrich's presence certainly did. One of us would win, one would lose. One would be the kid owner of the Dallas Cowboys, the other would not. These were the thoughts running through my mind as I jogged over to Coach Hubbard and Coach Vickerson to talk things over.

They had spent our last time-out to consider what our final play would be without Jackson Shockey in the backfield. Coach Vickerson looked angry, not at me, but at the gods of football for bringing us this close without a very good prospect to pull off a win in the end. Coach Hubbard looked frightened, not by losing, but by making the wrong call and opening himself up to criticism from others as the coach who couldn't finish the deal.

The three of us leaned into a mini huddle and Coach Hubbard gripped my arm tight enough to make me wince. "What do you think, Ryan?"

Bootlegs and throwbacks and double passes skittered across my brain, maybe a hook and lateral, something really big, something that would make me the hero and win us the game.

But then it came to me.

I didn't like it at all, but I could see no real choice.

I knew what we had to do.

I took a deep breath and looked up into the stands. There was Mr. Dietrich, on his feet training his binoculars right at me and my coaches. Not too far away sat my mom with her hands clasped like someone in church. Right next to her sat Izzy with her friend Mya.

I looked Coach Hubbard in the eye. "Estevan."

Coach Hubbard wrinkled up his face. "Estevan, what?"

I looked out onto the field at the forty yards between where the ball sat and the goal line we needed to cross. Everything I wanted was mine if I could just get that stupid funny-shaped leather ball across it, but it was too far for me to throw it. It just was. The truth of it was as painful as Jackson's hurt knee. I wanted to win and I wanted it to be me, but something Coach Hubbard said was rattling around in my brain.

When you want to win, he had said, *you put yourself second.*

"Estevan," I said, repeating his name. "You got to put him in for me."

"Wait, what?! You're taking yourself *out*?" Coach Vickerson didn't try to hide the disgust in his voice. To him, I was quitting, folding under the pressure and giving up on my team.

That made me mad. How could he question me after all I'd been through? But I realized that everyone else's reaction would be the same as Coach Vickerson's. It looked like a cowardly move on my part. Even if we miraculously got the touchdown we needed to win, I couldn't help thinking that Mr. Dietrich might give the team to Dillon anyway. After all, it wouldn't be *me* beating Dillon. It would be Estevan.

Coach Hubbard's words replayed themselves in my mind again. "Coach, I want to win this thing, just like you."

I jammed the end of my mouth guard between my teeth and bit down, spending my frustration and anger before I removed it to speak. "We got one play. Their corners have been jumping our routes the entire game. I know what their coaches told them, not to worry about the deep ball against me. I can't throw it deep. But Estevan *can*." I stared at Coach Hubbard. "From the old offense, the Hail Mary. Estevan can throw it. Griffin can catch it."

"What are you going to do?" Coach Hubbard asked, still not fully understanding.

I huffed. "I'm gonna stand here and watch with you. When you want to win, you put yourself second, right?"

I can't even explain the look on Coach Hubbard's face: the surprise, the wisdom, and the pride all at the same time.

312

"Okay." He nodded and gave me a hard wink and hollered for Estevan. Estevan bounced over with his helmet under his arm. His uniform was sweat-soaked as much as anyone's because Estevan was the starting free safety on our defense.

"You can throw it forty yards, right, Estevan?" I asked.

Estevan grinned. "You know I can, Ry-Guy."

I nodded at Coach Hubbard, who cleared his throat. "Okay, Estevan, Hail Mary play. Double slots. Throw it to Griffin's side. Just chuck it up there, whether he's covered or not. Got that? It's our last chance."

Estevan's face went instantly serious. "Got it, Coach."

I watched, standing there beside my coaches, second-guessing myself with every step Estevan took toward the huddle. I knew how dangerous a move this was. If we lost, I'd be painted as the kid who bailed in the final moments of a hard-fought battle, a total loser. If we won, I was hoping people would credit me for the self-sacrifice. That's not the way it works in football, though, especially in Texas. Estevan would be the hero and everything good I'd done would be forgotten.

It wouldn't be my win, it would be his. Dillon—and I had to believe Mr. Dietrich—would point out that I'd quit, pulling myself from the game and thereby losing the contest that my father's letter had said was between Dillon and me. I hadn't stopped to figure out any of this. I'd only been thinking of winning.

Either way, it was too late. Before I knew it, Estevan was jogging to the line with my offense, taking *my* snap and dropping back into *my* pocket.

Dillon came at him fast on a blitz, too fast, leaping over

the top of one lineman and swimming Bryan Markham like a stack of Jell-O.

Whether Estevan would even get the pass off was in serious doubt.

He reared back in total panic.

Just as Estevan's arm began its forward whip, Dillon hit him in the chops.

POW!

Estevan blew up. The ball flew into the air like a mortar, high but far. Dillon and Estevan lay in a heap. The only person on the field with a chance to keep the game alive was Griffin Engle.

Griffin must have known that, too. He darted forward from out of the end zone, stretching and reaching for the ball as it fell near the ten-yard line. Just before the ball struck the ground, Griffin scooped it in one beautiful motion, got one foot miraculously down on the ground, and kept going like a tightrope walker trying to stay upright. It would be like the miracle play I'd seen on ESPN Classic, Franco Harris scooping the ball and running it in to beat the Raiders in their famous rivalry of the seventies. Griffin had a long way to go, more than ten yards now with eleven Eiland defenders screaming toward him from every direction.

Griffin dodged and ducked, heading not to the end zone but sideways and backward to avoid being tackled. He looped around, then took off through the open space on the other side of the field. My heart rose in my throat because they looked like rodeo clowns scrambling after a crazy calf. All the possibilities flashed in my mind at once: us winning, me being celebrated as brilliant for my suggested play, Izzy and my mom being proud, Dietrich seeing things my way, and me owning the Dallas Cowboys without having to worry about that stupid Dillon messing with things.

Dillon.

Here he came, a lightning bolt, streaking toward Griffin in a blink, not like the rest of them, fumbling and bumbling, but like a heat-seeking missile. Griffin taking a false step to fake out a defensive back, ducking to avoid a hustling lineman. Fury blinded me. After destroying Estevan, instead of lying there in the grass to enjoy his kill, he must have gotten up unnoticed and taken off after Griffin, pursuing his prey all the way down the field. Dillon caught up with Griffin, pounced on his back, and swatted the ball from the crook of his arm with an iron paw.

The ball skittered and spun in the air.

It was now anyone's game.

If I were writing a fairy tale, Griffin, or even Bryan Markham—any Ben Sauer player—would have recovered his wits and flopped down on the ball in the end zone, securing our win, defeating my half brother and his unbeaten team. This isn't a fairy tale, though.

Dillon got the fumble. The whistle blew the play dead and ended the game.

The Eiland players went wild. Their fans screamed themselves silly. It was salt in our gaping wounds. I felt as if I'd been skinned alive. Everything hurt: the sun, the breeze, the noise, every footstep that brought me closer to the army of Eiland players when they'd settled down and lined up to shake our hands.

The person who thought of that hand-shaking business after a game must have never played in a game like ours, a game that left him feeling worse than a million toothaches in the center of his brain. When you lose a game like that, you want to just melt right into the earth and disappear without a trace. Instead, you hold your head as high as you can, keep your eyes fixed on the ground, hold out your slap hand, and mutter something sportsmanlike.

"Good game. Good game. Good game . . ."

Dillon brought up the rear of the Eiland team's line. Another nice possible ending: Dillon tells me he respected my incredible effort, wishes us luck the rest of the season, and suggests that two football players as dedicated and tough as him and me can certainly get along well enough to run an NFL football team together.

Instead, he said, "Good game." Like it was the punch line to a joke.

Turning to join his teammates, Dillon marched boldly toward our sideline and the fence beyond it that separated the Ben Sauer crowd from the field. He acted like he owned the place, like it was the Dallas Cowboys stadium. My first thought was that he'd lost his mind. Then I saw Izzy.

She stood there with her lower lip tucked under her front teeth, a look of concern. A look of confusion.

She wasn't alone. Mr. Dietrich stood there, too, smiling at Dillon. My mom appeared, not with them but behind them, clasping her hands and looking at me with the saddest face you could imagine.

Like a moth spiraling down into the flames of a camp-fire, I stumbled along after Dillon toward my own complete destruction.

I didn't hear what kind of greeting Izzy and Dillon traded.

It might have been "Hi" or it could have been "What's up?" Their eyes were locked, though, and I did hear Dillon's invitation to her quite clearly. "We're having a pool party at my house to celebrate. You should come."

Before Izzy could answer, Mr. Dietrich reached over the fence to shake Dillon's hand. "Outstanding, Dillon. Congratulations. That was some game. You win, Dillon. You won it all."

Then Mr. Dietrich saw me. "Ryan . . . very nice effort."

He held his hand out to me, too. I shook it. Dillon turned, sneering. "Smart move, taking yourself out on that last play. Knew I'd be coming on the blitz, huh?"

I hated Dillon more at that moment than I realized I could hate someone. He'd beaten me, at everything. Still, he had to rub it in, had to insult me, had to slice me open *and* stomp on my guts. My eyes felt hot and wet and I bit back the urge to cry, forcing my chin up. There was no answer I could give that would easily explain, but I had to say something. "No. We had to get the ball into the end zone. I don't have that kind of arm."

After a bark of delight, Dillon said, "That we know."

From the corner of my eye, I could see Izzy's face color with embarrassment for me.

Mr. Dietrich removed his sunglasses and tilted his head like he was peering into one of the cracks in my broken soul with those cold blue eyes. "What did you say, Ryan?"

I had no idea why Mr. Dietrich would torture me by dragging this out. To that point, I thought he might have actually sort of liked me, even if I wasn't going to be the kid owner. That he would instead be cruel to me was startling, and I blurted out the answer.

"I'm not strong enough. I'm not big enough. I don't have the arm." I crossed my arms. "There. Everyone happy?"

Mr. Dietrich waved his hand as if shooing a fly. "No, I know that, but why didn't you *try*?"

I didn't think I could despise anyone worse than Dillon until that moment. I hated Mr. Dietrich *more*. I couldn't hold back the tears; they spilled from my eyes, shaming me into a flood and a sob. Izzy grew foggy through the prism of salt water. Of all the people there, I wanted her to understand. I no longer cared about Mr. Dietrich.

"I wanted to *win*," I pleaded to Izzy, then turned to Mr. Dietrich. "You think I didn't want to be in there? To try? It made me *sick*, but I wanted to *win*."

A shred of laughter escaped from Mr. Dietrich's throat

before he finished my thought for me. "You wanted to *win*, so you took yourself out."

"It was supposed to be a Hail Mary play," I said.

Mr. Dietrich frowned. "You fell on your sword—so to speak—to win."

"And he lost anyway."

Dillon's smug smile burned like molten steel, soupy and orange, as he looked around.

My mom averted her eyes to the scoreboard. Jackson limped up behind me and laid a thick hand on my neck, saying nothing, just being there, like a true friend.

Izzy looked up from her feet and, to my surprise, glared at Dillon. "That's not even nice."

"*Nice?*" Dillon snorted. "I'm a football player."

Izzy fumed. "Well, I can't go to your stupid party, Dillon. I'm hanging out with Ryan. Even if I wasn't, I wouldn't go anywhere with you."

Dillon shrugged. "Whatever. This whole thing is a joke. Can you imagine? Him running the Dallas Cowboys?"

Mr. Dietrich cleared his throat. "Yes, I can imagine it. I can actually see it: Ryan Zinna, kid owner."

"What?" I don't know if I said that, or Dillon, or both of us at the same time.

"It's what this team needs. It's needed it for a long time." Mr. Dietrich looked at my mom and she nodded. "A team isn't about a bunch of stars. A team is about an individual working for the others. You can't have a coach and a general manager trying to get each other fired. You can't have players being favored because they show up at someone's birthday party. It's football. It's about winning. On the field."

Dillon's mom appeared suddenly, decked out in a snug black-and-orange shirt with expensive-looking sunglasses and tight jeans. Her voice was syrupy and sticky and sweet like a hot plate of pancakes. "Dillon, sweetie, you need to get to the buses. Your coach is asking for you."

Only then did she act like she'd even seen the rest of us.

"Oh, how are we? A nice little sending-off party?"

"It is a sending-off party." Mr. Dietrich slipped the sunglasses back on his face. "For you . . . and Dillon."

This confused her and she chuckled, but in a nervous way. "What are you talking about, Eric?"

"I'm voting my shares with Ryan, Jasmine. He'll be running things for the Cowboys from now on." Mr. Dietrich punctuated that with a nod.

Jasmine Peebles's smile morphed into a scowl. Her twinkling eyes burned like two house fires. Deep fissures appeared in her smooth skin, heaving cracks in her makeup. "You're joking."

"No," said Mr. Dietrich.

"You *said* this stupid game today was what mattered. You *lied*," Jasmine hissed.

"No," he said, "that was the truth. It was this game. I said I'd choose the kid owner based on who won. Those were your husband's explicit instructions. He said, 'Let the boys compete for it, then pick the winner.'"

"You don't even make sense, you old *fool*." Jasmine hooked her fingers into claws and I wondered if she might not pounce on Mr. Dietrich. "Dillon won!"

"I don't expect you to understand it, Jasmine, but it's done. It really is this time. My decision is final. Good luck to you and your son." Mr. Dietrich gave a little salute with the brim of his straw hat. "Oh, there is one thing I think Dillon got right."

Jasmine had gathered up her son, who seemed too stunned to even react, but she turned to snarl. "What's that?"

"Minority owners won't be welcome in the team areas, the sideline, locker room, practice fields . . . the complex, too."

Mr. Dietrich's face turned serious as stone. "And we *will* alert security."

Jasmine half dragged Dillon away. She had one red-nailed claw hooked to his shoulder pad. "I'll sue you into the dirt, Dietrich. You'll hear from my lawyer."

Mr. Dietrich sighed and spoke in a low voice. "I suppose I will." Then he perked up and looked at me. "Maybe we should get together after you're cleaned up. Talk about the details?"

"Would you like to come over later?" my mom asked. "We can barbecue some ribs."

"I like ribs." Mr. Dietrich touched the brim of his hat one last time, then turned and disappeared into the fading crowd.

My mom reached over the fence and gave me a one-armed hug.

I looked at Izzy. "We didn't win, so there's no bonfire after all. You wanna come over, too?"

"I said I was," she said.

"I know. I just didn't know if you only said it to make Dillon mad."

She grinned. "I said it because we're good friends."

"Really good," I said.

"Nice," said Jackson, patting me on the back.

"You two better get with your team," my mom said. "We'll wait for you outside the locker room."

Coach Hubbard stood in the middle of us, destroyed. He could barely talk, and all I heard were scraps of words here and there under his breath, things like "never quit" and "true winners" and "not over." Honestly, though, as much as I hated losing that game, I couldn't help feeling like I'd also won.

I had, after all. I was a way bigger winner than Dillon Peebles. I had friends like Izzy and Jackson. I had a coach like Coach Hubbard and maybe a secret coach in Coach Cowan. I had a mom like my mom, and a trustee like Mr. Dietrich. Plus, I owned the Dallas Cowboys. For real.

I am the kid owner.